The Calamity Café

"[A] delightful cozy mystery . . . that will leave you wanting more . . . You'll be drooling over the delicious Southern dishes Amy is serving up." —Fresh Fiction

"Leeson's first in a new series gives readers everything they could ask for in a pleasing summer read. Likable and relatable characters are in abundance, as is a fascinating mystery that needs to be solved. But the best part of the book is the addition of several good old Southern recipes in the back." —RT Book Reviews

"A good mix of suspense, laughter, and a touch of romance make this a pleasurable start to what looks like will be an amusing new series." —Mason Canyon

"We are treated to a murder mystery and some romantic overtones . . . If you're looking for a fun summer read, this would be a wonderful choice." —Book Babble

"Gayle Leeson has hit a home run with *The Calamity Café*." —Open Book Society

"A cleverly constructed plot, well-written characters, and a setting that feels like the town next door all blend together to form the perfect recipe for a new series!" —ReadingIsMySuperpower.org

Honey-Baked Homicide

A Down South Café Mystery

GAYLE LEESON

BERKLEY PRIME CRIME
New York

BERKLEY PRIME CRIME
Published by Berkley
An imprint of Penguin Random House LLC
375 Hudson Street, New York, New York 10014

ISBN: 9781101990827

First Edition: December 2017

Printed in the United States of America
1   3   5   7   9   10   8   6   4   2

Book design by Kelly Lipovich

To Tim, Lianna, and Nicholas

Chapter 1

I was working on breakfast prep when my cousin Jackie popped her head into the kitchen and said, "Amy, Stu Landon is here."

"Great. Thanks." I removed my plastic gloves and then went outside to greet the beekeeper.

Mr. Landon and I had just entered into an arrangement wherein I'd sell his honey on consignment to my patrons. I own and operate the Down South Café, one of Winter Garden, Virginia's only two restaurants.

It was a gorgeous August morning, and Mr. Landon, a tall, thin man with salt-and-pepper hair, was shading his eyes with his hand when I stepped out into the sunlight.

"Did you want me to bring the honey in through the back of the café or the front?"

"Just bring it into the dining room and put it on the counter, please," I said. "I've already cleared some shelf space on the back wall, and I plan to keep a jar by the register so people will be sure to notice it."

Mr. Landon opened the passenger side door of his olive green antique Chevy pickup truck and got out a small plastic crate containing half-pint jars of honey. I held open the door to the café for him and then followed him inside.

He placed the crate on the counter in front of the cash register. "This all right?"

"Perfect." I plucked one of the jars out of the crate. *Landon's Bee Farm, Pure All Natural Honey.* "I want to buy a couple of jars from you straight out to serve to my diners and one to take home to my mom and Aunt Bess."

I went around the counter, opened the register, and paid Mr. Landon for three jars of honey. I put a note in the register reflecting the transaction and then gave the consignment agreement I'd prepared the night before to Mr. Landon. I still had seven jars left to sell to Down South Café customers.

"Thank you, Ms. Flowers. I'll come around next week to bring you ten more jars." He took a dilapidated cap from the back pocket of his overalls, shook it out, and placed it on his head before leaving.

I turned to my cousin Jackie with a smile. "That one is a man of few words."

"Granny says he used to be some sort of secret agent."

Jackie's granny was my great-aunt Elizabeth, known to Mom and me as Aunt Bess. And since Aunt Bess is blessed with a vivid imagination, I wouldn't normally have given her theory on Mr. Landon more than a passing thought. But unlike most of the residents of Winter Garden, Mr. Landon didn't have much of a history here. He'd simply shown up one day about twenty years ago and taken up residence on the old Carver farm. He'd renovated the farm, started growing his own vegetables, and set up beehives. Since he kept to himself and wasn't very talkative, that's about all folks knew about him. Other than the fact that his honey was really tasty and that Mr. Landon swore that the stuff was good for everything from curing allergies to treating wounds. I didn't know how valid his claims were, but I did know that the honey tasted awfully good on a warm biscuit.

"Why in the world would Aunt Bess think Stu Landon was a secret agent?" I asked Jackie. "And what could the man have possibly been investigating in Winter Garden?"

She shrugged. "You'll have to take that up with Granny, but I believe she's under the impression that Winter Garden was merely his base of operations."

Dilly Boyd, one of our favorite café regulars, came through the door. She was a tiny lady with cottony hair and mischievous blue eyes. She wore a wide-brimmed sun hat that she swept off her head as she joined us at the counter.

"What have you got there?" She peered into the crate. "Ooh, Landon's honey. I'd like a jar, please."

"All right. I'll keep it here by the register for you and you can pick it up on your way out."

"Okay. When did you start selling Landon's honey?"

"Just this morning. It's our first batch, so to speak," I said with a smile. "I'm hoping to get even more of our local farmers to offer some of their crops on consignment."

"Maybe you should host a farmer's market here on Saturday mornings," Dilly said. "That'd be fun."

"That's not a bad idea, Dilly. I'll look into it."

4

Gayle Leeson

"Before we get completely off track, though," said Jackie, "what do you know about Stu Landon, Dilly?"

She frowned. "What do you mean?"

"We were just saying that we've known Mr. Landon all our lives, but we don't know much about him," I said.

"Well, he came here . . . oh, I reckon it was nearly twenty years ago now . . . from somewhere out West. Moved here alone and didn't go out of his way to socialize, other than with the Carvers, who live to the right of his place. That stands to reason, though, since he bought a farm from some of the Carvers. Some folks think they might be kin." She drew her thin, pale eyebrows together. "I always figured somebody had broken Stu's heart and that he came here to hide himself away. Some of us tried to fix him up with daughters or nieces or widows, but he wouldn't have any part of that nonsense, so we finally left him alone." She wandered over to her favorite seat at the counter.

"Scrambled eggs and biscuits?" I asked.

She nodded. "And some hash browns would be nice too."

"Coming right up." I went into the kitchen. "Jackie, would you mind shelving the honey, please? And leave a jar for Mom and Aunt Bess under the counter."

"No problem," she said. "Dilly, how's that raccoon of yours doing?"

Dilly didn't actually own a raccoon, but one came to visit her and get a biscuit every evening.

"He's as right as rain and as punctual as a clockmaker," she said. "He comes to my back door at sundown every single day."

"Wonder if he'd like some honey on his biscuit?" I called from the kitchen.

"I don't know whether he would or not. But if he thinks I'm wasting my good honey on him, the little beggar's mistaken."

We had a little lull in business just before ten that morning, and I was able to grab a cup of coffee and look around the café for a couple of minutes. I always try to remember to acknowledge my blessings every day, and the Down South Café was certainly a big one.

When I'd bought the café from Pete Holman, it had been a dive. I don't know how else to put it. The place was dingy—the floor was linoleum that should have been replaced twenty years prior, the fixtures were old and tarnished, and most of the stools and dining room chairs had tears. Thanks to my childhood friend—and Jackie's boyfriend—Roger, who had his own construction company, the floors were now gleaming and scuff-resistant bamboo, the walls were a cheerful yellow with blue trim, and we had new gray stools and dining room furniture, new light fixtures, and a patio for patrons to enjoy when the weather cooperated. We also had a refrigerated display case for pies, cakes, cookies, potato salad—whatever we thought our diners might want to take home with them. And we had a bakers' rack with shelves of jams, *Down South Café* T-shirts and aprons (blue with yellow lettering), and now Mr. Landon's honey.

Homer Pickens came in at ten o'clock, punctual as ever. He was always at the café at ten and always ordered a sausage biscuit. An eccentric, Homer chose a new hero every day.

"Morning, Homer!" I called from the kitchen. I'd finished my coffee and was preparing vegetables for the coming lunch rush.

"Hi, Amy. How are you this morning?"

"I'm good." I covered the bowl of lettuce I'd been shredding and went to speak with Homer properly. "Mr. Landon brought some honey this morning. We're selling it on consignment in addition to serving it to customers and using it in recipes. Would you like some?"

"No, thanks. I'm not a big fan of honey. I liked it when I was a little boy, but then one of my friends told me honey was bee puke. I never touched the stuff again after that."

"Some friend." I glanced around to make sure none of the other diners had heard his remark. If anyone had, it hadn't seemed to put them off their breakfast. "So who's your hero today?"

"Joseph Joubert, the essayist. Joubert once said, 'When you go in search of honey, you must expect to be stung by bees.' Appropriate for this morning, huh?"

"It sure is." I often wondered if Homer had a photographic memory. He was always at the ready with a quote from one of his heroes, and it often applied to the subject at hand. He'd grown up poor and had dropped out of school in the tenth grade to go to work. I wondered how far he might've gone had he been given the opportunity.

"What do you know about Mr. Landon?" I asked. "We were talking about him this morning, and we realized we don't know much about him except that he's a loner with a mysterious past."

"If being a loner makes a man mysterious, then I must

be an enigma myself." He took a sip of the coffee Jackie put in front of him. "After Mother died, I was completely alone. It had always been just the two of us. Of course, I dated now and then, but I never let myself get involved in a serious relationship."

"Why's that?" That behavior didn't sound like the warm, generous Homer I knew.

"I never wanted to marry and have children. What if I'd turned out to be like *my* father? He just ran out on us. I wouldn't have wanted that for any woman or child."

I was trying to think of something encouraging to say when Homer reminded me that he was awfully set in his ways. I took that as my cue to stop yammering and get him that sausage biscuit.

B y the time I closed the café that afternoon, I had only three jars of Mr. Landon's honey left, besides the one I'd bought for Mom and Aunt Bess. I decided to go by the farm to see if I could get more. The honey had sold better than Mr. Landon and I had anticipated.

Landon's Bee Farm was only about a twenty-minute drive from Winter Garden. It wasn't as hot as it had been—especially for August—so I drove with the windows down instead of using the air-conditioning. It dawned on me that if my yellow Beetle had more black on it, I'd resemble a giant bumblebee as I buzzed down the country road to see the beekeeper.

To get to the farm, I had to turn off the main road and climb a steep, deeply rutted dirt road. That's when I put up the windows and turned on the air. I didn't want a face full of dust.

No wonder Mr. Landon didn't get many visitors—this road was a nightmare. I drove as slowly as I could without losing the momentum to get up the hill, and I just hoped I didn't damage my car in the process.

When I finally parked near Mr. Landon's small brick house, I stooped down to make sure there were no fluids leaking from the undercarriage of the car. Fortunately, there weren't, but I made a mental note to check again—and to check my tires—before I left. I wondered how Mr. Landon's antique pickup truck survived the trek every day, but then I realized it was much higher off the ground than my little Bug.

I smoothed my hair back from my face and stepped onto the porch. I rang the bell, but Mr. Landon didn't answer the door. I went to see if he might be in the backyard.

Mr. Landon was striding toward the house with his veiled bee hat in his hand. He was still about a hundred yards away from me, but I could see that he was angry. I was beginning to regret dropping in unannounced; and if the man hadn't already seen me, I'd have been sorely tempted to leave.

When he was close enough, I called out, "Hi, Mr. Landon. I hope I'm not catching you at a bad time!" That seemed like a stupid thing to say since he was obviously upset, but I hoped that when I told him how well his honey was selling at the café, it might lift his spirits.

"What can I do for you, Ms. Flowers?" He went into a shed still a few yards away from where I was standing.

I eased forward but steered clear of the shed. I didn't want to crowd his space more than I already was. "I just came to let you know that we almost sold out of your honey today. I wondered if you might be able to spare a few more jars before next week."

Mr. Landon emerged from the shed without the veiled hat and wiped the sweat from his brow with a blue bandanna. "I'll need to put it into jars and drop it off tomorrow morning. Will ten more work?"

"Yes, that'll be great. Thank you."

We stood in awkward silence for a moment, and I was getting ready to say good-bye when Mr. Landon spoke.

"I was hoping to have quite a bit more honey by fall, but I won't if Chad Thomas has his way about it."

"What do you mean?"

"I just came from checking the hives," he said. "And you know what I found? Hundreds of dead bees."

I gasped. "That's terrible! And you believe this Mr. Thomas killed them?"

"I know he did. He wantonly sprays his crops whenever he takes a notion without regard for the safety of my bees." He shook his head. "Most of the farmers around here understand our mutual need to protect pollinators. They know I close the bees up at night and keep them there until noon. If I left them inside any later than that, the sun would cook them."

"How awful."

"Well, that's not going to happen, Ms. Flowers, because I take care of my bees. And most of my neighbors spray when the bees are closed inside their hives. But Chad—" He gave a low growl of disgust. "He's a different story. He sprays whenever he feels like it, and today one of my hives suffered for his flagrant disregard."

"Isn't there some sort of law in place to protect the bees? Aren't they an endangered species?"

"Not currently. But you can bet I'll be talking with Chad Thomas about what he's done."

"Maybe you should let the police handle it," I said.

"It's not their problem. It's mine. And I intend to take care of it."

Instead of going directly home, I drove on up to "the big house," where Mom and Aunt Bess live. You see, when my grandfather got out of the coal mining business in Pocahontas and built the house for Nana and himself here in Winter Garden—and Mom, because she was a little girl then—he also built a smaller guesthouse on the property. And that's where I live.

Nana and Pop lived in the big house until Pop died. Afterward, Aunt Bess moved in with Nana. After Nana died, Mom—who'd been living with me in the smaller house all my life—moved in with Aunt Bess. So, yeah, it's kind of a convoluted story, but suffice it to say that Mom and Aunt Bess live in a big house on a hill about three hundred yards from my house. As for the distance? My great-grandmother was the main guest in the guesthouse until Mom married my dad and moved into it. By that time, Great-Grams was in a nursing home. Pop didn't like his mother-in-law very much. Come to think of it, he didn't like my dad much either. And he happened to be an excellent judge of character—Dad left Mom and me when I was four years old.

When I got out of the car, I checked again to make sure I still had good air pressure in my tires and that no fluids were leaking.

Mom stepped out onto the wraparound porch, her short blond hair ruffled by the breeze. "What're you doing?"

"Making sure my car isn't broken. I went over to Landon's Farm after work, and the road leading to Mr. Landon's house is horrible."

"I went there once," Aunt Bess said. "It was about fifteen years ago. I don't remember the road being all that bad then."

Aunt Bess had walked out onto the porch beside Mom while I was looking underneath my car. The woman was eighty-two, a little on the plump side—though I'd never tell *her* that, and addicted to the Internet.

"Did you bring us some honey?" Mom asked.

"I did. I'm selling Landon's Farm honey on consignment now. Today was the first day, and the ten jars he brought are nearly gone. That's why I went to see him—to ask for more." I went up onto the porch, and the three of us sat on white rocking chairs. "Of course, Mr. Landon and his pre–Winter Garden life provided a lot of speculation today among me, the staff, and some of the regulars."

"Well, you didn't need to speculate," said Aunt Bess. "You could've come and asked me."

"I'm asking you now," I said. "Enlighten me about Mr. Landon's past."

Aunt Bess stopped rocking and leaned forward in her chair, delighted to have an audience—even if it *was* only an audience of two . . . or maybe one, since I wasn't entirely sure Mom was paying attention.

"I think he was a detective. Ever since Sherlock Holmes, detectives have been drawn to bees."

Okay, so I seemed to recall that Sherlock Holmes *had*

been a beekeeper, but I doubted that was evidence for Mr. Landon being a detective. Still, I didn't voice my thoughts aloud.

"Even more than that—he's a secret agent." Aunt Bess gave an exaggerated nod. "You know, he came to Winter Garden along about the time that Princess Diana died—God rest her soul. I cried when I added her to my Pinterest board *People I've Outlived*."

"Aunt Bess, are you saying you think Stu Landon had something to do with the death of Princess Diana?"

"I believe he failed to keep her safe. So he's been banished to Winter Garden to serve out his time doing intelligence work here in America . . . like that handsome Colin Firth."

"Colin Firth was only a spy in that movie we watched," I said.

"You believe whatever you'd like, dear. I myself feel just a smidge safer knowing that Colin Firth is on the job." She waved her hand. "But back to Stu Landon. The folks who used to live on that land where he has his farm were Carvers. The original Carvers died off or moved away ages ago, except for that one family that lives to the right of Stu's farm. Then Stu Landon comes along and takes over the land. Tell me that's not strange."

"It's not, Aunt Bess. I imagine the man bought it."

"Again, Amy, you think whatever you want, but I know the Carvers were a tightfisted bunch who'd never let anyone outside of family have their land . . . unless, of course, the British government strong-armed them into selling."

"But—" I began, but I noticed Mom give a slight shake of her head. She was right. Disagreeing with Aunt Bess was like trying to teach trigonometry to a pig—frustrating for you and confusing to the pig. "So, Mom, what do *you* think about Stu Landon?"

"I think his bees produce some awfully good honey, and I'm glad you brought us some." She smiled. "I also think it's great how you support the farmers in our region."

"Thanks. But poor Mr. Landon lost hundreds of his bees today. He said one of the neighboring farmers killed them. In fact, this afternoon he talked more than I've ever heard him. He was certainly riled up over it."

"Now why would anybody want to kill Mr. Landon's bees?" Aunt Bess wondered aloud. "I reckon they could be allergic. But in my experience, a bee won't bother you if you don't bother it."

"Mr. Landon thought the bees were killed by negligent pesticide spraying. I told him I thought he should report the incident to the police, but he said he'd handle the matter himself. I hope he doesn't get into trouble."

Chapter 2

When I got home, my little brown terrier Rory came running to greet me. He didn't particularly like being outside on these hot days, so he stayed inside enjoying the air-conditioning. He limited his backyard time to right after breakfast and again after dinner. And he had a blast chasing fireflies—or lightning bugs—just after dark.

I scooped him up into my arms, and he licked my chin. After cuddling him for a minute, I placed him back onto the floor.

I didn't see Princess Eloise. She was a white Persian cat that belonged to Mom. Unfortunately for both of them, Aunt Bess was allergic to cats and Mom hadn't been able to take the princess with her to the big house. But the two of them still saw each other fairly often.

More than likely, Princess Eloise was perched on a

windowsill napping or glaring out at her subjects. Probably napping.

I slipped off my sneakers and stretched out on the living room sofa. Napping sounded good to me. Apparently, it did to Rory too, because he hopped onto the cushion beside me and yawned.

"You and I should be going through our recipe books for some honey recipes instead of lying here like two sacks of potatoes."

His response was to sigh and roll onto his side.

"Oh, well, it won't hurt us to lie here for ten or fifteen minutes, will it?"

That was pretty much my last conscious thought until Princess Eloise pounced onto my chest and meowed that it was dinnertime. The sudden jolt startled Rory, so he scrambled off the sofa and ran barking into the kitchen.

I got up and followed him. Princess Eloise sashayed along beside me, tail twitching imperiously. I glanced at the clock and saw that almost an hour had passed since Rory and I had elected to take a nap.

I fed both pets and was looking in the cabinets to decide what I wanted for dinner when my phone rang. I'd left the phone in the living room on the coffee table, so I hurried to answer it.

"Hey," Jackie said. "Have you had dinner yet?"

"No, I haven't even decided what to have."

"Would you and Ryan like to join Roger and me for barbecue at that new restaurant in Bristol?"

"I'll check with Ryan and call you right back."

I'd been dating Deputy Ryan Hall since just after the Down South Café opened a little over a month ago. We'd first met when he was investigating the murder of my former employer, Lou Lou Holman. It had been a weird way to get to know someone, but I supposed the end result was the same.

I called Ryan, who'd just finished his shift, and he said he'd love to go. I let Jackie know and then went into the bedroom to figure out what to wear.

M y heart always did a little flip when I saw Ryan. He was tall, athletically built, and he had dark hair and eyes. And he had a deep, sonorous voice that kinda reminded me of Sam Elliott's. This evening he wore khaki pants and a navy polo.

"You look gorgeous," he told me as I met him on the porch.

I blushed as I thanked him, glad I'd chosen a floral-print sundress and had taken extra time with my hair and makeup. He looked gorgeous, too, but I didn't say so. I figured I shouldn't let him get too sure of himself, right?

He opened the passenger side door of his red convertible, and I slid onto the seat. I was glad the top was up tonight. I enjoyed having it down on occasion but not when I cared about how my hair would look.

After Ryan got into the car and we headed for Bristol, I asked him about Stu Landon. "You didn't get any calls to go out to Landon's Farm late this afternoon, did you?"

"No, why?"

I told him about my visit to the farm and how upset Mr. Landon was about his dead bees. "He seemed certain that a neighboring farmer's pesticide spraying was to blame. I told him he should call the police."

"Even if he had, there's nothing we could do, sweetheart. The farmer has a right to spray his crops."

"That's basically what Mr. Landon said. But then he told me he'd take care of the matter himself, and I was afraid he was going to confront the farmer," I said. "I was hoping Mr. Landon hadn't gone off half-cocked and done something to get himself in trouble."

"Well, if he did, I didn't hear about it."

Jackie waved to us when we entered the restaurant. She and Roger were an adorable couple. They were roughly the same height—around five foot nine—but Roger was stocky and muscular whereas Jackie was willowy. She had red hair and blue eyes, and Roger had dark blond hair and brown eyes. The two had been friends all their lives, and they'd finally started dating while Roger was renovating the café. In my opinion, it was high time. The couple had been flirting with each other for years but neither had wanted to spoil their friendship. I was glad they'd given their relationship a chance to grow. It was obvious how happy they were together.

Ryan and I weaved our way through the people and tables to get to Jackie and Roger's table. He pulled out my chair, and we sat down.

"Thanks so much for inviting us to join you," I told Jackie. "At the very moment you called, I was going through the cabinets wondering what I was going to have for dinner."

"Well, we hadn't met up for a meal in a while, and I thought we were due." She grinned. "Plus, having you here will keep Roger and me from arguing."

"No, it won't." Roger winked. "So what's new with you, Flowerpot?"

He'd given me the nickname when we were kids. He was the only person who'd ever called me that, thank goodness, but I didn't mind it coming from Roger.

Before answering, I glanced from one to the other of them. *Had* they been arguing? Or was Jackie only kidding? It was none of my business, of course, but Jackie was my best friend as well as my cousin—and I loved Roger too. I didn't want there to be any animosity between them.

Jackie read my expression. "We're fine, other than the fact that Roger is as hardheaded as a mule."

"You hadn't figured that out before now?" I asked.

"Well, yes, I had. But I still thought there was a chance he'd wear the sunscreen bracelet I bought him to remind him to reapply after he'd been in the sun for a while."

"I don't need to be reminded." He turned to Ryan. "You know how much my crew would make fun of me if I wore a stupid bracelet that went from white to purple when I'd been out in the sun for too long?"

"Oh, yeah." Ryan chuckled. "The only thing worse would be to have your mommy show up with the sunscreen and your superhero lunchbox."

"So caring about your health is childish?" Jackie asked. "Good to know."

"It's not the caring about my health that's childish. It's letting everyone else know I do that would cause the backlash." He gave Ryan a fist-bump. "Now back to my question. What's new, Flowerpot?"

"Well, we're selling honey at the café now. I imagine Jackie told you about that."

"She did. And I hear there was a lot of speculation this morning about where poor old Stu Landon had come from."

I smiled. "There might've been some of that."

Roger rolled his eyes.

"What?" I asked.

"Stu is a good guy. I did some cabinet work for him a year or two ago. Can't the poor man simply keep to himself and live on his farm in peace?"

"Apparently not." I relayed the tale of the dead bees and the farmer's thoughtless pesticide spraying habits believed to be the cause of killing the bees.

"Who was the farmer?" Roger asked. "Did Stu say?"

"Chad Thomas. Do you know him?"

Roger nodded. "I know *of* him, at least. I did some work for Chad's younger brother Bob a while back, and I found out that both brothers are hotheads. But Chad spent time in juvenile hall for assault and battery several years ago. From what I hear, he was lucky he was sixteen and not tried as an adult. I hope Stu has more sense than to confront the man."

"I'll make sure no calls came in when I go into work tomorrow morning," said Ryan. "And I'll look up Chad Thomas's record too. It never hurts to be fully aware of a situation . . . or even a potential situation."

The next morning, I was in the café making coffee when a distinguished-looking older gentleman came in. I was the only one there at the time, and normally I'd have locked the doors behind me upon arrival. But I'd been expecting Jackie to be there any minute, so I hadn't bothered with the lock.

"Good morning," I said to the man. "Welcome to the Down South Café. We're not officially open yet, but I can offer you some coffee as soon as it's ready."

"That'd be nice. Thank you." He wandered over to the display case and the shelves on the wall behind it. "Ah, you sell Landon's Farm honey."

"Yes, sir, we do. Would you like a jar?"

"Yeah, I think I might get a jar when I pay my bill. You must know the Landons then."

"I know Mr. Landon. He's the beekeeper."

"What's his first name?"

"Stu." I got out a cup as coffeepot number one finished filling. "Do you know Mr. Landon?"

"I think I might," he said. "I believe we used to work together. Could you give me directions to his farm?"

I was debating about whether or not to give the stranger directions to Landon's Farm when Jackie hurried breathlessly through the door.

"Sorry I'm late. What a morning! It was like I was the poster child for Murphy's Law or something." She noticed our customer. "Oh, hi. I'm Jackie. Has Amy already taken your order?"

"No, not yet."

"Actually, we were talking about Mr. Landon," I said. "This gentleman thinks they used to work together."

"Really?" Jackie stepped around the counter and deposited her purse on the shelf beneath the register. "It must've been a long time ago. I've never known Mr. Landon to work anywhere other than at his farm. Where do you think you worked with him?"

"Callicorp International." He extended his hand. "Walter Jackson."

"Jackie Fonseca." She shook his hand.

"And I'm Amy Flowers." I, too, shook Mr. Jackson's hand. "That coffee is ready. What would you like for breakfast?"

Mr. Jackson ordered ham and eggs.

I filled the cup with coffee and placed it on the counter in front of him, and he sat on one of the stools. Then I went into the kitchen to prepare his breakfast. I could still hear snatches of his conversation with Jackie.

"So you worked with Mr. Landon at Callicorp in—where—California?" she asked.

"I'm not even sure this Mr. Landon is the man I knew, but Callicorp is located in Oklahoma . . . although the name does lend itself to California more than Oklahoma, doesn't it?"

I heard his spoon clinking against the sides of his cup. I tried not to get distracted, but I was curious as to what this man knew about Stu Landon.

The door opened, and Jackie greeted Dilly. Dilly mentioned there being a slight chill in the air this morning to let us know that fall was on its way. Then she spoke to Mr. Jackson as she settled onto her favorite seat.

"I'm not ready for fall," Jackie told Dilly.

"You don't like fall?" she asked.

"Fall is okay. It's winter that I'm not crazy about."

"It's been so hot this summer that I'm ready for a bout of cooler weather. How about you, mister?"

"I appreciate any kind of weather. What if we were cooped up all the time and couldn't enjoy being outside? I imagine that would be a dreadful existence."

"I reckon it would," Dilly said. "I never looked at it like that. I don't recollect seeing you in here before."

"This is my first visit to the Down South Café."

"Are you from around here?"

"I'm originally from Oklahoma."

By that time, I'd plated Mr. Jackson's meal and took it to him. "Here you are. Is there anything else I can get you?"

He said there wasn't, so I moved down the counter to say good morning to Dilly.

"Hey, Amy." She jerked her head in the direction of Mr. Jackson. "Did you know this man came plumb from Oklahoma for a bite of breakfast?"

I smiled at her and then at Mr. Jackson. "I do now."

"So what do you reckon he's doing here?"

My eyes met Jackie's and she quickly hid a grin as she resumed stocking the napkin dispensers. Leave it to Dilly to talk about someone as if he wasn't sitting less than two feet away and couldn't hear everything she said.

"He's here for breakfast," I said. "You just said so yourself."

"I meant here in Winter Garden," she said.

"I'm in town searching for an old friend," said Mr. Jackson. "I think he might be Stu Landon, the beekeeper. I hoped to visit him yesterday, but he didn't answer when I phoned. I plan to try again this morning."

"It is a good idea to call first," Dilly told him. "He has hives not only at his farm outside Winter Garden but at different locations around the county."

Hmm, I hadn't known that.

"Thanks." Mr. Jackson went back to eating his breakfast.

Dilly looked at me. "I'm in the mood for pancakes this morning, Amy."

"Coming right up."

Mr. Jackson hadn't asked for directions to the farm again, and I was glad. If this man *was* Mr. Landon's old friend, he could call and Mr. Landon could give him directions to the farm himself. I didn't want to be the person responsible for sending someone who might be a stranger to Mr. Landon out to his farm. As private as Mr. Landon was, I didn't think he would appreciate that.

B etween the breakfast and lunch rush, I made sushi for the patrons to sample. That went over faster than a Southern belle with a too-tight corset onto a fainting couch. No one wanted to try a free mini sushi roll. They all thought I was offering them raw fish. I tried to explain that there were different types of sushi besides *nigiri*—the raw kind—and that the sushi I'd made for them to sample contained canned—not raw—tuna. Still, no dice. I couldn't even get Ryan to try a sushi roll when he came in for lunch.

"I . . . uh . . . I'm not a big fan of tuna," he said.

"Just try one bite."

"I'd really rather not." He picked up a menu. Even though he came here for lunch nearly every day, he actually picked up a menu. I knew it was to place a small, laminated wall between us—or, at least, between him and my mini sushi rolls.

Although I typically served the well-loved comfort foods I knew my patrons enjoyed, I often liked to try to get them to sample something a little healthier or more exotic. I'd test out a new recipe one day, and if the customers enjoyed it, I'd make it the next day's special.

"I guess I'll serve chicken salad for the special tomorrow," I said.

"Great. I love your chicken salad." Then he put aside the menu and ordered a bacon burger with a salad instead of fries. He smiled. "I thought I'd eat healthy today."

I turned to go into the kitchen to prepare his food, but he grabbed my hand.

"I almost forgot to tell you," he said. "I scored tickets to the Barter Theater for this evening. Would you like to go?"

"Sure. I love the Barter."

"I know it's last minute, but another deputy had the tickets. Something came up with him this morning, and he offered the tickets to me."

"I'm glad. Not that he can't go, but that he offered you the tickets. What's playing?"

He shrugged. "I have no idea."

"Oh, that's one of my favorites." I laughed and went into the kitchen. Before putting Ryan's burger on the grill, I put the container of mini sushi rolls into the refrigerator. They were a lost cause here if not even Ryan would sample them. Maybe Mom and Aunt Bess would like them. They were more intrepid than most and were willing to try most things I took to them.

The Barter Theater was located in Abingdon and had been in business since the 1920s. It was founded during the Great Depression in order to allow starving actors to be fed by local farmers, who bartered their crops and livestock for admission to the shows. Some of the illustrious Barter alumni included Gregory Peck, Ernest

Borgnine, Patricia Neal, Kevin Spacey, and Frances Fisher. That evening, the production was *Big Fish*, the story of a man reconnecting with his dying father who the son thinks is a liar. Ryan and I had a wonderful time.

We were on our way back home when we saw an old pickup truck speeding in the direction of Landon's Farm. In fact, it appeared to *be* Mr. Landon's truck, but neither Ryan nor I could see well enough in the dark to determine if it was.

Ryan drove until there was a wide enough space on the shoulder of the road to pull over. Then he took out his cell phone and called the police station.

"Hi, it's Ryan. I'm out on Route 11 just outside of Winter Garden. What appeared to be an antique Chevy truck just passed me going in the opposite direction. The vehicle is speeding, and I'd like for you to alert the officer on call—maybe contact the county dispatch as well."

He ended the call and placed the phone back in the car's center console.

"I'd hate for Mr. Landon to get a speeding ticket," I said.

"We're not sure that *was* Mr. Landon . . . or even if that was his truck. If it was, whoever was driving it took the expression *drive it like you stole it* to heart and deserves a ticket."

"I hadn't thought of that—that it could be his truck but not him driving. Maybe someone *did* steal Mr. Landon's truck. How awful."

Ryan picked up my hand and kissed it. "We don't know anything for sure right now. Given what we know about Mr. Landon, I doubt that was him or his truck."

"But we don't know for sure. There could be something

wrong. Let's turn around and drive out to Mr. Landon's place to see if we can help."

"We can't. I'm off duty, and we've already sent help his way. If anything's wrong, the police will get Mr. Landon the help he needs."

"I hope so," I said. "I've got a really bad feeling about this. I can't imagine Mr. Landon ever speeding down the road like that."

"Would it make you feel better to call the man?"

"No. He might think I was crazy to call him at this time of night to ask him if he was speeding down the road. And like you said, it probably wasn't him . . . or his truck."

Chapter 3

When I arrived at the café the next morning, I was surprised to see Stu Landon's truck haphazardly parked at the far right corner of the lot. I took my usual spot in the parking space farthest away from the front door to the left of the building. Gathering my keys and purse and stepping out of the car, I could see Mr. Landon sitting in the driver's seat of his truck. I gave him a smile and a wave, wishing he'd have let me know he'd planned on being here this early so I wouldn't have kept him waiting.

He didn't wave back, and I wondered if he was angry. Or maybe he hadn't seen me. Then again, he could simply be preoccupied.

I unlocked the door, put my purse under the counter, and waited for Mr. Landon to bring in the honey I'd requested yesterday. When he hadn't come inside after a couple of minutes, I went to check on him. Maybe he really hadn't seen me arrive . . . or noticed my car in the parking lot. Unlikely, but I guess it was possible.

I walked over to Mr. Landon's truck. No wonder he hadn't seen me. His straw hat had slid down over his eyes. Had he been waiting on me for so long he'd fallen asleep?

I rapped my knuckles lightly on the window. "Mr. Landon?"

When he didn't respond, I knocked a little harder. Still, no response. I was getting concerned. What if Mr. Landon had suffered a stroke or something?

I heard a car pull into the lot. I glanced over my shoulder and was glad to see Luis parking beside my Beetle. Luis was our busboy and dishwasher. He could help me get Mr. Landon out of the truck and inside the café if need be.

After knocking on the window again and still getting no response from Mr. Landon, I carefully opened the door of the truck. Mr. Landon began sliding out onto the pavement. Was that *blood* on his shirt?

"Luis! Can you help me?"

I heard Luis's feet pounding the pavement as he ran to us. "What's going on?" He gasped. "Amy, he's bleeding."

"I see that. And right now, he's falling out of the truck. Could you help me get him?"

"I don't think we should. Let's put him back inside the truck and call for help." He stepped between the door and Mr. Landon and gently pushed the man toward the passenger side of the truck.

Mr. Landon fell over and I could see that his throat had been cut. I was barely aware that I was screaming until I felt Luis's hands on my shoulders.

"I don't think there's anything we can do for him," he said. "Let's get you inside."

"No. No, we have to stay with him. We have to wait here until help comes."

I heard Luis talking, but it wasn't to me. He'd called 9-1-1.

"Thank you," I said as he returned his phone to his pocket.

"You shouldn't be looking at this." He gently turned me away from Mr. Landon's truck. "The man is dead."

We walked a few feet away from the truck.

"You're shaking," he said. "You need to sit down."

He needed to sit as badly as I did. Still, I wasn't about to leave Mr. Landon until after the paramedics arrived.

"I'm fine," I told him, knowing fully well that neither of us was fine.

I was relieved when I heard sirens approaching. Poor Mr. Landon was almost out of my incapable care.

Ryan and Sheriff Billings were the first to arrive. The sheriff quickly confirmed that Mr. Landon was dead and said that he appeared to have been in that condition for the past several hours.

"I'll get Ivy over here," he said to Ryan. "You secure the scene."

As the sheriff walked away to call his crime scene technician, Ryan hugged me. "Are you all right?"

I nodded and then shook my head. "I will be. I'll be okay."

"Do you need me to take you home? I'm sure—"

"I can't go home. I have to stay here."

"Amy, you're too upset to work."

"I need to. It'll help me to keep busy. Besides, someone might've seen something that will give us some insight as to what happened to Mr. Landon."

He sighed. "I'll check with Sheriff Billings and see if he needs for the café to be closed. But I still don't think you should be here."

"Today is Thursday. For some reason, it's our slowest day of the week. I think I'll be all right."

As Ryan went to speak with the sheriff, Luis said, "Jackie, Shelly, and I can handle the café if you need to go on home."

"No, Luis. But you can go if you'd like. You experienced the same thing I did." I realized I was being insensitive. "Maybe we *should* close the café today."

He shook his head. "You were right in what you said before—we might learn something today that will help the police figure out who did this."

Before Ryan returned, Jackie arrived. She quickly parked her car, got out, and ran to Luis and me.

"Are you guys all right?" She threw her arms around me. "When I saw the commotion, it scared me half to death. What happened?"

Luis explained the situation so I didn't have to. By the time he'd finished and had also gotten a hug from Jackie, Ryan had returned.

"Sheriff Billings says the café can remain open today. However, we'll need to cordon off a large part of the parking lot surrounding Stu Landon's truck."

"Of course," I said.

He nodded at Jackie and told her good morning.

"If it's all right with you and the sheriff, I'll go on inside and get some coffee made," she said. "I feel we could all use a cup."

"Good idea. Thanks." Ryan gently lifted my chin.

"You don't need to pretend you're made of steel, you know." He glanced at Luis. "And neither do you. You should both go home and get some rest."

"I'd rather be here where I can hopefully do something productive," I said.

"Me too," said Luis.

"Okay." Ryan squeezed my trembling hands. "Just no knife wielding for a while. At least, not until your hands stop shaking. Promise?"

"I promise."

By the time Homer arrived at ten o'clock, the paramedics had removed Mr. Landon's body. Ivy Donaldson was still examining every square inch of the truck, while the sheriff, Ryan, and two other officers were combing the parking lot and surrounding area.

Homer sat at the counter. "It appears something terrible happened out there."

I nodded. "It's Mr. Landon—he's dead."

"That's awful. Was it an accident?"

"I don't think so." I spoke quietly, even though everyone in the café had been whispering about the incident all morning. "So, tell me, who's your hero today?"

"The author Nathaniel Hawthorne. One of my favorites of his quotes is, 'Time flies over us but leaves its shadow behind.'"

I tried to smile. "Wonder what Mr. Hawthorne might have to say to us this morning?"

Homer considered my question for a few seconds. "I believe I know exactly what he'd say. 'We sometimes congratulate ourselves at the moment of waking from a troubled dream; it may be so the moment after death.' Is that a beautiful thought?"

"It is, Homer. Thank you for sharing it with me." I was able to muster up a smile after that. "I'll have your sausage biscuit right out."

"Thanks."

As I delivered Homer's biscuit and Jackie refilled his coffee cup, a young woman came into the café. She didn't appear to be much older than Jackie or me, but I didn't recognize her as someone we'd gone to school with.

"Hi, and welcome to the Down South Café. I'm Amy. Would—"

"What's going on outside?" The woman's wide brown eyes darted from me to Jackie to the windows and back. "Why are the police here?"

I didn't want to scare this woman any more than she already was. "We found a man unconscious in our parking lot this morning."

"Unconscious? Had he been here all night?"

I told her I didn't know.

"Who was he? Tell me his name."

"I'd rather you ask the police your questions." I didn't know this woman, and I had no idea if she'd merely stopped here out of curiosity or whether there was some other reason she was demanding information.

Before the woman could respond, Dilly burst into the café.

"Morning, everybody." She nodded to me, Jackie, and Homer. "I tossed and turned all night last night, so I slept in this morning. And it looks like I missed something exciting too! Why are the police going over Stu Landon's truck?"

The woman whirled to face Dilly. "Did you say Stu Landon?"

Dilly nodded. "He's the beekeeper, you know. So what's going on?"

"I *knew* that was Daddy's truck!" She brushed past Dilly and ran out to the parking lot.

"Did she say *Daddy*?" Dilly asked, before she quickly followed the woman outside.

That same question had just gone through my head, and I was pretty certain that *was* what the woman had said.

"'No man for any considerable period can wear one face to himself and another to the multitude, without finally getting bewildered as to which may be true,'" Homer quoted.

"Sure enough," Jackie said with a nod.

I was glad *she'd* understood what Homer was talking about. I guessed he meant that Stu Landon had obviously been hiding something—a daughter—but that only meant to me that he was private, not that he'd necessarily been *hiding* her.

Sheriff Billings brought the young woman back into the café. "Amy, could you please get some coffee for Ms. Carver and me?"

"Yes, sir."

"I'd like a cup too," Dilly said. She'd been part of the procession back into the café and now took a seat one table over from Sheriff Billings and Ms. Carver.

"Ms. Boyd, would you please move to the counter or to a table a little farther away?" the sheriff asked. "I need to speak with Ms. Carver privately."

"Well! If you're going to be that way about it, I don't want to sit near you anyway." The tiny woman got up and stuck her nose in the air. "As if I don't have anything better to do than to eavesdrop on people." She plopped down at the counter where she usually sat.

I served her coffee and patted her hand reassuringly before visiting the sheriff's table. "Is there anything else I can get you?"

"We're fine for now, Amy," said Sheriff Billings.

"Thank you," Ms. Carver added.

"It's so late in the morning, I can't decide whether I want breakfast or lunch," Dilly said. "I think I'll combine the two. Would you please get me a cheeseburger and a side of hash browns instead of fries?"

"Coming right up."

"Oh, and don't forget to make me a biscuit for the raccoon!"

As I went into the kitchen, Jackie strolled over to Dilly to chat for a minute. She undoubtedly wanted to make her feel better after the affront by the sheriff.

"Not now," Dilly hissed, shooing Jackie away.

Jackie shrugged and went to check on Homer.

It wasn't until after the sheriff and Ms. Carver left that Dilly let us in on why she hadn't wanted to talk with Jackie—she'd turned her hearing aids up so she could eavesdrop on Sheriff Billings and Ms. Carver.

"Dilly!"

"Hush," she scolded me. "At least, lower your voice until I get my hearing aids turned back down." She managed to lower the volume on the devices. "Now do y'all want to know what was said or not?"

At that time, Dilly was the only customer left in the café. Luis was in the back, and Shelly—our other regular waitress for the day—hadn't come in yet. Jackie and I shared a look.

"I want to know," Jackie said at last.

I glanced outside to make sure no one was coming in, and then I gave Dilly a slight nod.

"Now I didn't catch all of what they were saying, but that girl who said Stu Landon was her daddy? Her name is Madelyn, and she said Stu's name was Stuart Landon Carver before he changed it." She raised her cup. "I told y'all the other day that Stu Landon was a mysterious man. This proves it." She sipped her coffee.

"So why'd he change his name?" Jackie asked.

"I'm getting to that, Miss Impatient. He blew the whistle on the company he used to work for, and that's why he was hiding out here."

"Who'd he work for?" I asked, wondering if it was Callicorp, the company Mr. Jackson had mentioned.

"I don't know. I couldn't hear that part," she said. "I also didn't hear why the family didn't come here to live with Stu, if the sheriff even asked her that. But she did say that a man came to their house in Cookeville, Tennessee day before yesterday looking for her daddy. She came here to warn Stu."

"Why didn't she just call him?" Jackie asked.

Dilly shrugged.

"Do you think the man looking for Mr. Landon in Cookeville could've been the same man who was in here looking for him yesterday morning?" I got the coffeepot and topped off Dilly's cup.

"I don't know. That's when Sheriff Billings said he thought they should continue their conversation at the police station, where he was certain they wouldn't be overheard." She sighed. "I think he was on to me."

"No way," Jackie said. "You're too good of a spy for that. I think he was just being extra careful."

I thought Jackie was laying it on just a little too thick, but I merely smiled and nodded.

D illy had just left and the lunch rush was starting when Ryan came inside the café.

"How's it going out there?" I asked.

"It's coming along all right—slowly but surely. We're getting awfully hungry, though, especially given the tantalizing smells coming from your kitchen."

"Can't you take a break for lunch?"

"We can if only a couple of us eat at one time," he said. "I was hoping you could maybe set us up some sort of small buffet. The department will cover all your expenses, of course."

"I can handle that. Will burgers, hot dogs, chicken salad croissants—they're today's lunch special—cole slaw, potato salad, and an assortment of cookies do the trick?"

"That'll more than do the trick. It'll make my coworkers love you. Most of them have bologna or PB and J for lunch every day." He gave me a quick kiss.

"I'll have Jackie come and get you when the buffet is ready. But before you go back outside, I have something I need to tell you. Dilly overheard Ms. Carver tell Sheriff Billings that a man came to her home day before yesterday looking for Mr. Landon." A patron came in, and I greeted him as Jackie went to get him settled and to take his order.

"There was an older gentleman here asking about Mr. Landon yesterday morning," I continued, lowering my voice and leaning closer to Ryan. "This man's name was Walter Jackson, and he said he thought he'd worked with Mr. Landon at a place called Callicorp in Oklahoma. I have no idea whether or not it was the same man or if our visitor ever found Mr. Landon, but I think it bears looking into."

"Sure, it does. I'll give Sheriff Billings a call and let him know." He grinned. "I realize now why the sheriff and Ms. Carver had to go to the station. It was either leave or invite Dilly to pull up a chair."

"Pretty much."

As Ryan went back outside, Shelly came in, and I asked her to give me a hand in the kitchen. Even though the lunch rush was beginning, I felt sure Jackie could handle the orders and delivery while Shelly and I got the buffet set up for the officers.

Chapter 4

At just before three o'clock that afternoon, I was cleaning the grill. There were no diners in the café, and it was almost closing time.

Jackie came into the kitchen and leaned against the door frame. "All the tables have been cleaned, and Shelly is sweeping the floors. She said she'll mop while she's at it."

"Thanks," I said. "Will you help me wipe down the windows after I'm finished with the grill?"

"Sure. I'll go ahead and get started." She paused. "Do you think that sweet old guy who was in here the other day could be the one who killed Stuart Landon?"

"Anything is possible." I stood back to survey my work. The grill was gleaming. "After we finish up here, do you want to go to my house and see what we can dig up on Walter Jackson and Callicorp?"

"Yeah, let's do." She shivered. "It gives me the creeps

to think that someone who came in here looking for Mr. Landon could be responsible for . . . for what happened to him."

I knew she and I both were seeing Mr. Landon's body in our minds. To try to get us both thinking about something else, I opened the canister of window cleaning wipes and handed her one. "I guess we'd better get at it."

T he officers were still working as Jackie and I left the café, and I invited Ryan to come over for dinner. He accepted, saying he'd go home and shower and change when he was through at the café and that he should be there around six o'clock.

After we'd arrived at my house, I asked Jackie if she and Roger would like to join Ryan and me for dinner.

"No, thanks. You two could use some time to yourselves after the day you've had. And I think Roger and I could too."

"All right. Would you care for something to drink?"

She shook her head. "Not right now. Let's get down to business. After Mr. Jackson came looking for Mr. Landon yesterday and then given what Dilly overheard about Stu being a whistle-blower, I want to find out what Callicorp is all about."

I went into the fancy room and got my laptop. The fancy room is pretty much a den or sitting room. Before she moved out, it was Mom's room. Roger had helped me renovate it—he added floor-to-ceiling bookshelves and helped me find a rolltop desk—and I exchanged the bed for a white fainting couch and a peacock blue chair with matching ottoman. It was girlie and wonderful, and I loved it.

When I got back to the living room, Rory was happily perched on Jackie's lap. I sat down beside them on the sofa, turned on the computer, and searched for *Callicorp*.

Callicorp had been one of the largest pest control product manufacturers in the south central United States, but the company had closed its doors in early 1996. The article we'd pulled up stated that the corporation had not been able to weather the fallout from the scandal of 1994.

Jackie and I exchanged glances, and I typed *Callicorp Scandal of 1994* into the search engine. The first article in the list was from an Oklahoma newspaper. I opened the article and read that Stuart Carver, an entomologist for Callicorp, came forward and announced that Callicorp was using a chemical deemed harmful to humans—in particular, unborn children—and devastating to honeybee populations. The chemical had replaced one that had been in use by the company for the past fifty years. The original chemical had been nearly as effective as its replacement but caused no known damage to humans or pollinators. The replacement chemical was said to have been chosen for its lower price and increased effectiveness, and the company argued that there was no solid proof that the chemical was harmful to humans.

Upon further investigation, it was discovered that Callicorp vice president Walter Jackson had received research indicating that the chemical could, in fact, be detrimental to unborn babies but that he had buried the research because he was receiving kickbacks from the chemical's parent company. It was too advantageous monetarily to both Jackson and the chemical company to have Callicorp use their product, so both parties turned a blind eye to potential hazards.

When the two-year investigation was concluded, Callicorp was shut down and Walter Jackson was sentenced to eighteen years in a federal penitentiary.

I looked at Jackie. "An eighteen-year prison sentence? That might be enough to make a man come looking for revenge."

"Yeah, especially when Mr. Jackson lost not only his freedom, but his livelihood, company, and who knows what else?"

"But he seemed so *nice*," I said. "Maybe this isn't the same Walter Jackson. He didn't look like a hardened criminal to me. Besides, I doubt they'd have made him serve his entire sentence."

"Look him up, and see what else we can find out about him."

I searched for *Walter Jackson, Callicorp, Oklahoma*. What I found wasn't pretty. The Walter Jackson in the newspaper photographs could certainly be the man who'd strolled into the Down South Café the day before yesterday. The eyes were the same, the facial features were similar, just younger . . . and not as weathered.

From all accounts, Mr. Jackson wasn't sorry he'd endangered the people—and bees—of the south central United States. He was just sorry he'd gotten caught. It had been his contention that the chemical "wasn't all that bad" and "how many pregnant women would be inhaling the stuff anyway?"

"This certainly doesn't sound like the Walter Jackson we met," Jackie said as she read the article.

"No, it doesn't. Maybe it's not him."

"Oh, I'm pretty sure it's him."

"But the man we met seemed so warm and friendly," I said.

"He was probably warm and friendly to his coworkers

too." Jackie blew out a breath. "Well, except for Stuart Landon . . . or Carver. And no one announces himself to be a psychopathic killer out for revenge. Right?"

"I don't know enough psychopathic killers bent on revenge to poll them. Do you really think Mr. Jackson would hold a grudge for almost twenty years, come all the way here to Winter Garden, Virginia, and kill Stuart Landon Carver?"

She shrugged. "I guess stranger things have happened."

"And what about Stu's daughter? Wonder why she was living in Cookeville, Tennessee—nearly four hours away from her dad?"

"Maybe she was attending school there," Jackie said. "Are there any colleges in Cookeville?"

"You're missing my point. Madelyn was living four hours away from her father. It would appear that no one in Winter Garden even knew Stuart Landon Carver had a daughter." I keyed *Madelyn Carver* into the search engine, but there were too many results to sort through. "Do you think Madelyn moved here from Oklahoma to be closer to her dad?"

"I have no idea, but I'm sure you're bound and determined to find out." She waggled her fingers. "Like a good stew, the plot thickens."

I was grilling boneless, skinless chicken breasts when Mom came to the back door. I let her in, and she enveloped me in a hug.

"Jackie told Aunt Bess and me what happened. Are you all right?"

"I'm fine." I wasn't really, but I didn't want Mom to worry.

"Why didn't you call me? Why did you stay there and work? You should've closed the café and come home. The place would have been all right for one day. Everyone would've understood."

I tried to backtrack and answer her questions. "I didn't call you because I didn't really think about it. I believe I must've been in shock at first, and then people were coming in and we were working. It was a hectic day. As for why we kept the café open, we thought someone might've seen something and that they'd stop in and talk with us about it. But that wasn't the case. Besides, the officers needed food and drinks. They were there all day."

"I know," she said. "I just worry about you." She hugged me again. "What a terrible thing to have seen."

I gently extricated myself from her arms. "I need to turn the chicken."

"Jackie said you were making dinner for Ryan. What're you having?"

"Chicken Alfredo."

"That sounds good."

I didn't really want to—but I felt obligated—to invite her and Aunt Bess. "We'll have plenty."

"Oh, no. That's fine. I was already planning on heating up a lasagna. But thank you."

After I turned the chicken breasts, I took out a pot and filled it with water.

"Are you sure you're all right?" Mom asked.

"I guess so." I sighed. "Did Jackie tell you about Madelyn Carver?"

"Stu's daughter? Yes, she told us." She barked out a laugh. "Of course, Aunt Bess swore up and down that she knew all along that Stu Landon had a secret family."

"I feel terrible for that girl. I really need to talk with her. I mean, I suppose she's Mr. Landon's—or Carver's—heir, and I should give her the remaining honey and the proceeds from the honey I sold."

"Hmph. That sounds like you're looking for an excuse to be nosy."

I put the pot on the stove, turned on the burner, and looked at Mom. "It's a legitimate concern! I don't want to have Mr. Landon Carver's money and honey at the café when it should go to his estate."

"Of course, dear. I understand."

"Now you're patronizing me."

"I'm not," she said with a smile. "I'd like to talk with her too. Just . . . be sensitive."

"Aren't I always?"

"I'd better get back before Aunt Bess tries to bake the lasagna herself."

"Wait," I said. "You don't think I'm sensitive?"

"You are under normal circumstances. But I think that you sometimes lose sight of the gravity of a situation."

"Mom, the girl's dad was murdered. I get that."

"I realize that, but I also know that you have a million questions about Stu Landon, where he came from, where she's been all these years, why they didn't live together, what happened to her mother . . ."

"All right, all right. I probably won't even talk with her. I'll probably get her dad's property to her through the police or something."

She put her hand on my shoulder. "Please don't be miffed at me. I mean well."

"I know. I'm just tired. It's been a rough day."

* * *

I was still feeling sorry for Madelyn Carver but less sorry for myself when Ryan arrived. I'd showered and changed into a linen skirt and a knit short-sleeved shirt. My hair was still damp, but I'd pulled it back in a barrette at the nape of my neck.

Ryan's hair was still damp from the shower too. He looked—and smelled—yummy. He held me for a long moment after he walked through the door, and I clung to him. He felt so strong, so safe, so comforting.

"I'm glad you're here," I whispered.

"Me too." He pulled back and cupped my face in his hands. "I know that seeing Mr. Landon—Carver—like that this morning was probably the worst sight you've ever seen."

"It was. I'm sorry Luis had to see him that way, but it was nice to have him there to help me."

"I'm sure. Have you talked with him? How's he holding up?"

"Like the rest of us, he handled the situation better when he was working. I haven't called him since I've been home, but I will if you think I should."

"Does he have family? A roommate?"

"Yes, he still lives at home with his parents and his sister."

Ryan nodded. "He should be all right then. I just wanted to make sure he had a support system in place."

I gave him a peck on the lips. "You're awfully sweet, you know that?"

"I'm glad you think so."

"Are you hungry?"

"Famished. I didn't think I would be after the lunch I ate—thank you for that, by the way. Everybody appreciated it."

"We were glad to do it." I took his hand and led him into the kitchen.

"Smells great. What are we having?"

"Chicken Alfredo. I hope you like it."

"Love it," he said.

I walked to the refrigerator and took out a pitcher of iced tea. "Is this okay, or would you prefer something else?"

"Suits me fine, thanks."

After I'd filled our glasses and our plates and we'd sat down to eat, I broached the subject of Madelyn Carver.

"I owe Mr.—well, *Stu*—some money, and I'll need to return the honey he left at the Down South Café," I said, deciding it was easier to call the beekeeper Stu rather than Mr. Landon, or Mr. Carver, or Mr. Landon Carver. "Could you see that his daughter gets that?"

"Of course, if you want me to."

"Has she gone back to Cookeville already?"

He shook his head. "No, she's spending at least tonight in Abingdon, and she'll probably stay for another day or two. She said she was going to call her brother and have him come up to join her."

"Her brother? How old is he?"

"She didn't say."

"And does he live in Cookeville too, or is he out in Oklahoma?" I asked.

He raised a brow. "You've been doing homework."

"Kind of. Jackie and I were really curious about Wal-

ter Jackson—the man who came into the café looking for
Stu—and his company, Callicorp, so we looked them up
on the Internet. We learned that Stu was a whistle-blower
in that company and that the resulting investigation led
to the downfall of the company and to the arrest of Mr.
Jackson."

"And you call that *kind of* doing homework? What
would you call actual homework?"

"Hunting down Walter Jackson, of course." At Ryan's
appalled expression, I laughed. "I'm just kidding. That's
your job." My smile faded. "I just find it so hard to believe
that this seemingly sweet old man came here and murdered Stu Landon Carver."

"Well, we don't know that he did. At this point, he's
simply a person of interest."

"Have you found him?"

Ryan inclined his head. "You know I can't discuss an
ongoing investigation with you. However, if Mr. Jackson
should happen to come into the café again, please call
me immediately and don't approach him on your own."

So, no, the police had not yet located Walter Jackson.

"Why didn't Madelyn Carver stay at her father's
house?" I asked. "Wouldn't it make more sense for her to
stay there than at a hotel twenty minutes away from Winter Garden?"

"It might once the house is reopened . . . if she feels
safe enough to stay there, that is. Officers are still going
over it to see if they can find anything that will help lead
to—and ultimately convict—Mr. Landon's killer. Excuse me, Mr. *Carver's* killer. I can't get used to calling
him that."

"Neither can I. He'll always be Stu Landon to me." I

sipped my tea. "It's hard to believe we knew so little about him. Don't you agree?"

"Actually, as a police officer, I learned very quickly that the face people show the public is seldom the face they wear in private."

"That's sad. I am who I am all the time. I'd like to think the majority of other people are as well."

"Maybe you're right," he said, reaching across the table to take my hand. "I guess I just let my job make me cynical sometimes."

"What's in Cookeville?" I asked. "I mean, why was Madelyn Carver there rather than here in Winter Garden?"

Ryan weighed his answer carefully, deciding what he could reveal to me that wasn't a part of Mr. Landon Carver's murder investigation. "From what we were told, the Carvers moved from Oklahoma to Cookeville when Madelyn was a toddler. Sometime after that, Stuart Landon Carver moved to Winter Garden and took up residence on his family's old farm. But he visited the family in Cookeville several times a year."

"Did they ever come here?"

"Ms. Carver didn't say."

"They couldn't have," I said. "If they had, someone would've seen them and would have blabbed all over town that Stu had a family." I gasped. "I realize Stu moved here because he was in hiding. But why leave his family behind? Did he leave them in Cookeville and change his name in order to protect his family from the person or persons who were after him?"

"I have no idea, sweetheart."

"But if Mr. Landon Carver moved away from Cookeville while Mr. Jackson was still incarcerated, then Mr. Jackson wasn't the person—or, at least, not the *only* person—Mr. Landon was concerned about."

Ryan smiled. "We need to put you on the force, you know that?"

"No, you don't. You're way ahead of me, I'm sure. That's why officers are searching Mr. Landon Carver's house."

He didn't respond.

"Where will he be buried?" I asked. "Cookeville, or here in Winter Garden?"

"I don't think Ms. Carver has made the arrangements yet. Besides, there will be an autopsy, so it will be a few days before the body is released to the family anyway."

"Of course." I frowned. "Did Ms. Carver say anything about her mother?"

"Not to me, she didn't."

I went back to eating my pasta, but I wondered what had happened to *Mrs.* Stuart Landon Carver. Was she still living? Had she and Stu divorced when he moved to Winter Garden from Cookeville? It would make sense that they had—how could they maintain a relationship while living so far apart? And why had Stu never brought his children to Winter Garden? The man had been mysterious in life. He was no less an enigma in death.

Chapter 5

As soon as I pulled into the parking lot of the Down South Café on Friday morning, a small silver sedan veered off the road and parked beside me. It frightened me at first, and then I realized that the driver of the car was Madelyn Carver.

I got out of my car and waited on her. She stepped out of her vehicle and slid her palms down the sides of her jeans. We introduced ourselves, though I already knew who she was—she was Stu Landon Carver's daughter.

"I'm sorry just to drop in on you like this," she said. "I mean, I know the café isn't even open yet, but I'll be happy to wait until it is. I'd like to get some coffee before I go to Dad's house. He never drank the stuff when he was visiting us, so I doubt he has any."

"I'm so sorry for your loss. Come on inside. I should be able to get a cup of coffee ready in no time. Do you prefer regular, French vanilla, or decaf?"

"Regular, please." She walked with me to the door. I unlocked it, flipped on the lights, and we walked inside.

"This is such a beautiful little café." Madelyn stood in the center of the dining room, taking everything in. "I really like it. It's welcoming."

"Thank you."

"Did my daddy come here a lot?" She ambled slowly over to the display case and gazed at the shelf that held her father's honey.

"Sometimes. I'd recently begun selling jars of his honey on consignment. In fact, I have some money for you . . . proceeds from the honey that has been sold already," I said. "And you're welcome to take the remaining jars with you."

"I'd rather leave them here, if you don't mind. Just keep to the arrangement you had with him for now."

"All right." I dropped my purse behind the counter and then began readying the coffeepots. "Are you thinking of staying here in Winter Garden then?"

"I don't know what I'm going to do. It's really too soon to think about that. But someone needs to tend the hives." With a sigh, Madelyn dropped onto a stool. "Daddy had a map to all of them on his refrigerator . . . left in case something happened to him, I suppose. One of the police officers gave it to me, and I checked on the hives yesterday evening before going to Abingdon."

"So you know all about beekeeping too?"

She nodded. "Daddy passed on his love of bees and beekeeping to both me and my brother, Brendan. In fact, we have hives of our own in Cookeville."

"Is that where you grew up—Cookeville?"

"Yeah. My parents and my grandmother left Oklahoma

when Mom was pregnant with me. They bought a house in Cookeville, and that's the only home I've ever known. I think Mom still misses Oklahoma, though."

"You've never considered going back there?" I asked.

"No. Granny—my Mom's mother—came with us, and we had no other family out there. I guess there was really no reason for us to return." She smiled slightly. "The police wouldn't let me go into Daddy's house yesterday. It'll be cool to see how he lived here on his own."

"You've never visited your dad here in Winter Garden?"

"Nope. Hard to believe, huh?" She spread her hands. "See, Daddy got it in his head after I was born that the people who'd been running Callicorp were going to come after him. That's why he dropped his surname and moved here to his parents' farm. It was supposed to be just for a little while . . . just until he knew we were all safe. But it became a full-time situation when I was around five or six years old."

"That must've been hard."

"We adjusted. And by *we*, I mean Brendan and me. Mom never did. Even though Daddy came to visit as often as he could, Mom couldn't handle the long-distance relationship and finally divorced him. She remarried about eight years ago."

The coffee finished brewing, and I got Madelyn a cup. "Do you like your stepdad?"

"He's all right." She dumped a packet of creamer into her coffee. "Brendan is closer to him than I am." She glanced up at me. "He thought Daddy was either some kind of paranoid conspiracy nut or that he used Callicorp as an excuse to live here in Winter Garden on his own without the responsibility of caring for his family on a day-to-day basis." She stirred in a packet of sugar. "I guess he feels pretty stupid now."

"Did the police talk with you about Walter Jackson, the man who came here looking for your dad?"

"They did. He's the same man who came to Cookeville looking for him. It scared me half to death. I called Daddy over and over, but cell service at the farm is practically nonexistent and Daddy seldom checked his landline because we'd always call and leave him messages on his cell knowing that he'd get back with us when he got the messages."

"But he never returned your calls?" I asked.

"Not this time. That's when I got scared, hopped into the car, and headed up here." She closed her eyes. "And I was too late. I should've left sooner . . . or called to have the police check on him, or—or something."

"I'm sure you did everything you could do. Besides, if Mr. Jackson struck you as being as harmless as he struck us . . ." I let the thought simply hang there.

"No. I knew he wasn't harmless. Daddy had been warning us about this moment all our lives."

"I can't imagine you told Mr. Jackson where your father was living," I said.

"Of course I didn't."

"So you couldn't know the man would find him so quickly. You thought you had plenty of time." I patted her hand as her eyes filled with tears.

"I suppose. I just wish I'd have called the police and had them go out to the farm and talk with Daddy in person . . . to tell him what was going on. There's no way Mr. Jackson was working alone. That man was far too frail to get the jump on someone as strong as my dad."

"I have to agree with you there. Mr. Jackson was the first suspect to spring to my mind, but—like you—I decided he was too old and feeble to hurt your dad. Have the police been able to locate Mr. Jackson yet?"

She shook her head. "They hadn't found him as of last night. Hopefully, that'll change soon."

"I hope so too. I can't begin to imagine how hard this is for you. If there's anything I can do to help, please let me know."

"Thank you."

As Madelyn Carver was finishing her coffee, Jackie breezed in.

"Good morning." Her smile encompassed both me and our guest. "I think I could've slept until noon if my alarm hadn't blasted in my ear."

"Then I'm glad it blasted you," I said. "I need you here."

"Spoilsport." She stepped around the counter, got an apron, and tied it around her waist. "I see Amy has already got you started with some coffee. Would you care for some breakfast?"

"No, thank you," said Madelyn.

"You sure? We make some awfully good pancakes around here."

"I have to pass. I have a lot to do today. And Brendan should be here soon." She stood. "Thank you for the coffee, Amy. What do I owe you?"

"It's on the house."

"Thank you."

Madelyn left, and Jackie raised her brows at me.

"Before you even ask, no, I didn't arrange a meeting with her. She was apparently passing by on her way to her dad's farm when she saw me pull in. She wanted some coffee, so I invited her inside."

"And?"

I quickly clued Jackie in to what I'd learned.

"So you think Madelyn might be staying here in Winter Garden permanently?" Jackie asked.

"It's too soon to say. I think at this point she's merely curious about the life her dad led here."

"That's really weird, don't you think? I mean, why wouldn't he bring his entire family with him if he thought they were in danger in Cookeville?" She shook her head. "I'm thinking the stepfather might be right—that whole *someone's out to get me* thing might've just been a way for Stu Landon to escape his responsibilities."

"I'm not so sure, now that his past has caught up with him," I pointed out.

"You mean Walter Jackson?" She scoffed. "That poor old guy wasn't in any shape to cut another man's throat. I just don't think he had it in him."

"Then who do you think killed Stu?"

"I don't know. Maybe it was just a random thing. You said you and Ryan saw his truck speeding down the road the night before. It could be that someone carjacked Mr. Landon, made him drive them somewhere, and then killed him when they got back here so he wouldn't call the police on them."

"I suppose that's possible," I said. "But if it really *was* a random killing, we'd all better be looking over our shoulders when we get here in the mornings."

"It's not the mornings that scare me." She gave a little shudder. "It's the nights."

*   *   *

During the lull between breakfast and lunch, I began preparing Parmesan-crusted pork chops. They were the special of the day. I hadn't tried them out on the Down South Café patrons beforehand, but I figured they'd go over well with many of our customers.

I'd mixed the Parmesan, bread crumbs, garlic powder, and other seasonings together in a shallow bowl and was lightly dredging the pork chops through a plate containing olive oil and then coating them with the Parmesan mixture when Homer came in and took his usual spot at the counter.

"That looks good," he said. "I might have to come back for lunch today."

"That'd be great." I smiled. "Who's your hero today?"

"Jason Silva, who reminds us that 'there's always going to be the circumstances you can't plan for.' Like yesterday. Silva says there's always the unexpected relevance and the serendipity."

My smile faded as I searched the recesses of my mind for the name *Jason Silva* and came up blank. "Who's Jason Silva?"

"He's the host of that show *Brain Games*. Ever watch it? It's fascinating."

I chuckled. Here I was expecting a philosopher, and I got a television show host. "I haven't seen it, Homer, but I'll watch for it."

"Do that. You'd enjoy it."

Jackie got Homer some coffee. "I've seen it. It's cool. It gives the viewer insight into how the human brain works."

I put the coated pork chops into my prepared baking pans and popped them into the preheated oven. Then I removed my gloves, washed my hands, put on another pair of gloves, took a sausage patty from the refrigerator, and put it on the grill.

Luis brushed past me with a dishpan to bus the table of the diners who'd just left.

"How are you both—you and Amy, I mean?" Homer asked Luis. "I know you witnessed a terrible thing yesterday."

"I can only speak for myself, Mr. Pickens, but I'm as well as can be expected. I had a hard time sleeping last night, but my dog Hada came and got in bed with me. I fell asleep after that."

"You just needed the comfort of having her there with you," Homer said. "Dogs know when you need them."

"Yes, sir, they do."

I felt a stab of guilt. I'd asked Luis how he was when he came in this morning. He'd said he was fine but was otherwise noncommittal. I felt I should've said something more to draw him out the way Homer had been able to.

"Doesn't Mr. Silva have some wisdom befitting a situation like this to impart?" I asked Homer.

He frowned slightly. "No, dear. He's a television host, not a psychologist."

Before leaving the café that afternoon, I took a small box and filled it with desserts, side items, and some leftover Parmesan-crusted pork chops. I didn't know how diligent Stu had been in his grocery shopping, and I thought I'd take the box of food by his house for Madelyn . . . and for her brother, when he arrived.

But I wasn't about to take my car over there again. So I went up to the big house and swapped vehicles with Mom. I told her—out of Aunt Bess's earshot—that I'd tell her everything when I got back.

Leaving my Bug there for Mom in case she needed to go anywhere, I got into Mom's SUV, waved good-bye, and headed for Landon's Farm.

When I pulled into the driveway, I didn't see Madelyn's car. I was afraid she wasn't there and wished I'd called first. I was sitting there wondering what to do when I saw the curtains move. Maybe Madelyn was inside after all. It wouldn't hurt to go up and knock on the door.

I got out of the SUV and went to the door. Before I could ring the bell, Madelyn flung the door open.

"Amy! I'm so glad it's you."

"I apologize for not calling first," I said. "I just wanted to drop some food off for you. I left it in the car—I was afraid I'd missed you."

"My car is in the garage. I didn't want to advertise that I was here alone."

I went back to the car, got the box of food, and brought it to Madelyn.

"Thank you. I appreciate that," she said. "I'm sorry I didn't recognize you at first since you weren't driving your yellow Beetle."

"I swapped cars with my mother because the road up here is so rough."

"It sure is," said Madelyn. "I wonder why Daddy never bothered to pave it."

"I'd say paving that road would be a hard and expensive task to undertake. Plus, he had that pickup truck. I guess the ruts didn't bother him."

"Guess not. Come on inside."

I followed Madelyn into the house. I tried to be non-chalant, but it was interesting to see inside the home of a man who'd been so reclusive that not even his children visited him there.

The living room contained a brown leather sofa with a matching recliner. There was a television sitting on a small entertainment center in the corner of the room, and newspapers and magazines were scattered about near the recliner—which had apparently been Mr. Landon's favorite seat. There was a table between the sofa and the chair. It held the television remote, a couple of hardcover novels, and a telephone.

I was surprised—though I probably shouldn't have been—to see that there was no dining table. Instead, there was a single stool sitting at an island in the middle of the room.

Madelyn sat the box on the island and began unpacking it. "Oh, wow. All this food looks delicious. And Brendan will be thrilled with these pies. He has a big-time sweet tooth."

"If there's anything else you need, please let me know. I'm so sorry for your loss, and if a little food helps bring you some comfort, it's the least I can do."

She finished putting the food into the refrigerator, and I was getting ready to say good-bye when she asked if I'd like to go with her to check on the hives.

"Sure," I said.

"Have you ever seen a working beehive?"

"No, I haven't."

"Then you're in for a treat. Come with me." She went out the back door, and after I'd followed her, she locked it behind us. "I'm afraid not to be cautious."

"I don't blame you there."

She stopped by the garden shed and got us both a veiled hat. "We don't need the full regalia today. I'm only checking to make sure they're all right and to lock them inside for the night. Daddy had made a note that he was concerned about this particular hive because of the neighbor's pesticide spraying habits."

As we walked up the hill behind her father's house, she spoke about her life in Cookeville. She told me she was a paralegal and that she liked the firm she was with, but that if she could find a job in this area, she might be willing to stay.

"Daddy's house is really nice, and I could maintain his legacy with the hives if I stayed in Winter Garden," she said. "Of course, Brendan might want to sell the house and split the profits. If that's the case, we'll have to sell— I don't think I could come up with enough money to buy him out."

"Wouldn't you be afraid to live here?"

She shook her head. "Not really. I'm a practical woman. Just because someone held a grudge against my dad doesn't mean they'd have any reason to harm me."

As we approached the hive, I saw that it was larger than I'd expected it to be. And louder.

"It's big," I said.

She laughed. "Yeah, there are about sixty thousand bees in there."

She walked closer to the hive and muttered a curse under her breath. "Can you believe this?"

I stepped closer and saw what she was talking about— hundreds of dead bees littered the outside of the hive. "Oh, no!"

"Daddy was right. Somebody around here is using a pesticide detrimental to pollinators. There's no doubt about that."

I told Madelyn what her father had told me about Chad Thomas. "I urged him to call the police, but he said there was nothing they could do."

"He's right. But most people care enough about the bees—and the environment—to do a more considerate job of spraying." She looked down at the bees and sadly shook her head. "If this is a common occurrence, the hive could really be diminishing."

"Your dad told me he was afraid of losing the hive."

"I wonder if he talked with this Chad Thomas about his spraying."

"I have no idea," I said. "He talked as if he planned on it, but . . ." But I'd never gotten to talk with him again after that. I didn't finish the thought, but Madelyn understood.

She shut up the hive, and we slowly walked back to the house.

"I wonder if I should say something," she mused. "Maybe he'd listen to me better than he would have my dad. Daddy could get fighting mad over his bees. I can too, but I've learned to control my anger better than he could."

I simply shrugged, feeling that I shouldn't offer an opinion on the matter. "If you want to get the police involved, I'm sure they'd be happy to send someone to talk with Mr. Thomas too."

"Yeah, maybe. I'll—" She broke off.

We could see the house now, and there was a newer model pickup truck parked in the driveway.

"It's Brendan." She smiled. "He's younger than I am, but he has a good head on his shoulders. I'm really glad he's here."

She and I hurried the rest of the way to the house, where Brendan was sitting on the front porch.

"Where've you been?" he asked. "I was trying to call you."

"I left my phone inside. Besides, cell service is lousy out here. You know that." She strode onto the porch and hugged her brother. "Brendan, this is Amy."

"Amy who? What's she doing here?"

"Amy owns the Down South Café, and she was kind enough to bring us some food," said Madelyn.

"Down South Café . . . That's where Daddy was found?"

She nodded. "Yes, it is."

"I think we need to go in and talk all this over," Brendan said. "Just you and me."

"I was just leaving." I waved to Madelyn. "Thank you for showing me the hive. If there's anything I can do for you, please let me know."

"Thanks, Amy."

I got into Mom's SUV and tried to avoid looking at the porch as I turned the large vehicle around. Madelyn talked about Brendan as if he was a great guy, but he certainly hadn't been friendly toward me. Did he think I had something to do with his dad's death?

Chapter 6

When I got to the big house to swap vehicles with Mom, she was sitting on the porch.

"How'd it go?" she called.

I walked up onto the porch and sat on the rocker beside her. "Where's Aunt Bess?"

"Inside pinning stuff to her *Lord, Have Mercy* board." She lowered her voice. "Why? What is it you don't want her to know?"

"Nothing really. I'd just rather talk with you alone." I told her about Madelyn—how nice she was, that we'd visited the hive, and that I was surprised at how many bees there actually were—and then about Madelyn's brother showing up and practically throwing me out. "Do you think he believes I had something to do with his father's death?"

"He might, sweetheart. People have strange reactions sometimes when their loved ones die. You were there for Madelyn. That's what matters."

"Yeah. She talked as if she might be moving to Winter Garden and taking over her dad's farm."

"Really? That's interesting."

"Very," I said. "Especially considering that today was the first time she'd ever set foot on the place."

"Hmm . . . and yet she took you straight to the hive?"

I nodded. "Her dad had a map to all his hives prominently displayed in case something ever happened to him, I guess. Talk about dedication. Anyway, Madelyn went to see about the hives yesterday, but she hadn't been inside the house until today. She said nothing was decided yet about what she'd do, but she said she wanted her dad's legacy to live on. But, of course, she has to take her brother's wishes into consideration."

"And dealing with family members over a loved one's property can be tricky. I hope Madelyn and her brother are able to work everything out amicably."

"Me too." I stood. "I hate to hurry off, but I've invited Ryan, Sarah, and John to dinner this evening, and I've got to get cooking. That's another reason I'm glad Aunt Bess is occupied—when she knows I'm making dinner, she expects to be included."

Mom laughed. "I know. We're having chef's salads and baked potatoes."

"That sounds good."

"Not better than what you're having, I'm sure."

"Fingers crossed," I said. "I haven't made chicken scaloppini since I was in culinary school." I gave her a quick kiss, hopped in the Bug, and drove down the hill to my place.

I quickly fed the pets, washed up, and got out the ingredients for the tiramisu cake I wanted to serve for dessert. I was really tapping into my Italian roots—even though I was fairly certain I had none. Still, I loved the food.

The cake's recipe called for a pint of coffee-flavored ice cream, so I sat that on the counter to be softening while the oven was preheating. I sprayed a Bundt pan with nonstick cooking spray and then put a vanilla cake mix into the bowl on my stand mixer. I added eggs and then had to put the ice cream in the microwave for ten seconds before including it in the mixture. I blended the ingredients on low until they were adequately combined and then beat the batter for another two minutes on medium speed. I then poured the batter into the pan and popped the cake into the oven. I set the oven timer for 35 minutes.

As most chefs will tell you, the hardest part of making a Caesar salad is getting the dressing right. Unfortunately, that's something else I hadn't done since culinary school. But I was confident I could get it right.

I minced cloves of garlic and anchovy filets and added them to a small bowl of mayonnaise, Parmesan cheese, Worcestershire sauce, mustard, and lemon juice. I seasoned the mixture with salt and pepper and then covered the bowl in plastic wrap and put it in the fridge.

I cubed a loaf of Italian bread I'd picked up at the grocery store and sautéed the cubes in a pan of olive oil and a little garlic. When they were browned, I put them on a plate and sprinkled them with salt and pepper.

Along with the lettuce, I put Parmesan and Romano cheeses into a large glass bowl and placed the bowl in the refrigerator to chill. Closer to the time for my guests to arrive, I'd toss the salad with the dressing and croutons.

Last but not least, I prepared the risotto. Since it baked at the same temperature as the cake, I slid the dish in to bake beside the Bundt pan.

By the time I had done all this prep work, Rory had eaten his dinner, gone outside to play in the backyard, and had come back in again to see what I was doing. I walked into the living room, sat down on the sofa, and patted the cushion beside me. He dived onto my lap and licked my chin. I laughed and kissed the top of his head.

"So, have you had a good day today, Rory?"

His tail wagging furiously, he hopped back down, ran from the living room into the kitchen and back to the sofa as fast as he could go. And then he leapt back onto my lap.

"That good, huh? I'm glad."

Ryan arrived as I was stirring the capers and butter into the broth to pour over the chicken breasts. He called to me from the porch, and I invited him to come on in. He brought me a lovely bunch of white flowers—roses, daisies, snapdragons, and dahlias. It wasn't the first time he'd given me flowers, so he knew where I kept the vases. He filled one with water and placed the flowers in it.

Then he came over, put his arms around my waist from behind, and kissed my cheek. "How was your day?"

"Well, I'm not going to race around the house like Rory did, but it was better than yesterday."

"I imagine so."

"I went over to Stu Landon Carver's house to take

Madelyn some food after work today," I said. "She's really sweet, and I like her. She told me she's thinking about keeping the farm, depending on what her brother wants to do. He didn't strike me as the nicest person on the planet."

"Wait. He's here?"

"Yes, why?"

"He was supposed to check in with Sheriff Billings when he got into town," Ryan said, stepping away from me and taking out his phone. "What time did he arrive?"

"I'm not sure. He was there when Madelyn and I walked back to the house after checking on the hive nearby. I guess it was about four o'clock."

Ryan called Sheriff Billings and let him know that Brendan Carver was in town. When he ended the call, he looked at me. "Thanks for telling me about Madelyn Carver's brother. The sheriff is sending someone over to question him now."

"Why are the police questioning Brendan?"

"He's family. He might know something his sister doesn't about any enemies his dad might've had . . . things like that."

"Oh. You don't consider him a suspect then."

He shrugged. "At this point in our investigation, Walter Jackson is our main suspect, but we can't rule anyone out yet." He stepped over to the counter and gazed longingly at the freshly iced cake. "This looks good." He held out an index finger.

"Don't you dare!"

He laughed. "I won't. Probably. It looks and smells awfully tasty, though. What kind is it?"

"Tiramisu cake."

"That's new. Or, at least, it's new to me."

"Trust me—you'll love it."

He did love the cake, and so did Sarah and John. We lingered over it and espresso after our meal and talked about Sarah's job—she worked for Billy Hancock, Winter Garden's only attorney—and John's classes—he attended the Appalachian School of Law in Grundy, which was only an hour and a half away, so he usually came home on weekends. And, of course, the conversation eventually turned to Stu Landon Carver.

"That was so terrible," Sarah said, giving my hand a squeeze. "I'm sorry you had to be the one to find him."

"Thank you. It was . . . horrifying." I shook my head as if doing so would remove the memory. "The truly strange thing is that on Wednesday night, Ryan and I saw a truck that we believed to be Stu's truck speeding away from town. And then I found him sitting in the truck in my parking lot the next morning. I honestly thought he'd arrived early to bring me more honey and that he'd fallen asleep."

"Was Thursday his typical delivery day?" John asked.

"Actually, no. Wednesday was," I said. "And this past Wednesday, I received the first order. But the honey sold so well that I went over to the farm to ask Stu if he could spare a few more jars."

"So you saw him on Wednesday," Sarah said. "Did he act upset about anything?"

"As a matter of fact, he did. A bunch of his honeybees were dead, and he was afraid that if he kept losing bees like that, his hive would collapse. And more bees were dead when Madelyn and I checked on the hive today."

"Did Mr. Landon—or, Carver—know what had caused the bees' death?" John sipped his espresso.

"He suspected it was careless pesticide spraying by a neighboring farmer, Chad Thomas."

Sarah groaned. "That guy is a Class-A jerk. He and his brother came into the office a while back and demanded that Billy represent the brother, Bob, in court *the next day.* Can you believe that? The hearing was the next day! Billy had no information about the case, and he didn't appreciate the men's attitude in the slightest. So he refused to take the case and asked the Thomas brothers to leave."

"I bet that went over well." John rolled his eyes. "Chad was always getting suspended for fighting when he was in high school. He was known for his temper. I think he even went to juvie for fighting once."

"Oh, he and his brother both got so belligerent with Billy, that I had to threaten to call the police before they'd leave." Sarah looked at Ryan. "Have you guys had trouble with them before?"

Ryan gave her a tight smile. "I'm not privileged to share that information."

"I can understand that," said John, "but if the sheriff hasn't spoken with Chad Thomas about his whereabouts on Wednesday night, he should."

"Point taken." Ryan pushed away from the table. "How about I clear the table and we play some cards?"

After Sarah and John had soundly thrashed us in Rook and had left us alone with our messy kitchen—at my insistence—I leaned against Ryan's chest.

"Let's go cuddle on the sofa. I'll clean up the kitchen in the morning."

"You have to work in the morning," he said. "You go cuddle up on the sofa, I'll clean the kitchen, and meet you there."

"No, that's no fun. I'd feel guilty the entire time." I began putting dishes in the dishwasher. "Besides, it'll go quicker with both of us working."

"Tonight was fun."

"It was," I agreed. "And the meal went over well."

"The meal was fantastic."

"I'm glad you enjoyed it. Take the rest of that cake home with you."

"And gain twenty pounds?" he asked. "I'd better not. I need to be able to fit into my uniforms."

"All right. Take maybe one piece for breakfast then? I'll share the rest with Mom and Aunt Bess. Aunt Bess loves her desserts."

"Hey, when I'm eighty-two, that might be my only food group." He laughed.

Ryan rinsed the dishes and handed them to me to load into the dishwasher. We worked in silence for a minute, and then I said, "I'm sorry we got off on the subject of Stu Landon Carver's murder. I feel like Sarah and John kinda put you on the spot."

He shook his head. "Nah, they both realize I can't discuss confidential information. They're in law themselves. Everybody's just curious. But between you and me, the sheriff has spoken with Chad Thomas."

"So he *is* considered a suspect?"

Ryan dropped a quick kiss on my lips. "Right now, the department's main focus is on finding Walter Jackson."

* * *

The next morning, I found myself wishing there was some sort of reward out for information on Mr. Jackson's whereabouts because he came ambling into the Down South Café as if it was the most natural thing in the world for him to do.

Just like the first time he'd visited the café, he got there early—even before Dilly Boyd. I had just prepared the coffeepots, turned, and he was getting ready to walk through the door. My heart pounded in my ears. I didn't know what to do. I needed to call Ryan. But I didn't want to freak out Mr. Jackson and have him bolt.

Luis was in the kitchen refilling salt shakers, Jackie had the day off, and Shelly wasn't there yet. Could I call to Luis and get him to phone the police before—

"Good morning, Mr. Jackson! How nice to see you again!" Had Luis heard that? Was he aware that the police were looking for Mr. Jackson? I thought he was, but maybe not.

"Hello, Ms. Flowers. Isn't your sweet smile a blessing today?"

Great. I'm conniving to call the police on the man, and he's telling me my smile is a blessing. But he might've killed Stu Landon Carver!

"Thank you. What can I get for you?"

"I'd like coffee and—" He wrinkled his brow. "I'm not certain. What do you suggest?"

"I'll get you a menu." I shoved a menu across the counter toward the man. "While you're looking it over, I'll run into the kitchen and check on the . . . stuff in there."

I hurried over to Luis and whispered, "Call the police. Tell them Mr. Jackson is here having breakfast."

Luis got out his phone.

"No," I hissed. "Do it outside. I don't want him to hear you."

Luis nodded and then went out the back door. All this cloak and dagger stuff was not his forte . . . nor was it mine, if you want the truth.

I stirred in an empty saucepan with a wooden spoon so Mr. Jackson would think I was actually doing something productive in the kitchen. Although if he believed I was making that kind of noise preparing breakfast for someone who wasn't even at the café yet, he might have left by the time I returned to the dining room.

With that thought in mind, I returned to the dining room. And I pasted on another of those blessing smiles.

"Hi, again," I said. "So what did you decide on?"

"I believe I'll have the buckwheat pancakes."

"Excellent choice. I'll get started on them right away." Still smiling, I went back into the kitchen. The man must think that making buckwheat pancakes was my favorite thing in the world. Actually, it was pretty fun, but I didn't usually grin like a nitwit while I was stirring them up and pouring the batter on the griddle.

Luis came back inside as I was whisking together buttermilk, butter, and eggs.

"It's done," he whispered, like he was my wise guy and I was his mafia boss.

Would that make me the godmother?

"Thanks. Go talk with him while I'm mixing up these pancakes so he doesn't leave." *Make him an offer he can't refuse.*

"Why would he leave?"

"I don't know. I just don't want the police to come and have their elusive suspect be gone again."

Luis nodded. "What should I talk about?"

"The weather," I suggested.

Luis walked into the dining room. "How about this weather, huh?"

"Yes, it's beautiful here."

"Yep. We've sure been having a lot of sun. Of course, it's summer. We usually have a lot of sun in the summer. But sometimes it rains, you know. Which is good. We need the rain for the crops and to keep the lakes from drying up and stuff like that. What's the weather like where you're from?"

"Um, we have sun in the summer too, son," said Mr. Jackson. "Am I keeping you from something?"

"No, no, no. I was just refilling the salt shakers before, but I'm done now. That's not a bad job, but it's a little tedious. You're afraid you'll spill it, and you don't want to waste any—but I usually don't have any spills. I use a little funnel."

"Funnels are good."

"Yep, they sure are. They keep you from making messes."

"Right." By this time, Mr. Jackson had apparently concluded that Luis was a tad on the nitwit side himself—that the Down South Café was a virtual madhouse. How could the man possibly know Luis was simply terrified that he was talking to a murder suspect and was trying to keep him from escaping the police? The next thing Jackson said was, "I imagine Ms. Flowers is a special employer, isn't she? She treats you well, makes sure no one is harsh with you . . . Am I right?"

"Yeah, Amy's great."

Oh, no. Poor Luis.

I finished mixing the pancake batter, and poured out three pancakes onto the griddle. I then stepped into the dining room to assure Mr. Jackson that his pancakes would be ready momentarily.

Before I could speak, Mr. Jackson said, "I normally wouldn't do this, but there's something about you, young man." He reached into the inside pocket of his suit.

Luis held up his hands. "Please, no!"

Mr. Jackson took out his wallet and looked from Luis to me in utter confusion.

"It's all right," I said. "Luis, you may return to the kitchen now. Mr. Jackson, your pancakes will be ready in just a couple of minutes."

"Thank you," he said. "I'm sorry I frightened the boy."

"He's . . . um . . . he's a little high-strung." I scurried back to the kitchen to find Luis flipping the pancakes.

"He thinks I'm nuts," Luis muttered. "But I thought he was on to us and that he had a gun."

"I understand. Thank you for not letting those burn."

"You're welcome. I can also tie my own shoes, by the way."

I patted his shoulder. "Sorry."

"It's all right."

"If it's any consolation, I believe he thinks I'm something of a babbling idiot myself." I plated the pancakes, put an orange slice garnish on the side, and took the plate out to Mr. Jackson. When asked what type of syrup he'd like, he went with blueberry.

"Excellent choice," I said. I got him the syrup, topped

off his coffee cup, and then rushed back to the kitchen and allowed him to eat in peace. I was as nervous as Luis, but I had a hard time picturing this sweet little old man as a murderer.

On the other hand, I imagined Robert Durst came across as a sweet little old man to some people.

It wasn't until Mr. Jackson was almost finished with his breakfast that Sheriff Billings strolled into the café.

"Good morning, Amy," he said. "I'd like a coffee, please." He took the seat beside Mr. Jackson. "Hello."

"How are you?" Mr. Jackson asked.

"I'm fine. As a matter of fact, I'm better now. I've been looking for you."

"You have? Whatever for?"

"For questioning in the murder of Stuart Landon Carver."

Mr. Jackson paused with his fork halfway to his mouth. "Stu has been murdered? That's terrible." He carefully lowered the fork back onto his plate, his appetite apparently gone. "But it does explain why I couldn't find him."

"I'd like for you to come down to the station and have a chat with me," said Sheriff Billings.

"Of course. Just please allow me to pay my bill."

"Take your time."

I placed Sheriff Billings's coffee in front of him and slid the sugar and creamer over to him.

"Thank you, Amy."

Mr. Jackson picked at his pancakes a bit more, but he didn't eat. I thought it likely he was contemplating his trip to the police station to answer questions about the search for Stuart Landon Carver that had led him from

Oklahoma to Cookeville, Tennessee to Winter Garden, Virginia. Meanwhile, Sheriff Billings drank his coffee like a man who was definitely not about to ask his questions in front of me or anyone else.

Chapter 7

&D illy came into the café just as the sheriff and Mr. Jackson left. She watched Mr. Jackson get into the police car with Sheriff Billings, and then she turned to me.

"Hey! Isn't that the man who was in here the other day—the day before Stu Landon turned up dead?"

"Yes, that's Walter Jackson," I said.

"What's Billings talking to him for? He didn't do anything."

"How do you know?"

"Well, for one thing, he has nice eyes," said Dilly. "Killers don't have nice eyes. Plus, they don't come back to the scene of the crime. If he'd murdered Stu Landon right out there in the parking lot, he'd have kept going. He wouldn't have come back here nosing around."

"In the movies, the bad guys always return to the scene of the crime," Luis pointed out.

"Honey, this ain't the movies." Dilly patted his arm. "And Walter Jackson didn't strike me as being that stupid when I met him the other day."

Dilly had made an excellent observation, but there remained too many unanswered questions.

"But, Dilly, Mr. Jackson was in here looking for Mr. Landon the day before Mr. Landon was killed," I said, dropping the *Carver* in order to refer to the man as Dilly was . . . as we'd all originally known him. "Plus, he specifically asked where Mr. Landon lived. That certainly makes him look guilty."

"Maybe, but he'd have to be a dummy to come in here and say he was looking for a man he aimed to kill." She glanced toward the window.

We both watched as Madelyn and her brother, Brendan, got out of Madelyn's car and headed for the door.

"Now there's one that bears watching," she said.

"Who?"

"Whoever that boy is." She squinted toward the window again before looking back at me. "That one has killer eyes. Madelyn Carver—she's the one I saw talking with the sheriff the other day—she has nice eyes. But that boy with her sure doesn't."

The door opened, and I turned my sunniest smile on Madelyn and old Killer-Eyes Brendan. "Good morning!"

"Hi, Amy," Madelyn said, coming over to the counter and sitting with one empty seat between her and Dilly. "Brendan and I wanted to come by and thank you for the food you brought yesterday. It was delicious. Wasn't it, Brendan?"

"Yeah." His voice was flat. "So where was dear old dad found?" He turned to look out the window. "Oh . . .

I suppose it was out there where the police tape is at. How can you stand to come here, Maddy?"

"It's the only place in town. And Amy has been kind to us." Her cheeks reddened. "And we wanted to get some breakfast. We have a full day ahead of us planning Daddy's funeral and everything."

"*Your* daddy's funeral," Brendan muttered. "I'm missing a fishing trip with my dad because of this mess Stuart got himself into."

Madelyn looked down at the table. "He was your father too."

"Stuart was never much of a father to me—or to you either, for that matter. I don't know why you stayed loyal to him. Douglas has been the only dad I've ever really known—the only one who counted. And he's been good to you too."

"May I go ahead and get you both some coffee?" I asked brightly.

"Please," Madelyn said, nodding but not raising her eyes to look at me.

Dilly certainly did, though. She rolled her eyes and jerked her head toward Brendan in a not-so-subtle way of telling me *I told you so*. Of course, Brendan acting like a jerk didn't make him a killer. I had to agree with Dilly on one count, though—his eyes did look a little soulless. Or maybe I just thought so because I'd never seen them when they weren't glaring at me.

"Have you gone out there and looked at the crime scene yet?" Brendan asked his sister.

"No. And I'm not going to."

"Why not? I might, since we're already here and everything. And since you've buddied up with some stranger on whose property your dead dad was found."

"Brendan, stop it. You're being cruel."

"Aw, I'm just messing with you. Chill out."

I got Madelyn and Brendan their coffee, took Dilly's order, and was relieved to see Shelly hurrying through the front door.

"Morning!" she trilled. "I'll be with y'all in just a minute."

"Thanks, Shelly," I said. "I'll get started on Dilly's order while you take care of Madelyn and Brendan."

"All right."

I gratefully escaped to the kitchen. There was too much drama in the dining room for me this morning.

Dilly wanted eggs, bacon, biscuits, and gravy—which was a lot of food for her. I figured she was either really hungry or she wanted to linger over her breakfast so she could eavesdrop on the Carvers.

I was frying Dilly's bacon when Shelly brought Madelyn's order into the kitchen. "She said she'd like to have two eggs over easy and two slices of whole wheat toast."

"Got it. And what for him?"

She flipped her palms. "He said he's fine with the coffee. She tried to get him to eat something, but he won't."

"Fine. Thanks, Shelly. I'll get Madelyn's breakfast out to her as soon as I can."

"Anything I can do to help?"

I shook my head. "I'm fine. Thanks."

Luis overheard our exchange. "No matter what that man thinks, everyone around here knows you had nothing to do with Stuart Landon's death."

"I appreciate that, Luis." *Why would he say that? Were people talking? It wasn't as if Brendan had come right out and accused me of anything.*

"Maybe you should tell the Carvers about Mr. Jackson coming in this morning," he suggested.

"I don't think so," I said. "That's the sheriff's job. I don't want to get any more in the middle of this situation than I already am. Brendan seems to think I'm already poking my nose where it doesn't belong."

"I understand." He took a box full of ketchup bottles into the dining room to see if there were any empties that needed to be swapped out.

We weren't terribly busy yet for a Saturday morning. People generally liked to sleep in on Saturdays. Still, I remained in the kitchen until Madelyn and Brendan Carver had left. Something about Brendan really unsettled me.

I continued to be out of sorts all morning, and that's how Homer found me.

"Why so glum this morning?" he asked. "You aren't letting the day run you instead of the other way around, are you?"

"I don't know. Maybe. Did that come from today's hero?"

He nodded. "Jim Rohn. He said that either you run the day or the day runs you. And it looks like your day is about to get the best of you, and you haven't even made it to lunchtime yet."

I got Homer a cup of coffee and then returned to the counter. Then I told him about taking food to Madelyn the day before, her brother showing up and practically asking me to leave, and then about their visit this morning.

"I don't understand why he's acting so belligerent toward me," I said. "Of course, I realize this is the place where his father was . . ." I glanced around the café. "You know . . . But I had nothing to do with that."

"His attitude probably has nothing at all to do with you, Amy. He could still be going through the stages of grief—one of those is anger, as I'm sure you're aware— or he might have unresolved issues with his dad."

"Well, I did hear him tell Madelyn that Stuart hadn't been much of a father to him and that Douglas—I'm guessing that's the stepfather—was the only real dad he'd ever known."

"I can understand that," said Homer. "I resented my dad until my mother explained to me how blessed I was to have her and my grandparents. But that old grudge would still rear its ugly head once in a while—especially when I saw other kids spending time with their dads."

"I'm sorry you had such a rough time."

"You're missing my point. I was able to move on. I adopted the hero-a-day thing, accepted the blessings that I did have rather than dwell on the ones I lacked, and I built a good life for myself." He spooned sugar and cream into his coffee. "It sounds like Madelyn was able to forgive her father for moving here and leaving her behind, but Brendan wasn't. Stu abandoned him, and he abandoned Stu."

"Yeah. Well . . . I'll get your sausage biscuit."

"Take your time," he said.

I knew better. I'd already cut into his schedule by talking about the Carvers.

Ryan called as Shelly, Luis, and I were doing our final cleanup work of the day. They were both wiping down the tables while I cleaned the windows and the front of the display case.

"I know you're busy, so I won't keep you but a second," Ryan said. "I'd like to make you dinner tonight."

That was a change. I was always the one who made dinner. I'd only been to Ryan's apartment once.

"So, what do you say?" he asked.

"Um . . . yeah! Yes, I'd like that."

He chuckled. "I really caught you off guard, didn't I?"

"You sure did. Is there anything you need me to bring?"

"Actually, I'm running low on butter. Would you mind stopping by the grocery store on your way and getting some?"

"I'll do it," I said.

When I ended the call and put the phone back into my jeans pocket, I noticed that both Luis and Shelly were grinning at me.

"What?"

"He's invited you to his place for dinner?" Shelly asked.

"Yeah. So?"

Luis nodded at Shelly. "This is getting serious."

"Oh, guys, it is not." I could feel my face flushing and quickly resumed cleaning the display case.

I didn't know how *serious* it made our relationship, but this was something new for Ryan and me. I was nervous, excited, and I wondered what he was making for dinner. Also, I couldn't stop smiling.

In fact, I was still smiling when I pulled into the parking lot of the grocery store late that afternoon. I'd dressed casually—a jean skirt, a peasant blouse, and sandals—and I realized I was going to get to Ryan's place a little early. I decided to take my time with that butter. I didn't want to seem too eager to get there.

I wandered around the store, checking out the produce, seeing what cuts of meat they had available, on the look-out for any new products the store might have in stock that I might want to use at the café. I was surprised to see that this particular store carried basmati rice, and I was trying to decide if there were any dishes I could sample to my patrons that called for it when I heard a man's voice behind me.

"Excuse me, miss."

I turned and felt as if I were looking at a solid wall of cotton. My eyes traveled up to the man's stubbly face and dark eyes. "I'm sorry. I didn't realize you were there."

"That's all right. You were awfully absorbed in trying to pick out some rice."

"Yeah," I said with a smile.

He picked up a bag of the basmati rice like the one I held. "What's so special about this kind? I've never seen it before."

"Basmati rice is an aromatic grain that comes from India. When you're cooking it, it kinda smells—and actually tastes—like popcorn."

"Weird. How do you know so much about it? You don't look Indian."

I opened my mouth to answer, but he interrupted.

"Wait, I know! You're Amy Flowers, the gal who bought and redid Lou's Joint," he said. "Turned it into the Southern Café? Is that the name?"

"The Down South Café. And yep, I'm Amy."

"My wife and I have been meaning to come in there.

We've heard the food is out of this world. But we typically have dinner whenever we go out to eat and you're always closed by then."

He had me at a disadvantage. He knew me—or knew *of* me—but I had no idea who he was. Still, I smiled and told him they should stop in sometime.

"You know what? I'm off on Monday. Are you open on Mondays?"

"Yes, sir. We're open every day except Sunday."

"Well, I'll do my best to bring my wife over there for lunch on Monday," he said.

"Thank you. I'll look forward to seeing you both." I began walking away, but he stopped me.

"Um . . . the . . . uh . . . the parking lot is all cleaned up and everything . . . right?" He frowned down at me. "I mean, I heard that Stu Landon's body was found there."

"The parking lot is fine. You'd never know such a terrible thing had happened there."

"It was terrible, all right. I couldn't believe it." He shook his head. "Stu and me . . . we were neighbors."

"Really?"

"Yeah. My farm is right next to his."

"Oh." Could this be Chad Thomas? *The* Chad Thomas with the terrible temper? "What's your name? I'd recently started selling Mr. Landon's honey on consignment. Maybe he mentioned you."

"Chad Thomas." He watched my face carefully.

I hoped I didn't give anything away as I said, "No. But then, Mr. Landon wasn't much of a talker. He generally left most of the talking to me."

He chuckled. "Nope, Landon didn't say much. He sure

loved his bees, though. I think he liked bees better than he did people."

I merely nodded.

"There's been somebody staying at his place for the past day or two," Mr. Thomas said. "Have you heard anything about who that could be?"

"It's Mr. Landon's daughter and son. I took them some food yesterday."

"So are they living here while they make their dad's arrangements, or are they planning to make Winter Garden their home now?"

"I have no idea," I said. "I'm afraid I don't know them well. I feel just terrible for them, being here for the first time under such tragic circumstances."

"First time? Huh. I reckon that explains why I didn't know Landon had any family. He's lived next door as long as I can remember—my farm was my dad's before he passed on and handed it down to me—and I never knew Landon to have a wife or kids," he said. "Where've they been?"

"I believe his daughter said she drove up from Tennessee." I lifted my shoulders. This conversation was making me uncomfortable. I'd never met Chad Thomas before today, had heard some very unflattering things about him, and didn't want to discuss Stu or his family with someone who'd probably killed a bunch of the man's beloved bees.

Once again, I turned to leave.

"You haven't heard anyone say anything about what they plan on doing with the farm?" he asked.

"No." I'd already answered this question. Why was he asking it again?

"I'm just really curious about it because if they want to sell, I'd sure be interested in buying. If you hear that they're selling, would you ask them to talk with me first?"

"I honestly don't know his family," I reiterated. "I only just met them."

His eyes hardened.

"But if I hear anything, sure, I'll let you know," I said.

He smiled. "I appreciate that. You have a good weekend now, you hear? And me and the missus will do our best to make it in on Monday."

"I'll look forward to it." I hurried to the dairy case.

Ryan had a corner unit in his apartment building. The buildings were white with burgundy trim. Each apartment had its own small covered porch on the front and a deck on the back. Ryan waved to me from the deck, where he was grilling.

"Hi," he called. "Come on up. The steaks are almost done!"

I walked around to the back and came up the stairs to the deck. I held out the bag. "Here's your butter."

"Thanks. We'll need it for the rolls." He gave me a quick kiss before taking a pair of tongs and turning the steaks. "Are you okay? You've got sort of a dazed and confused look on your face. You're not *that* surprised by my invitation, are you?"

"No. I just met Chad Thomas in the grocery store."

"What?"

"Yeah . . . I was looking at rice, and he came up behind me. I thought I was in his way, but then he started talking to me. He was probably just trying to be nice."

"He probably wasn't," Ryan said. "I haven't had any personal dealings with this man, but from what I've heard, he's someone to be avoided."

"I've been hearing the same stories you have—well, other than what you've seen in police records and stuff—but he was friendly with me, albeit nosy. He said he and his wife had been wanting to check out the café and that they might be there Monday for lunch."

"What else? I mean, what was he nosy about?"

"He started talking about Stu Landon. That's when he told me he was Mr. Landon's neighbor," I said. "And he asked me *twice* what Mr. Landon's children intended to do with his farm."

"Why's he so interested? Did he say?"

"He said he was interested in buying the place. I suppose he wants to expand his farm."

Ryan removed the steaks from the grill and placed them on a porcelain serving tray. "So that's what he was getting at—he wants to buy Landon's farm, and he thought you'd put the word out for him."

"I guess. I told him I'd only just met Madelyn and Brendan."

"Get that door for me, would you?"

I opened the sliding glass door, and we stepped into Ryan's kitchen.

"And given his behavior every time he's been around me, Brendan would do the exact opposite of anything I'd suggest," I said. "That guy has taken a real dislike to me. Homer says that it might not be me but his dad that Brendan has such animosity toward. But it sure feels like that hostility is being directed at me."

Ryan sat the tray on the butcher block table, which he'd set with china, silverware, napkins, and candles.

I smiled as he lit the two taper candles. "This is beautiful. Thank you for doing all this for me."

"You're welcome. And I know it's easier said than done, but try not to take Brendan's behavior too personally. He's young, he's just lost a dad who didn't live with the family, and he's likely suffering more loss than he even realizes at this point."

"Now I feel like a jerk," I said. "I shouldn't have been a baby and whined about Brendan not liking me and possibly blaming me for his father's death."

He smiled as he pulled me in for a hug. "You're the least jerky person I know. You just worry too much sometimes. But tonight we aren't going to worry about anything."

"Okay."

"Promise?"

"I promise," I said.

After we ate dinner and cleaned up the kitchen, we went into the living room. It had light-colored wood flooring, a dark brown leather sofa, a maple and bronze coffee table, and matching end tables. On each end table, there was a lamp with an amber shade. There was a basket in the center of the coffee table containing magazines—the top one was *Law Enforcement Technology*—and the television remote. The television was located on the wall above the stone fireplace directly across from the sofa. A ficus grew in a large blue vase placed near the window, and there was a bronze-framed mirror above the sofa. I remembered his telling me that his mom had decorated it for him.

We sat on the sofa and Ryan draped his arm around my shoulders. I rested my head against him.

"Thanks for dinner," I said. "I love to cook, but it was nice to have someone prepare a meal for me for a change."

"I'll have to do that more often then."

Chapter 8

I slept in until nearly nine o'clock Sunday morning. Actually, I woke up at my regular time but snuggled back under the covers and dozed off again. And again. I finally dragged my butt out of bed at nine. Then I took a quick bath, had a granola bar with my coffee, and then got dressed and headed for the big house, where Jackie and I always made Sunday lunch for Mom and Aunt Bess. The menu for the day was barbecued chicken breasts, zucchini potato casserole, a garden salad, garlic cheese biscuits, and banana pudding.

Jackie was already there when I arrived. She was sitting at the kitchen table chopping zucchini. I got another knife and started on the onions. Mom and Aunt Bess were sitting at the table too, and Mom offered to help. I put her to work shredding lettuce for the salad.

"Jackie was telling us about a man who's been nosing around trying to find gas," Aunt Bess said.

I gave Jackie a questioning look.

"Roger was working at a construction site when a man from Ives Oil and Gas came by and asked to test the property for natural shale gas," Jackie explained. "Of course, Roger told the man he'd have to get permission from the owner, but then the man went on to tell Roger that Appalachia has one of the United States' five largest potentially undiscovered shale gas reserves."

"Really?"

She nodded. "That's what he said. He told Roger that the Appalachian Shale Basin is at the top of the list but the area is hampered by the mountainous regions."

"I had no idea we could be sitting atop a basin of natural gas," I said.

"Neither did I," said Aunt Bess. "And now I'm afraid our house is right over one of those gas pockets and that we're all gonna blow up!"

"I doubt there's even any gas around here," said Mom. "From what I've heard, that company has been poking around Winter Garden for several days now, and they must not have found a thing. If they had, more people would be talking about it."

"Will you call up that Ives man to make sure there's no gas underneath our house?" Aunt Bess asked.

"Of course I will."

"I'll go in here to my computer and see if I can find a phone number for them." Aunt Bess pushed away from the table and strode to the living room.

"I'm really sorry I opened that can of worms," Jackie said softly. "I had no idea it would make Granny freak out about the house blowing up like that."

"With Aunt Bess, you just never know," said Mom.

"Later on, she could decide that having gas on our property could make us as rich as Jed Clampett and that I could take up with Dash Riprock."

"Don't be silly, Mom. You know Aunt Bess is the one who'd land Dash—especially if she's telling the story."

"Well, there is that."

"Hey, guess what?" I asked brightly. "I got to visit one of Stu Landon's beehives on Friday with his daughter, Madelyn. I was really surprised by how many bees were in the hive."

As I was speaking, Aunt Bess returned with a scrap of paper. She slipped it into Mom's pocket. "There. Now you can call them in the morning."

"All right. I will."

"Is his daughter planning on staying and taking over the farm?" Aunt Bess asked.

"She's not sure. She told me she'd consider staying on but that her brother might want to sell the place."

"What's she like—Stu's daughter? Is she mysterious?" Her eyes brightened. "Is she foreign? Does she speak with an accent? That would make sense, him probably being a spy and all. It would be like James Bond having a baby with one of those weird foreign women he used to get tangled up with."

"Um . . . she's lived in Cookeville, Tennessee her whole life, so she talks like we do," I said. "And she isn't mysterious, as far as I can tell."

"Well, just the same, I hope she stays . . . for the bees, if for no other reason. What would happen to the bees if she left? Would they die?"

None of us could answer Aunt Bess's question then, so I looked it up online when I got back home late that afternoon.

I found one beekeeper forum in which a man said he'd been a beekeeper for four years and had eight hives. According to him, the bees practically took care of themselves. Of course, Stu had a different circumstance in that Mr. Thomas's pesticide spraying forced him to keep his bees locked in their hives overnight.

Another beekeeper on this same forum reported that a few feral hives and those abandoned by a beekeeper did well on their own but that the majority failed within two years due to disease or queen failure. The British Beekeepers Association advised that honeybees shouldn't be left unattended for any length of time. The association recommended weekly inspections to prevent swarming between the months of April and August, treatments for parasites in August and September, and feeding during the winter months.

While learning about honeybees, I also discovered that one should move slowly and wear light-colored clothing around bees because they apparently associated dark colors with predators. And ants, raccoons, skunks, birds, and bears could disrupt your hives. I had a sudden image of Winnie the Pooh—silly old bear.

But thoughts of cartoon bears aside, there was a lot that could go wrong with the hives should they be abandoned. They would likely collapse soon. I wondered, if Madelyn decided not to stay on in Winter Garden, whether she could possibly relocate the hives. I realized she had more important things on her mind at the moment—her father's arrangements, her sullen brother—but the bees had been so important to Stu Landon Carver. I knew he'd want them cared for. More than likely, Madelyn knew that too.

After doing all that pointless research on honeybees—especially since I couldn't tell Aunt Bess what I'd found without having her worry about them—I updated the Down South Café website. I put the specials for the upcoming week onto the home page. Then I went over to social media. Although most of our regular patrons were older, I'd seen an uptick in traffic among younger people and working professionals since becoming more active on social media. I posted an offer of ten percent off a customer's total bill if they mentioned the ad when they came into the café.

O n Monday morning, Madelyn came in for breakfast. Brendan wasn't with her, and I was glad. Of course, I tried not to let on that I was.

I got her some coffee and asked if she'd be dining alone this morning.

"Yeah. Brendan couldn't get up. He tends to stay up until dawn and then sleep like the dead." She looked over at the display case. "I might take him a cookie or something to have when he wakes up." She smiled wanly. "I know he hasn't been very nice to you—and I can't understand why for the life of me. He's usually such a sweetheart. But he does have a lot on his mind."

"I know," I said, handing her a menu. "You both do. I'll let you look that over, and I'll be back in a jiffy."

"That's okay. I know what I want. I'd like an omelet with ham, onion, and green peppers, a biscuit with some of Daddy's honey on it, and a side of hash browns."

"Coming right up. Your dad's honey is delicious. I'm guessing you've had it before?"

She nodded. "It's not like ours from home. I won't say Daddy's is better, just different. The bees here seem to draw from a wider variety of trees and flowers than they do at home."

"I know you have much more pressing things on your mind right now, but what will happen to the bees if you decide to sell the farm?"

"I'd try to relocate Daddy's hives to our house. Or see if I could find another beekeeper in this area to take them over."

"I wish you luck," I said. "And if there's anything I can do to help, just say so." I went into the kitchen to prepare her breakfast.

A group of students from a nearby college came in and ordered coffee and pastries to go. The pastries had already been made and were in the display case, so Jackie was able to serve them without requiring anything from me. She did slip into the kitchen to tell me that they used the ten-percent-off coupon, so that was good. The advertising was working.

When I delivered Madelyn's order to her, I mentioned that there was talk about Ives Oil and Gas Company sending someone to scout local properties for natural gas.

"My poor Aunt Bess thought the house might blow up, so she's having my mom ask the company's representative to come out and test," I said. "I don't think there's anything there, but you never know."

"Actually, someone from the oil and gas company came out and spoke with Daddy," she said, sprinkling pepper onto her hash browns. "He was positively not interested in letting them test his property. He was afraid they'd upset the bees."

I smiled. "He was awfully protective of those bees, wasn't he?"

"He sure was."

Homer came in and sat at his usual spot at the counter. "Good morning, Amy!"

"Hey there, Homer. How are you?"

"Doing well."

I introduced him to Madelyn. "Madelyn is Stuart Landon Carver's daughter."

Homer told her he was glad to meet her and studied her face for a second. "I can see it now. You have your father's eyes."

Madelyn blushed. "That's what everybody tells me . . . well, everybody who knew us both."

"Mr. Landon was a good, hardworking man," Homer said. "And I'm sorry for your loss."

"Thank you, Mr. Pickens."

"Homer, I'll get that sausage biscuit ready for you," I said.

"And I've got your coffee right here," Jackie told him.

After Madelyn left, I asked Homer who was his hero for the day.

"Andrew Smith," he said. "He's an author of young adult fiction, and frankly, I'd never heard of him until I ran across one of his quotes. I looked him up after that."

"Cool. Have you heard that someone from Ives Oil and Gas has been checking out property here in Winter Garden to see if there are any natural gas reservoirs?"

"I am aware. The man came by my house and asked if he could test. I told him to have at it, and he tested some rocks. Unfortunately, he didn't think there was anything to be extracted from my place, or you might be looking at one of Winter Garden's upper echelon."

"I *am* looking at one of Winter Garden's upper echelon," I said. "Besides, Aunt Bess is afraid that there's gas under our property and that it'll somehow make us all blow up."

"'People fear what they don't understand and hate what they can't conquer,'" he said.

"Andrew Smith?"

He nodded. "That's the quote I liked."

"I like it too," I said with a smile.

There were more people than usual in the café for lunch, and almost all of them mentioned the social media ad. I was happy that the promotion was going so well. I just hoped Jackie and Shelly didn't quit on me. But they seemed to be handling the traffic all right, and the people seemed to be generous tippers. That always helped a server's mood.

When I realized that the initial traffic increase wasn't just one large group but a steady stream, I asked Luis to call Donna—our part-time waitress—and ask her to come in so Jackie could help out in the kitchen. Donna had arrived—eyes wide at the crowd—and Jackie was helping me keep an eye on the grill while we both chopped vegetables.

Shelly popped her head into the kitchen. "Hey, Amy, there's somebody out here who wants to see you."

"Who is it?" I asked. "Can't it wait?"

She shrugged. "It's a big, husky guy here with a woman who I'm guessing is his wife."

I remembered running into Chad Thomas in the grocery store. I sighed.

"Go ahead," said Jackie. "I've got this."

"Okay. I'll make it quick." I took off my plastic gloves and discarded them before going into the dining room. I spotted the couple right away, although you couldn't have asked for a couple more mismatched than this one. Whereas Chad was, as Shelly had aptly described him, big and husky, his wife was tiny and birdlike.

Chad waved to me as I stepped out behind the counter, as if I might've forgotten him already.

"Hi," I said as I approached their table. "I'm so glad you could make it."

"We wanted to let you know the food was really good. Wasn't it, Fern?"

Inwardly, I let out a sigh of relief.

"It was." Fern spoke so softly that I had to lean forward to hear her. "I hope we get to come back here again sometime."

"We will, darlin'. We will," he said. "I just wanted to introduce you two. I told Fern about meeting you in the grocery store, so Amy, this is my wife, Fern. Fern, Amy."

Fern and I shook hands, and I told her it was nice to meet her.

"It's a pleasure to meet you too. I came in here once when the place was called Lou's Joint, and I didn't like it at all."

"I'm glad we've improved the place," I said.

"You sure have done that."

"Well, I need to get back into the kitchen, but it was truly an honor to meet you. Please tell Shelly to take ten percent off your bill when you go up to pay."

"You don't have to do that," said Chad.

"I want to," I said. "We have to keep good customers like you and Fern coming back."

As I turned to head back to the kitchen, I nearly ran into a newcomer. "Excuse me," I said to the man.

"Excuse *me*." The tall, balding man with a slight paunch smiled and held out a hand to Chad. "Mr. Thomas, good to see you again."

"Pull up a chair," said Chad.

I went on back to the kitchen.

Upon pulling into my driveway after work, I found Rory barking his head off, a large white truck parked between my house and the big house, and the man I nearly slammed into in the restaurant poking dart-like things with red tops into my yard.

"May I help you?" I called as I got out of the Bug.

"I'll be with you in just a second."

Just a second, my eye. I hurried over to where he was working.

"Watch your step, please," he said without looking up.

"What are you doing? This is my house."

He finally looked up. "Oh, hey! I remember you from the restaurant. Nice seeing you again." He took a card from his shirt pocket. "I'm Calvin Dougherty, a geologist with Ives Oil and Gas Company. Your mom called and asked me to come out and check your property for gas reserves."

"Have you found anything?"

"Not up on the hill. I'm testing down here just to make sure," he said.

"I imagine Aunt Bess was relieved that there were no gas deposits up there."

"She was. But she's still afraid your place will blow up." He chuckled and smoothed his comb-over to the left. "I tried to explain to her that it doesn't work that way, but . . . well, I don't think she was convinced."

"I know better than you how hard it is to convince Aunt Bess of anything once she has her mind made up. Would you like some water or iced tea?"

"No, I appreciate it, but I'm about to finish up here and call it a day."

"I understand you've been looking at a lot of property around Winter Garden," I said. "Do you think there's a possibility that you'll find *any* natural gas reserves around here?"

"It's possible. I've come across one or two places where I'd like to run some additional tests, but I'm waiting on the go-ahead from my company. There's always the mandatory red tape, you know." He went to the truck, stayed a few moments, and then came back to retrieve the darts he'd placed in the ground. "Well, it was good seeing you again. I'll have to stop back in your café again for lunch sometime. The food was delicious."

"Thank you. I appreciate that." I began walking toward the house but stopped and turned back. "Mr. Dougherty, how would it affect the residents of Winter Garden if you should happen to discover that there's a gas deposit around here?"

He shrugged. "It could make one or two of them set for life."

Chapter 9

    I went inside and fed the pets and then I walked up to the big house. Mom was sitting on the front porch enjoying a glass of lemonade.

"I see you met Mr. Dougherty," she said. "Would you like some lemonade or iced tea?"

"No, thanks. I'm fine." I sat on the rocker beside hers. "What were those dart-like things Mr. Dougherty was putting into the ground?"

"He told Aunt Bess that they were geophones and that through some kind of recording equipment he has in his truck, they tell Mr. Dougherty whether or not the land should be tested further."

"Does Aunt Bess feel better now that she knows we're not sitting atop a gas well?"

"Yeah." Mom smiled. "She went to take a nap as soon as she learned all was well. She didn't get much sleep last night."

"Whoa. She was more worried than I'd thought." After rocking and watching a pair of blue jays flit from limb to limb on a maple tree for a few seconds, I asked, "What did you think of Mr. Dougherty?"

She groaned. "You aren't trying your hand at matchmaking, are you?"

"No. I genuinely want to know your opinion of the man."

"I thought he was okay . . . clean-cut . . . fairly nice looking, although I wish he'd just let himself go bald already and forget about combing what little hair he has over to the side . . . He seemed kind." She gave me a sharp look. "If you aren't matchmaking, why do you want to know what I thought of him?"

"I don't know. I just get kind of a strange vibe from him."

Her brows shot up. "Did he do or say something inappropriate to you?"

"No, not at all. And maybe it's not really the man himself I'm suspicious of—maybe it's this whole situation. Don't you think it's weird? This man comes to Winter Garden alone. He doesn't have a team with him. And he's investigating the possibility of there being natural gas somewhere beneath the town." I spread my hands. "What is he—some kind of wildcatter or something?"

"I don't think he's working alone," Mom said. "I believe he's just the initial investigator. When I called Ives Oil and Gas and asked to speak with the representative they had working in Winter Garden, Virginia, they put me through to him right away."

"I still think it's odd that he just showed up here one day and started trying to find gas in Winter Garden.

Wouldn't someone have to suspect they had gas on their property and call Ives Oil and Gas to ask them to look into it?"

She shrugged. "Maybe someone did. Besides, you heard Jackie say that Mr. Dougherty told Roger that they believe the Appalachian Shale Basin is at the top of the list of possible undiscovered reserves. It could be that they're just now getting around to exploring Winter Garden."

"I guess."

Mom reached over and patted my arm. "You're still shaken up over Mr. Landon's death."

"I know. I saw Madelyn this morning, by the way. She said Ives Oil and Gas had approached her dad about testing his land, but he wouldn't let them. He was afraid they would disturb the bees."

"Do you think Madelyn will allow Mr. Dougherty to test the property now?"

"I don't know. Mr. Thomas sure was chummy with Mr. Dougherty today, though." I explained to Mom that Chad Thomas and his wife came in for lunch and that they asked to speak with me. "When I was going back to the kitchen, I nearly ran into Mr. Dougherty, although I didn't know who he was at the time. He was walking over to the table to speak with Mr. and Mrs. Thomas."

"Wouldn't you imagine Mr. Dougherty has met a lot of people since he's been in Winter Garden?"

"Yeah." I blew out a breath. "Maybe you're right. I'm letting what happened to Stu affect the way I look at everything around me. But how can I not, Mom? The man died in my parking lot."

"I know, sweetheart."

"Did I mention that Roger had told us that Chad Thomas had a terrible temper?"

"I don't think so," she said. "When was this?"

"This was just after Stu told me he thought Mr. Thomas's pesticide-spraying habits were killing his bees. Ryan and I met with Jackie and Roger, and Roger told us that Stu should be careful about confronting Mr. Thomas because both he and his brother had quick tempers. He knew this from when he'd done work for Mr. Thomas's brother."

"So you're afraid Mr. Landon confronted Mr. Thomas and that Mr. Thomas . . . killed him?"

"The thought had crossed my mind, but when Mr. Thomas was in the café with his wife, Fern, you couldn't have asked for anyone to have been any nicer," I said. "When I first ran into him in the grocery store, he came across as a bit overbearing, but he didn't strike me as ill-tempered. Do you think Roger could've been mistaken?"

"That's possible. Roger was around this man and his brother, though, right? People are usually more themselves around family. They don't have their guard up or feel the need to be as polite as they might be in social situations." She smiled slightly. "Or it could be that you've simply not made the man angry."

Rory and I were watching a movie and sharing a bowl of popcorn later that evening. Even Princess Eloise was in the same room with us, albeit in the chair across from the sofa watching us with narrowed green eyes. The movie was a comedy, and although Rory didn't really get all the jokes, he appreciated the popcorn. Princess Eloise found nothing amusing about the situation whatsoever.

My phone rang, and I paused the movie. Rory hopped off the sofa to go into the kitchen and drink some water from his bowl.

I answered the call and smiled when Ryan told me he just wanted me to know he was thinking of me.

"That's sweet," I said. "Thank you. What's going on in the underbelly of Winter Garden tonight?" He was on patrol.

"Absolutely nothing. It's been a boring shift. But given recent events, that's a good thing."

"It *is* a good thing." I paused. "By the way, was it ever determined whether or not that was Stuart Landon Carver's pickup truck we saw speeding out of Winter Garden on our way home from the Barter?"

"No. It was really too hard to tell, given that the truck was going so fast. And you'd think a truck that old wouldn't be your first choice for a road race."

"That's true, especially with the wear and tear going up and down that driveway to Stu's house every day had to have on it."

"Ivy's still processing Mr. Carver's truck, though, so if there was anyone else in it the night he died, I feel fairly confident that she'll find out."

"Me too. She's really good at her job."

"I'd better get back out on patrol," he said. "Are we still on for dinner tomorrow evening?"

"You bet. See you then."

"If not before. I might make it in for lunch tomorrow."

"That would be great too," I said.

We ended the call. Rory—apparently full of popcorn—lay on the floor beneath the coffee table, and I resumed the movie. It was hard to concentrate on the goofy plot, though. I still had my mind on the night Stuart Landon Carver was murdered.

Had Ryan and I seen Stu fleeing for his life? Was there something we could've done to help him?

Finally, I gave up on the movie and called Sarah.

"Hey, girl, what's up?"

"I was watching a movie with Rory and Princess Eloise—okay, Rory—but I started dwelling on Stu Landon Carver," I said. "Would you like to go get a cone of ice cream with me?"

"Sure. I'd already got comfy for the night, but let me put on a bra, and I'm good to go."

I laughed. "Be there to pick you up in about fifteen minutes."

"See you then." A note of seriousness crept into her voice. "You okay?"

"I'm all right. Just too much time to think this evening."

"I heard that. See you in a few."

On my way to Sarah's house, I looked into my rearview mirror and saw an old pickup truck coming up behind me way too fast. It was dark and the truck's lights were shining in my eyes, but it reminded me of Stu's truck.

I blinked my eyes a few times and then adjusted my mirror so the lights wouldn't blind me. I really was letting Stu's death get to me. But he'd been such a nice man, as far as I could tell. And I was the one who'd opened that truck door. I gave an involuntary shudder at the unwelcome remembrance of that moment.

The truck followed me all the way to Sarah's house and then sped past me as I pulled into her driveway.

"Slow down!" she called angrily as she stepped off her front porch. She opened the passenger side door of the Bug. "Are you all right? You look as pale as a ghost."

"I'm okay. That truck just scared me. He was tailgating me, and the truck reminded me of the one Stu Landon Carver drove."

She nodded. "It *is* like that one almost. It belongs to Joey Carver." She slid into the car. "Apparently, his great-grandfather was big into those kinds of trucks and passed the love of them—or the actual trucks, I don't know—down through the family."

"Wait, you said *Carver*. Is this Joey related to Madelyn and Brendan?"

"Mr. Landon's—or as we now know—Mr. Carver's children? Yeah. Joey would be their first cousin."

"I wonder if they know each other," I said.

"Hard to say. We know the kids never came up here to visit Stuart, but he might've taken Joey or some of the rest of the family to Cookeville to see them on occasion." She shrugged. "It sounds to me like they were a very strange family."

"Me too. My cousin is like my sister." I grinned. "But then, so are you."

I dropped Sarah back off at her house after we'd gotten ice cream, and then I called Ryan.

"Hi there, beautiful. I hope you're not calling because you're as bored as I am."

"Well . . . um . . . I was, but then Sarah and I went and got ice cream."

"And now you're calling to rub it in?"

I chuckled. "No, I wanted to tell you about Joey Carver." I explained about the tailgating truck and how I thought it looked like Stu's truck. "So, of course, I thought my mind was playing tricks on me because I'd been thinking about Stu. But when I got to Sarah's house, he sped past, and Sarah yelled at him to slow down."

"You should have called me then. I could've made him slow down."

"I know. But when Sarah got in the car, she told me it was Joey Carver. He's Stuart Landon Carver's nephew, I guess—and apparently, the Carvers come from a long line of old truck enthusiasts . . . same make, same model."

"So you're telling me you think it was Joey Carver who was hightailing it out of town Wednesday night," he said.

"I thought it would bear looking into."

"It will. I'll get on it right now and let you know what I find out."

"Thanks."

"Hey, either way, maybe it'll help us solve our case."

"I sure hope so."

As was her custom, Dilly was one of the first patrons through the door on Tuesday morning.

"Good morning, Dilly. How are you today?"

"Better than my raccoon, I can tell you that much."

"Oh, no! Did something happen to him?"

I was genuinely concerned, as was Jackie, who hurried over to hear about Dilly's furry friend.

"Well, yesterday evening, he was favoring one little paw," said Dilly. "It was one of his front paws. He kept holding it up and wouldn't walk on it. And he's typically right-handed—he always takes his biscuit with that paw—but last night, he used the left one."

"Do you think you should call a veterinarian?" I asked.

"Nah. It's likely he's just bruised it somehow. I'll keep an eye on him for a couple of days and make sure it doesn't get worse." She shook her head. "He is a sad little thing holding that paw up, though. It made me feel so sorry for him that I nearly gave him two biscuits last night instead of one. But I thought if I did that, he'd never put that paw back on the ground again."

"You're probably right about that," said Jackie. "Animals know how to manipulate us sometimes. Let me get you some coffee."

Jackie went to get Dilly's coffee, and I asked her how well she knew the Carvers.

"I know them fair to middling, I reckon. Or rather, I *knew* them. All the older ones have died out or moved away. And I don't know any of their younger generation." She squinted. "I should've known that Stuart Landon was a Carver. But I just never made the connection. Back when he first came here, I was probably too busy living my own life to give his much attention. I had a lot more going on then than I do now."

Jackie returned and placed the coffee on the counter in front of Dilly.

"Thanks, hon." She spooned sugar and cream into the cup and stirred it. "If I'm not mistaken, Stuart's daddy must've been Gerald. I know Gerald moved out West right out of college. He got some kind of agricultural job out there. Did pretty well for himself, from what I heard."

"That would explain why Stuart came here from Oklahoma," I said.

"Yeah. I guess it would. And how he ended up owning the Carver farm and his granddaddy's old pickup truck. I thought he'd bought both at an estate sale or something."

"Both?"

"The farm, the truck, maybe some of the furniture . . . I don't know. I did realize he didn't get both of those pickup trucks. Jimmy Carver got one of them, and I believe he's passed it on down to his son."

"Joey?" I asked.

"Yeah, that's him. He's kinda reckless with it, if you want my opinion. His great-granddaddy probably rolls over in his grave every time that young'un goes flying off down the road. Oh, well, you never know how life's gonna turn out, do you?" She tilted her head. "You think I should go with eggs or pancakes this morning?"

"Live large—have one of each."

"Good idea. But make it two of each. And don't forget my biscuits."

"We won't," Jackie said. "Don't you forget to keep us posted on how your little buddy is doing."

"Oh, I couldn't forget that. It's odd, you know. I never had any pets—didn't really want any. I figured I had enough to take care of with my husband and myself. But now he's passed on, we never had any children, and that goofy raccoon has become . . . not really a pet, but a friend, I guess. Someone I expect to see every day." She smiled. "I've even told my neighbors that if anything happens to me—if I should have to go into the hospital or something—to put a biscuit out for that furry beggar."

"You're sweet," I said. "Your raccoon is lucky to have you. And so are we."

Our cordial conversation was interrupted when a young man in ripped jeans and a dirty red T-shirt stormed through the front door, looked at me, and demanded, "Are you the one that called the cops on me?"

"I beg your pardon," I said. "I don't even know who you are."

"You drive that yellow Bug out there?"

"Yes."

Jackie took a protective step toward me. I didn't feel I needed her help, but I appreciated the gesture.

"I'm Joey Carver. And you called the cops on me last night 'cause one of them came to my house and asked me a bunch of questions."

I didn't know what to say. I hadn't exactly "called the cops" on Joey Carver, but I had told Ryan that he owned a truck similar to that of Stuart Landon Carver and that he'd been tailgating me.

Jackie saved me from having to say anything. "I don't think anybody here called the police on you last night, but I'll call them on you right now if you don't get out of here."

"Fine." He jabbed an index finger in my direction. "But don't think this is over."

Chapter 10

After Joey left, Dilly and Jackie began talking at once, and Luis came from the back to see what was going on.

"Nothing's going on," I said. "Everything is fine. It was just some guy who came in accusing me of calling the police on him. And . . . I . . . I guess I kinda did." I told them how the truck had been tailgating me the night before. "When I got to Sarah's house, she recognized the driver as Joey Carver, and I mentioned it to Ryan because we saw a truck that looked like that racing out of town on the night before I found Stu Landon Carver in the Down South Café parking lot."

"And now you're thinking it was Joey you saw instead of Stu," Jackie said.

"It makes more sense. Dilly says the kid is always driving too fast."

"He *is* always driving too fast," Dilly insisted. "It's a

wonder he hasn't wrecked that truck by now. I'm glad Ryan talked to him. Maybe it'll make him think twice about speeding again."

"Yeah," said Jackie. "It might just save the kid's life."

I nodded, more shaken by Joey's visit than I wanted to let on. I wondered what Ryan had said to him and why he was so angry with me. People who didn't have anything to hide weren't that defensive and angry, were they? Nor did they issue veiled threats.

On the pretense of getting a breath of fresh air, I slipped out the back door and called Ryan. When he answered, I told him about my visit from Joey Carver.

"I didn't mention any names." He paused, obviously thinking about what he had said to Joey Carver the previous evening. "I did say he was seen tailgating a yellow Volkswagen and traveling at a high rate of speed. I'd looked up his driving record prior to leaving the station and had learned that he'd been cited twice for speeding and once for reckless driving. But the main reason I went to talk with him was because I wanted to know whether or not that was him we saw on the night Stu Landon Carver presumably died."

"Was it?"

"He says it wasn't, but I don't know whether to believe that or not. I mean, he denied everything else, so why not that? And we know he was tailgating you last night."

"Unless someone else was driving his truck," I said. "But according to Dilly, Joey is always driving recklessly."

"Well, maybe if nothing else, my warnings will slow him down and force him to be more careful. And if he steps foot back in the café behaving aggressively, call the station immediately and someone will be there to deal with him."

"Thanks."

"You didn't do anything wrong, and you don't deserve to be treated that way," he said.

"Well, I know that, and you know that, but I'm not sure Joey Carver does."

"Do you want me to have another talk with him?"

"No." I forced out a chuckle to show Ryan how not scared I was. "It'll be fine. I doubt he'll be back."

I could put on a brave face, but that didn't mean I'd fool everyone. I certainly didn't fool Homer. When he walked into the café and saw me scanning the parking lot as I poured his coffee, he asked me who I was expecting.

"Excuse me?" I asked.

"Who are you looking for? You're watching the parking lot like a hawk. I didn't think your beau usually came in until lunchtime."

"He doesn't." I sighed. "Someone came in this morning, and he was angry because something I said to Ryan got the man questioned by the police."

Homer smiled. "I don't know anyone who is particularly delighted to get an official visit from a police officer, but if he did something wrong, then he deserved it."

"He was tailgating me and driving recklessly. But that wasn't why I mentioned the incident to Ryan. I mean, people drive like that all the time. The reason was because the guy was driving a truck similar to the truck driven by Stuart Landon Carver." I explained to Homer that on the night before I found Stu in the parking lot, Ryan and I saw a truck that looked like Stu's speeding away from Winter Garden. "We thought maybe something was wrong. Ryan wanted to question the young man—Joey Carver—because he wanted to find out if it was him we saw instead of Stu."

"And did Ryan get an answer?"

"He got an answer. He just doesn't know if Mr. Carver was telling the truth."

"I don't understand why this situation is still concerning you if it happened this morning," said Homer.

"Before he left, Joey Carver told me, 'This isn't over.' I don't know what he might be intending to do. Maybe nothing. But I don't know him, and I'm afraid to let my guard down."

"My hero of the day—the author Arnold Bennett, by the way—once said, 'Your own mind is a sacred enclosure into which nothing harmful can enter except by your permission.' So I'm advising you not to give this young man permission to destroy your peace today. Be watchful, but don't fight imaginary threats."

"That's good advice," I said. *Also easier said than done.*

"And after I eat, I'll go by Phil Poston's bookshop and see what he can tell me about Joey Carver. If I'm not mistaken, Phil's granddaughter goes to school with the young man."

"All right. I'll get your sausage biscuit." As I strode back into the kitchen, I realized that Homer had a point. I was nervous—and had been all morning—about what a high school kid had stormed in here and said to me during what amounted to a temper tantrum. Joey Carver had wanted to scare me, and he'd succeeded. Because I'd *let* him succeed! Well, that was ending now.

I lifted my chin, took a sausage patty from the refrigerator, and prayed that Joey Carver wouldn't kick in the back door and kill me before I could get Homer's biscuit to him. Because, knowing Homer, he'd be distraught but he'd darn well want that biscuit.

M adelyn came in for lunch late that afternoon. She waved to me and then sat at a corner table. I murmured to Jackie that I'd take Madelyn her menu.

When I walked over to her table, Madelyn asked if I could sit for a minute.

"Sure." I pulled out a chair, sat, and placed the menu I carried onto the table.

"I just wanted to let you know that I'm going back to Cookeville for a couple of days," she said. "It's going to be at least that long before the medical examiner releases Daddy's body, and I need to check on things at home."

"What about Brendan? Will he be going with you?"

"I don't know." She huffed. "He didn't come home last night. I'm guessing he stayed at Joey's place."

"Joey?"

She nodded. "Joey is our cousin. We don't know Joey's parents all that well, even though they were related to my grandfather's brother, but Dad used to bring Joey with him when he came to stay in Cookeville sometimes during the summer. I imagine it was because Joey's mother needed a break more than anything—that kid could be a handful. I think he still can be."

"You mean, in terms of mischievous kid things or . . ."

"For the most part, they were harmless," she said. "He'd pull pranks like gluing our books shut or replacing the crème filling in our cookies with toothpaste. Sometimes my tolerance level for Joey was zilch, and I'd get furious and threaten to tell Daddy on him. When he slashed my bike tires, I learned to keep my mouth shut and just hide anything I didn't want him to destroy."

"Wait—he slashed your bike tires? How old was he?"

"About twelve or thirteen."

"Was he mean like that to Brendan?" I asked.

"No. I think Joey thought the sun rose and set for Brendan. Still does. Brendan is three years older than Joey, and Joey found his cooler, older role model in Brendan." She shrugged. "I was just *the girl*."

I made a mental note to keep an eye on my tires for the next couple of days. Here at the café, I didn't think Joey could sabotage them without anyone seeing. And I didn't know whether or not he was brazen enough to try to slash them at my house. But now that Madelyn had put the thought in my head, I felt it better to take precautions— like leaving the porch light on all night.

"The reason I came by," Madelyn continued, "was to give you my cell phone number in case anything happens that I might need to know about. The police have my number . . . and Brendan does, of course, but he's been acting weird ever since he got to Winter Garden."

"Weird, how?"

"I can't exactly point to any one thing. He's just been belligerent, running wild with Joey. He tries to pretend he's not affected by Daddy's death, but I know he is. He has to be."

I nodded, even though I had no insight into Brendan Carver's feelings whatsoever. "They say people deal with grief in different ways."

"Right." She slid a piece of paper across the table to me. "Anyway, here's my cell number. Please call me if there's anything you think I should know or if anyone here should need me."

"Will do." I slipped the paper into the pocket of my jeans.

Madelyn picked up the menu. "So, what's the special of the day?"

"Spaghetti, meatballs, and garlic breadsticks."

She handed me the menu. "I'll have that and a glass of tea, please."

"Coming right up."

If Madelyn's visit hadn't already made me nervous enough about Joey Carver, Homer's news when he returned just before closing would've done the trick.

"I went to see Phil Poston," Homer said, agreeing to a complimentary slice of apple pie à la mode as payment for his investigative work. "His granddaughter, Emma, not only goes to school with Joey Carver, but the two of them dated."

"How old is Joey?" I asked.

"He'll be a senior when school starts back this year— I guess that won't be long now, will it? Anyway, Phil says the boy's a hothead. Emma stopped going out with him because he scared her with his driving and road rage, plus he tried to be very controlling of her."

"You're not the first person I've heard bad things about Joey Carver from today."

He paused, spoon halfway to his mouth. "Who was the other?"

"Madelyn, his cousin." I told Homer about Madelyn stopping by and telling me about the pranks Joey used to play.

"If I were you, I'd definitely leave the porch light on tonight. Maybe even leave a light on in the living room and the television on low if you can sleep without the noise bothering you," Homer said. "Tires are expensive."

"Yes, they are."

"I'd tell my honey about it too, if I were you."

My lips twitched as I tried to hide my smile. "My honey?"

"Don't play coy with me. You know who I'm talking about."

"True. But telling my honey is what got me in trouble with Joey Carver in the first place."

"Well, there is that." Homer took another bite of pie, and then he rested the spoon on the side of his saucer and placed his hand over mine. "You be careful, Amy. Some of these bad seeds like Joey Carver think they can get away with just about anything because they're not eighteen yet."

I gulped. "I hadn't thought of that."

"Just be vigilant."

"I will."

He went back to eating his pie.

"You know, there's something else that's troubling me," I said. "When I first met Madelyn, she couldn't speak highly enough of her brother. But today she gave me her cell phone number because she's afraid she can't depend on him enough to call her if need be."

"She said that? That she's afraid she can't depend on him?"

"Not in so many words." I thought back to what exactly Madelyn had said. "She said that Brendan has been acting weird, being belligerent, and running wild with Joey since he came to Winter Garden."

"Then it might not be that she's afraid she can't *depend* on him to call." He dabbed at his mouth with his napkin. "It might be that she's scared someone will have to call her *about* him."

"I hadn't thought of that. She must really be worried about him."

"It makes me wonder if he has changed that much since coming here to Winter Garden, or if he was really *running wild* as she called it all along and she simply didn't want to admit it."

"And I keep wondering about his and Madelyn's mother," I said. "Even if she and Stu were divorced and she's remarried, shouldn't she be here in some way for her children?"

He lifted his shoulders. "Maybe she is. Just because she isn't here in person doesn't mean she's not supporting her children."

"True. I'm sorry."

"No need to apologize for thinking out loud. Besides, maybe the mother isn't being supportive at all," he said. "I'm just glad Madelyn made a friend in Winter Garden when she needed one so badly."

*   *   *

When I got home, I took a desperately needed snuggle break with Rory. Then I turned on the television. As a talk show droned in the living room, I took the little dog into the bedroom.

"So what am I going to wear for my date this evening?" I asked, placing him on the bed before opening my closet door.

He pranced on his front feet and let out a high-pitched woof.

"Really? A dress?"

Rory barked again.

"Which one?"

He leapt off the bed and ran out of the room. Within seconds, he was back. I seriously doubted any dress in my closet would make me feel like doing sprints. I decided on the denim shirtdress with the brown basket-weave belt and a pair of tan espadrilles. Not sprinting material, but comfy enough that I could jog if I had to. Hopefully, that wouldn't be necessary.

By the time Ryan arrived, I'd fed the pets, taken a bath, and made myself presentable. Maybe even more than presentable. According to Deputy Hall, I looked "incredible." And he was an officer of the law, sworn to uphold truth, justice, and the American way. Right? Or was that just Superman? Either way, I was taking the man at his word . . . mainly because I wanted to.

I was having the fleeting thought that I would likely wind up as wild as Aunt Bess in sixty years when Ryan asked me something. I completely missed his question to me.

"Excuse me?"

"I asked if you'd like me to turn the TV off," he said.

"Uh . . . no. No, thank you. I'm leaving it on for . . . Rory."

He arched a brow.

That was the other thing about dating a police officer. That upholding the truth thing must come with a built-in lie detector test.

"You've never left the TV on for Rory before. Spill it."

"I just . . . I'd rather not leave the house . . . you know . . . obviously empty this evening."

"Why not?" he asked. "What exactly did Joey Carver say to you today?"

"It wasn't Joey . . . at least, not directly." I told Ryan what Madelyn said and what Homer had found out from Phil Poston. "If Joey thought it was a prank to slash Madelyn's bicycle tires when she threatened to tell her dad about his bad behavior, then he might think the same scare tactics will work on me."

"For one thing, when Madelyn's tires were slashed, she should've gone straight to her father and had him deal with Joey. Why didn't she?"

I merely shrugged.

"And for another," he continued, "that young man needs to realize that he's not hiding behind pranks anymore. There are serious consequences to his bad behavior. I tried to impress that notion upon him last night, but I apparently didn't get through to him after all."

"It's okay."

"No, Amy, it's not. You're afraid to go to dinner without leaving your TV on because you want this guy to think someone is home. That's the opposite of okay."

"Well, he hasn't threatened me. I'm just letting my imagination get the best of me. Maybe Homer said it best earlier today." I rolled my eyes heavenward trying to recall what he'd said. "Your mind is a sacred enclosure . . . something, something . . . Basically, no one can scare you without your permission."

"Then why have you not only given Joey Carver permission to scare you, you've all but sent him an engraved invitation?"

I blew out a breath. "You're right. I know that. It's just that he and Brendan are—as Madelyn put it—running wild together. I get the impression that Brendan blames me for Stu's death since he was found in the parking lot of the Down South Café. And I doubt either Brendan or Joey would swerve to miss me if I happened to be standing in the middle of the road. Add to that the fact that it was probably Joey we saw racing out of town on the night Stu was killed, and I have to wonder if he had anything to do with Stu's death."

"Why? That's quite a leap in logic to make."

"Brendan has made it clear that he didn't particularly like Stu. He preferred his stepfather. Joey has a serious case of hero worship for Brendan; so if Brendan didn't like Stu, Joey probably didn't either. What if Joey had something to do with Stu's death?"

"What's his motive?" Ryan asked. "What would he gain from Stu Carver's death?"

"I don't know." I shook my head. "You're right—I'm jumping to conclusions. If conclusion jumping were an Olympic event, I'd be a gold medalist."

He kissed my forehead. "No, you wouldn't. You're just on edge. After everything you've been through this past week, you have every right to be."

I placed my head against his shoulder and let him hold me for a moment. Then I pulled back and said, "I'm really hungry. Let's go eat."

"I'm all for that."

I turned and started to shut off the television.

"Why don't you leave that on for now? It'll keep Rory company."

I smiled. It was nice to be understood.

Chapter 11

I woke up Wednesday morning before the alarm clock sounded. I lay there in bed for a minute listening to the unintelligible sounds coming from the television still playing in the living room and wondering what having the set on all night would do to my electric bill.

For some reason, I was also thinking about figs. I had no idea why figs were on my mind, but they were. Glancing at the clock, I saw that I had time to linger over a cup of coffee with my recipe books and see what I could find that called for the fruit.

After turning on the coffeepot, I went into the living room and turned off the TV. I hoped it hadn't allowed any poltergeists into the house. Funny—I hadn't seen that movie in years, and yet the thought of that little girl sitting in front of the television with nothing on the screen except "snow" had popped into my head. These days, every channel played twenty-four hours a day. So maybe the poltergeist doors were all closed. Not that I believed in poltergeists, but this morning I wasn't taking any chances.

I stepped into the fancy room and picked out a few cookbooks that might contain some interesting fig recipes. Then I went back into the kitchen, poured myself a cup of coffee, and sat down at the table.

Rory came running in from the backyard. I patted his head and got him a dog treat. He lay down at my feet and I went back to thumbing through cookbooks.

I stumbled upon a recipe that my patrons might actually enjoy—baked fig crostini—but the recipe listed fresh figs, and they were almost impossible to find around here. In Richmond, I believed there was a Mediterranean grocer who sold fresh figs in August, but Richmond was five hours away. I'd have to keep looking for something a little more practical.

I actually got so engrossed in my cookbooks that I was nearly late for work. I glanced at the clock, did a double-take, and nearly turned my chair over getting up. I ran into the bedroom with Rory at my heels.

"I shouldn't have been lollygagging," I told him.

He hopped around me in little circles, eager to play whatever game it was we were playing.

I threw on my clothes, brushed my teeth, pulled my hair up into a ponytail, and put on some lipstick. I grabbed my purse and hurried out the front door.

I didn't even think about having the television on all night—or why. I was just eager to get into the car and get going.

And then I saw the truck slowly driving by my house. Joey Carver's truck. After he passed the house, he braked and backed up.

"Good morning!"

I saw that it wasn't Joey driving the truck, but Brendan.

"Hi, Brendan." I still kept my distance. "Is there something I can help you with?"

"Nope. Joey and I just thought we'd stop and say hi . . . see how you're doing."

Joey leaned forward from the passenger seat and waved to me.

I slowly raised my hand in greeting. "I'm sorry to rush off, but I'm going to be late for work if I don't."

"So what?" Brendan asked. "You own the place, don't you?"

"Yes, which is all the more reason to get there on time. If I'm not there to unlock the door, no one can work."

"I hadn't thought of it that way. Had you, Joey?"

Either Joey didn't answer or I couldn't hear his response.

Eager to end the conversation and get away from these two, I said, "Come on by the café later for coffee and doughnuts. Bye!"

I quickly unlocked the door, got inside, and unobtrusively locked myself in. Then I started the car. Thankfully, Brendan drove on off.

As relieved as I was that my tires weren't slashed and that the young men didn't make any veiled threats today, they'd rattled me. Why had they been driving by my house so early in the morning? How did they even know where I lived? Or had it been a coincidence that they were driving by and spotted me? They could've seen my car, I supposed—there weren't that many yellow Beetles in Winter Garden. In fact, mine might've been the only one.

Either way, I was fine. My car was fine. I was now on my way to the café—which I was pretty sure would also be fine. I refused to let these boys scare me. I was determined to take Homer's advice to heart about your mind being a sacred place that no harm could enter without permission. I guess it was originally that other guy's advice—the author whose name I couldn't remember—but the sentiment was the same. I marveled again at how Homer could remember quotes from all those different people and yet I couldn't even recall who his hero had been yesterday. I chose to chalk it up to stress. And then I decided not to have any more stress today because my mind was a sacred place and all that jazz.

When I pulled into the Down South Café parking lot, I saw Ryan standing there beside his police car. He was leaning against the driver's side door with his arms folded across his chest. And he was smiling. I don't know when I'd ever been happier to see anyone.

I put the car in park, got out, and sprinted over to hug him.

He laughed and so did I.

"What's that all about?" he asked. "If I'd known you'd be this glad to see me, I'd drop by the café every morning."

"Come on in, and I'll fix you some breakfast."

"Seriously, is everything all right?"

I smiled up at him. "Everything is great." I saw no need to tell him about my *other* early morning visitors.

We went inside, and as I was getting the coffee ready, I asked Ryan how things had gone with Mr. Jackson. "I kinda forgot about him with everything else that's been going on around here. Was he arrested?"

Ryan shook his head. "There wasn't any evidence to hold him, and he denied all charges. Sheriff Billings let him go but asked him to keep us apprised of any plans to leave town."

"Do you think he left for Oklahoma—or wherever he planned to go next—as soon as he was released?"

"I don't think so. He told the sheriff he was staying at the Fairbanks Hotel in Abingdon and would be there until after Stuart's funeral."

"That's odd, don't you think?" The coffee finished dripping into the pots, and I got us both a cup. "If he *was* guilty of murder, he'd have gotten out of town as quickly as he could. Don't you agree?"

He shrugged, spooning creamer and sugar into his coffee. "Maybe he thinks he'll look less guilty if he stays."

"He will, in my opinion."

Ryan smiled. "The jury is still out, Ms. Flowers. Please don't exonerate or convict the suspect until we've gathered the sufficient evidence."

"Yes, Deputy. Any word on how soon the funeral might be?"

"The regional medical examiner should be sending the body back tomorrow or the next day. We requested that Mr. Landon's—or rather, Carver's—body be given priority not only due to the fact that the victim was murdered but also because his family is from out of town. We don't want to create an unnecessary burden on the Carvers."

It was sweet how Ryan slid into and out of *official police mode* so easily.

"Madelyn has already made all the arrangements, hasn't she?" I asked.

He nodded. "The funeral director said they'd finalize everything as soon as the body is returned from the ME."

Determined to shake off our depressing conversation, I asked, "What else can I get you for breakfast?"

"I'd love a couple of eggs and some whole wheat toast."

"Coming right up," I said with a smile.

As I went into the kitchen, Jackie and Luis came in. They were chatting with Ryan as I prepared Ryan's food, and my mind wandered back to Walter Jackson. I really wanted to talk with Mr. Jackson—get his side of the story.

Why had he come to Winter Garden to find Stuart Landon Carver? Had he wanted revenge? And even if he had, I found it hard to believe that he'd actually killed Stu, especially in the brutal way Stu had been murdered. It seemed to me that it would've taken a younger, stronger person to wrestle Stu, cut his throat, and place him into the truck.

I hadn't taken time to examine the truck, but I hadn't seen a lot of blood there. I could be mistaken, of course, but I got the feeling that the murder might've happened somewhere else and that Stu had been put into the truck afterward.

Mr. Jackson simply didn't strike me as being that strong. It was possible he'd drugged Stu before cutting his throat, but it still didn't explain how he'd lifted him into the truck . . . unless he'd had help. I made up my mind then—although I most definitely intended to keep my plans to myself—to go talk with Mr. Jackson that afternoon. I knew there was a slim chance Mr. Jackson was a murderer, but I figured he wouldn't do anything in the lobby of his hotel . . . in broad daylight . . . with (hopefully) lots of witnesses around.

* * *

The rest of the morning was uneventful but pleasant. Dilly reported that her raccoon friend seemed to be doing better—he was still favoring the injured paw yesterday evening, but not as much as he had been the day before. Homer's hero was a skydiver named Don Kellner. And there was no sign of the Carver cousins.

Lunchtime was a little more interesting.

Calvin Dougherty came in—black leather portfolio in hand—and gave me a smile and a wave. He sat at a corner table, and Jackie went over to take his order.

She came back, leaned through the window separating the kitchen from the dining room, and said, "Get this. The Ives Oil and Gas Company fellow just ordered two cheeseburgers, two orders of fries, and four soft drinks."

"He's obviously expecting someone to join him."

"Yeah, but not only that. He doesn't want them to be disturbed. He ordered two meals and *four* drinks, so I don't have to keep refilling their glasses."

I peeped around Jackie to where Mr. Dougherty was sitting. He'd opened up the portfolio and was writing something.

"I'll get right on those cheeseburgers," I said.

"I'm eager to see who joins him."

I nodded as I took two beef patties out of the refrigerator and put them on the grill. I, too, was wondering about who Mr. Dougherty was meeting. I mean, I acknowledged that it was none of our business. But the fact that he was meeting with someone and wanted a smidgeon of privacy made me think he might've discovered a natural gas reserve on someone's property. That could be exciting . . . maybe . . . or bad . . . for Winter Garden, depending on how you looked at it. Some people wanted Winter Garden to grow and become a boomtown. Others liked our sleepy little town just the way it was. I'd have to say I was in the latter camp.

Chad Thomas came in, wiped his palms down the sides of his pants as he quickly scanned the dining room, and then strode over to Mr. Dougherty's table. Mr. Dougherty stood and shook Mr. Thomas's hand, and then the two sat and immediately put their heads together to quietly talk.

Jackie came into the kitchen. "So now I guess we know who that other burger is for. Wonder what they're talking about?"

"Maybe Mr. Dougherty found something promising about Mr. Thomas's property while performing his tests."

"I don't know. I think the oil and gas guy might be trying to pull one over on some of Winter Garden's more gullible residents." She turned and surveyed the pair's animated discussion before whirling back around to me. "Maybe he's trying to convince people to pay for some bogus but expensive tests with the hope that he'll find gas beneath their property and get rich."

"What makes you say so? He didn't try to swindle Mom and Aunt Bess. Or Homer either, for that matter."

"Yeah, Amy, but they're too smart to fall for anybody's hogwash. Besides, their main goal isn't to strike it rich."

"Is that Chad Thomas's main goal?" I asked.

"I believe it very well could be. And it could be a goal for the majority of people in this town. I mean, who doesn't want to be filthy, stinking rich?"

I flipped the burgers. Before I could answer Jackie,

two customers came in and she ducked out of the kitchen to hand the women menus. As I continued grilling the burgers, I thought about what she'd asked. Sure, I'd like to have a bit more money . . . maybe upgrade my wardrobe . . . but I didn't care anything about being "filthy, stinking rich."

Since opening the Down South Café, I'd become much more aware of money. I now had payroll, supplies, utilities, taxes, and additional insurance to think of. So, yes, more money in the bank to provide a cushion for those things would be terrific, but I wasn't ready to fall for anyone's get-rich-quick scheme. And I doubted many other Winter Garden residents were either.

I glanced into the dining room, where Calvin Dougherty and Chad Thomas were smiling and nodding.

At least, I *hoped* there weren't many other Winter Garden residents that ready and willing to be fooled.

After work, I didn't even go home first. I drove to the Fairbanks Hotel in Abingdon, where Walter Jackson was staying. It wasn't one of the fancier hotels in town, but it was clean and reasonably priced. The automatic front doors whooshed open, and I stepped into the cool lobby.

A desk clerk looked up from his computer. "Good afternoon. Welcome to the Fairbanks. How may I help you?"

"I'm waiting for a friend." I took a seat on the sofa. Now that I was here at the hotel, I wasn't sure how to approach Mr. Jackson. I mean, if I had the clerk call up to Mr. Jackson's room and tell him I was here to see him, what would I say?

Um, hi, could you call Walter Jackson's room and let

him know Amy Flowers is here to see him? What? He's
asking why I want to talk with him? Um . . . I'd like to
ask him if he's guilty of murder. By the way, do you have
any complimentary water? Thanks.

Maybe this had been a bad idea.

Maybe? The little voice inside my head taunted. *It was*
definitely *a bad idea.*

But now if I simply got up and left, I'd look like an
idiot. Should I look at my phone and pretend I got a text
from my so-called friend?

What would Ryan say if I got killed here? What would
Mom *say? And how sad it would be for Aunt Bess to have*
to add me to her People I've Outlived *Pinterest board.*

Okay, this was stupid. No matter what the desk clerk—
someone I'd never met and would likely never see again—
thought, I was leaving. I dropped my phone into my purse
and stood.

The front doors whooshed.

"Why, Ms. Flowers. What a nice surprise."

Naturally, it was Walter Jackson.

"Hi, Mr. Jackson."

"What are you doing here?" he asked.

"Actually, I'd like to talk with you. Do you have a
minute?"

"Of course. Shall we go into the restaurant and have
a coffee?"

I nodded. "That would be nice."

As I accompanied him to the hotel's restaurant, I re-
flected that he looked just as I'd remembered—white hair,
slightly stooped shoulders, thin, average height, carried
himself with a humble dignity. There was no way this
man could be a killer. I hoped.

We sat at a table near the bar and ordered coffee. The waitress brought us our drinks, told us to let her know if we needed anything, and then returned to the bar.

"So what was it you wanted to speak with me about, Ms. Flowers?"

"On the morning that we first met, you were searching for Mr. Landon—or as we now know, Mr. Carver. I simply wondered if you'd found him."

He raised his bushy eyebrows.

"I'm not here to accuse you of anything, Mr. Jackson. It just seemed to me that it was really important to you that you talk with Stu Landon Carver . . . and I hope you were able to do that."

"I did get the opportunity to talk with Stu."

"Good." I sipped my coffee. "I'm glad."

"So am I. Although, I have to admit, I wish my timing had been better. But I did get to make my peace with the man."

I merely nodded. I wasn't going to prompt him to tell me anything else. I'd already decided that coming here was a mistake. Talk about your bad timing.

Mr. Jackson, on the other hand, was in a talkative mood.

"I'm going to tell you a story, young lady. And I hope it will be a lesson to you."

I said a silent prayer that it wouldn't begin, "Once upon a time, there was a young lady who poked her nose into other people's business . . ."

It didn't.

"Years ago—long before you were born, I'm sure—Stuart Carver and I worked together at a company that made pesticides. Stu was an entomologist with the company—Callicorp—and although I started out as an accountant, I moved up the ranks to chief financial officer and then vice president."

"That's impressive," I said.

"Thank you. I'd like to say it was all due to my hard work and dedication, but there was more to it than that. I took shortcuts. I didn't always behave with integrity. And that came back to bite me."

I knew what he was talking about because Jackie and I had found the articles online, but I remained silent.

"You see, our company was known for being environmentally conscious and safe for bees while discouraging aphids, flies, and mosquitoes from eating crops," he continued. "It was safe but it wasn't as effective as the pesticides our competitors were using, and we were losing market share."

The waitress returned to see if we were okay or if we'd decided we'd like to order something to eat.

"I'm fine," said Mr. Jackson. "Ms. Flowers?"

"I'm okay too," I said. "Thank you."

Mr. Jackson drank his coffee and looked around the otherwise empty dining room until he was certain she was out of earshot.

"I authorized technicians to swap out one chemical in our pesticide for another—one that was cheaper for us to use and much more effective but that could be harmful to humans." His lips curved into a small, sad smile. "But I think what bothered Stu about it most was that it was devastating to honeybees. Wherever the pesticide was sprayed, the bees either died or left." He raised his eyes to mine. "I accepted a bribe to switch the two ingredients. I went to prison for eighteen years."

For lack of anything better to say, I mumbled, "I'm sorry."

"It was my mistake, and I paid for it. I didn't have to serve the entire time, but I don't want to discuss that. Suffice it to say, I came out of the experience a changed man."

I nodded and took a sip of my coffee. It was bland.

"I didn't come to Winter Garden to kill Stuart Landon Carver, Ms. Flowers. I came to apologize to the man. I hadn't realized the magnitude of what I'd done until I had a while to really mull it over."

"But why did you feel the need to apologize to Mr. Landon Carver?"

"I've actually felt the need to apologize to a number of people for what I did back then. With Stu, I felt that I owed him an apology for my flagrant disregard for his bees," said Mr. Jackson. "Oh, they weren't *his* bees, of course, but our pesticide certainly led to a marked decrease in the honeybee population. So much so that Stu felt that he had to dedicate the rest of his life to building it back up to the extent that he could."

"That must be why he started all those hives when he moved to Winter Garden."

"Indeed. He became consumed with repairing what he'd helped destroy."

Chapter 12

$\mathcal{E}\mathrm{A}$fter leaving Mr. Jackson, I got into the car and pulled up a cake recipe on my phone. I intended to make the cake to serve tomorrow and needed to go by the grocery store for some of the ingredients I didn't have on hand. I noted the items I needed and headed for the store.

I couldn't get what Mr. Jackson had told me out of my mind. He said he hadn't come here for any sort of vengeance on Stu Landon. He'd had a lot of time to think in prison, and he'd sought out the man to apologize to him. He'd been looking for Stu on and off for several years.

So Stu had been right in his assumption that someone from Callicorp might come looking for him someday. But he'd been certain that when that day came, it would be by someone out for revenge. Was Mr. Jackson the person Stu had been afraid of? Or was there someone else—or more than *one* someone else—that Stu feared would harm him and his family? I knew from the article that Mr. Jackson wasn't the only Callicorp executive to face ramifications from Stu's whistle-blowing.

When I arrived at the grocery store, I was lucky enough to find a parking spot fairly close. Yes, it would've been healthier for me to walk a longer distance, but I'd been on my feet most of the day and was glad for the serendipity that had made whatever car had been in this primo space leave just before I'd arrived.

As I was walking into the store, Fern Thomas was walking out.

"Oh, hi," I said.

She looked vaguely confused.

"I'm Amy Flowers . . . of the Down South Café. You and your husband had lunch there on Monday?"

The fog lifted from Fern's face, and she smiled. "Yeah. It's nice to see you again."

"You too. I'm sorry you weren't able to come to lunch with your husband again today."

The smile faded. "Chad was there to talk business with Mr. Dougherty. Chad doesn't like for me to be around when he's discussing business."

Not for the first time this afternoon, I was at a loss for words. So I merely said, "Aw, it was probably boring stuff anyway, right?"

"Oh, no. If Chad found it important enough to talk about, then I doubt it was boring."

"Well, hey, either way, if Mr. Dougherty finds gas reserves on your property, you'll be a rich woman." I forced a little laugh.

Fern did not laugh. She said, "Yes, Chad would be wealthy. He'd like that."

Now it was my turn to look confused.

Seeing the incredulity on my face, Fern hastened to add, "He's a good husband. He takes care of me and gives me just about anything a wife could want."

"That . . . that's nice," I said. "Gee, I shouldn't keep you any longer. I don't want your groceries to spoil. I hope to see you back at the café again soon."

"Me too." She stood there looking rather lost for a second and then scurried on out into the parking lot.

I chose a shopping cart and strolled on through the store. It was apparently my day for odd encounters. Okay, so I'd invited the first weird chat, but this second one was even stranger and completely unexpected. What wife said her *husband* would be wealthy rather than *they* would be wealthy? Apparently, Fern Thomas.

I shook my head and concentrated on getting the ingredients I needed to make my chocolate pistachio pudding cake. I wanted to make the cake this evening, so I could take it in to work tomorrow morning.

While I was at the store, I picked up a few staples, replenished my supply of pet food, and browsed the magazines. The magazines that featured headlines like *World's Most Decadent Cheesecake* and *Lose Ten Pounds This Week* on the same cover always made me smile. As if someone could buy the magazine, prepare and eat the cheesecake, *and* lose ten pounds in a week. Barring a tragic accident or a terrible illness, I didn't think that was going to happen.

I paid for my groceries and was on my way out of the store when I saw Calvin Dougherty walking toward me.

"Good afternoon, Ms. Flowers. Do you have something there that you're planning to offer for tomorrow's special of the day?"

"Not exactly," I said. "I am making a chocolate pistachio pudding cake to take in, though."

"Sounds delicious. I'll have to stop by."

"Please do."

"I'm trying to bring all of my Winter Garden contacts to the Down South Café. The ones who haven't tried it yet are dutifully impressed, and the ones who've been there already know it's the best place in the region to eat." He patted his stomach.

I smiled but wondered why he appeared to be schmoozing me. "I appreciate that, Mr. Dougherty." Since he might be fishing for information, I supposed I could do the same. "I saw that you had Chad Thomas in today."

"Yes, ma'am."

"Didn't you find it odd that he didn't have his wife join you?"

Mr. Dougherty rocked back on his heels. "I take it that Mr. and Mrs. Thomas have a—what's the phrase I'm looking for—an old-fashioned relationship. He handles all the business affairs, and she is the dutiful homemaker. She keeps a lovely home. She really does."

"Huh. And do you think there's a natural gas preserve beneath their land?"

"I really couldn't say. At this point, it's all just speculation. We need to perform more tests."

"But you must've seen something promising there," I said. "I mean, you didn't recommend further testing for our land."

"Nope, I didn't. That's just the way it goes sometimes.

You'll see something in one plot of land and think you've hit the jackpot, but then you'll test the plot next to it and find nothing."

"I see. So it's just the luck of the draw."

"That's it, Ms. Flowers. I'm sorry if you were disappointed."

"Oh, I wasn't. I wouldn't want my home destroyed." I smiled. "And, of course, Aunt Bess was relieved."

He chuckled. "She was, wasn't she? She's a sweetheart."

I agreed with him and then said I needed to get home and get started on my cake. He said he hoped to stop by and try a piece tomorrow, and I pressed the button on my key fob to unlock the car door.

I loaded the groceries into the car and called Sarah before I started home. She agreed to come over for homemade pizza and a game of Scrabble. I was glad. I'd like to get her take on Mr. Jackson.

Two hours later, Sarah and I were sitting at my kitchen table eating slices of ham pizza while puzzling over letters printed on small wooden tiles. We also had pita chips with hummus and a fruit tray, so we could sit there all night if we had to.

At the moment, my thoughts were divided between, one, what word I could make using the letters X, Z, Y, N, L, P, and H given the existing vowels on the board, and two, the possible duplicitous nature of Mr. Jackson. I was considering using my turn to exchange tiles, but I wasn't ready to commit to that move yet. So I landed on the topic of Mr. Jackson.

I told Sarah how I'd gone to see him at his hotel.

She slowly lifted her head, eyes wide and mouth open. "You did what?"

"Yeah, I know. When I think about it now, it seems like a totally crazy thing to have done."

"You think?"

I huffed. "Do you want to know what he said, or not?"

"Of course I do."

"He said he came here to make amends with Stuart Landon, not to have it out with him."

"And yet, Mr. Landon—Carver, whatever—is dead," Sarah said. "He isn't walking around with a new BFF."

"I know, but don't you think Mr. Jackson could've simply been in the wrong place—Winter Garden—at the wrong time—the day of Stu's death?"

Sarah gave me a look that plainly said, *Say that sentence over again to yourself.*

"Okay, okay," I said. "So he arrived the day Stu was murdered. He found him, made his peace with him—"

"And then disappeared to where the police couldn't find him for two days."

In frustration, I swiped a pita chip through the hummus. I bit the chip and debated this while I chewed.

I swallowed. "But Mr. Jackson didn't know the police were searching for him. If he had, he might've been on his way to turn himself in instead of stopping by the Down South Café for breakfast. He didn't appear to realize Stu was dead."

"He doesn't read the newspaper? Watch the news on TV? Why are you so determined that this man is innocent?"

Flipping my palms, I said, "I don't know. I just feel in

my gut that he didn't do this. Do you ever get gut feelings about your clients at the law firm?"

"Sometimes. And they're fifty-fifty. I've been shocked before at what some of Billy's clients have been convicted of—and later confessed to—doing. Remember, Ann Rule refused to believe that Ted Bundy was guilty up until almost the very end." Sarah pulled out her phone. "Here's what I'm talking about." She came around to my side of the table and placed the phone between us.

She'd brought up an article written in *The Washington Post* in 2015 after Ann Rule's death. In the article, Rule was quoted as having said in 1999 that people could completely fool you. Ms. Rule had been a cop and had years of education in psychology, but Ted Bundy's mask had been perfect. She said it was scary that you could never be a hundred percent sure you knew someone.

"And it *is* scary, Amy. Some people really can make you believe anything they want you to. Please promise me you won't seek this guy out again. He might appear to be a harmless little old man to you, but there's a strong chance that he's a killer. I don't want you to be his next victim."

"Okay."

"I'm serious. Promise me."

"I promise."

She looked down at my tiles; picked up *L*, *Y*, *N*, and *X*; and made *lynx*. The *X* in *lynx* came under an *A* to make *ax*. The word began on a Triple Word Score space and wound up being worth fifty-one points, given the 9 points for *ax*. "You're welcome." She picked up her phone and returned to her chair.

"Thanks. That's why you're the Scrabble Queen."

"You know it." She popped a grape into her mouth and surveyed the board. "You gonna tell Ryan?"

"That you were whipping my butt in this game but then took mercy on me and helped me play catch-up?"

She arched a brow.

"Okay, no. Given your reaction, I'm definitely *not* going to tell Ryan that I went to talk with Mr. Jackson."

She simply shook her head and ate a strawberry.

"And given *your* reaction, I won't tell you the next time I do something crazy either," I said.

She picked up a grape, threw it at me, and it hit me on the forehead. "Ow! What was that for?"

"How about this? Don't do anything crazy!"

That night, I took a relaxing lavender-scented bubble bath. When I got out of the tub, I put on my favorite summer pajamas and snuggled into bed. I read a cooking magazine until my eyelids got heavy and I couldn't concentrate on the words. Then I put the magazine on the bedside table, turned off the light, and went to sleep.

It seemed that immediately afterward, I heard Rory barking like crazy in the backyard. I sat up in bed, heart racing. It wasn't unusual for Rory to use his doggie door in the middle of the night, but he didn't normally go bananas like this.

I looked at the clock. It was two a.m. What on earth could be the matter with him at this hour?

I threw off the covers, stepped into my slippers, and eased toward the kitchen. I needed a weapon. Anything—or anyone—could be out there. I took the cleaver from the knife block.

If I could just get Rory inside and make sure he was safe, then I could get back into the house and lock the door. And push something in front of the doggie door. Of course, if the threat was small enough to fit through the doggie door, I could probably handle it. At least, I could with the help of this cleaver.

I looked through the window of the door, but it wasn't big enough for me to see much of anything. I couldn't even see Rory.

I moved to the windows over the sink. Now I could see Rory; he was scratching at the fence as if he wanted out. Did that mean that whoever or whatever was out there was on the other side of the fence? If so, that was a positive sign. It meant that it wasn't likely to be a person after all. The fence didn't lock. Anyone could open the gate. Whatever Rory was barking at must be an animal.

Still, I kept the cleaver in my hand. I slowly unlocked the door and stepped onto the stoop. I was being as quiet as I possibly could, but of course, Rory heard me.

The dog ran halfway between the fence and the door. Then he turned back to the fence as if he wanted me to either let him out or go with him to investigate. Neither was going to happen.

"Rory! Come here!" I hissed.

He started back toward me, but then there was a soft thump against the gate.

Rory started barking with renewed fervor, went back to the fence, stood on his back legs, and scratched furiously.

There was another thump. Was there an animal on the other side of that gate trying to get it open? What if it *did* come open? Or what if the animal—coyote, fox, bear?—found a way to climb over the fence?

My heart pounded so hard I could feel it in my throat. Could there be a *person* on the other side of that fence? Someone toying with me before coming into the yard?

"Come on, Rory," I said loudly. "You know I haven't fired this gun in a long time, but I'm still an excellent shot."

Okay, so Rory knew that I'd never used a gun in my life and that the cleaver I held was in no way, shape, or form a firearm. But, one, he wasn't telling. And, two, it sounded better to say I had a gun than to threaten to cleave anyone who might come through the gate.

Whether he was satisfied that we had the threat under control or he could hear the anxiety in my voice, Rory did as I asked and came to me. I scooped him up in one arm, fled into the house, and locked the door behind me. And I braced a chair under the doorknob.

I looked for something to put in front of the doggie door because I was afraid that someone could reach through it and dislodge the chair. I went with the cast iron skillet. It was heavy, and if someone knocked it over, Rory would hear it and sound the alarm.

Leaving the cleaver on the counter, I left the kitchen light on and went back into the bedroom. I peeped out the bedroom window, but I couldn't see anyone or anything out of the ordinary. I was glad.

I was still unsettled, though. I locked the bedroom door, got Rory into bed with me, and pulled the covers up to my chin.

Through all this commotion, I didn't see or hear Princess Eloise. That wasn't unusual, though. I believe that cat would sleep through a bombing and then come prissing into the war zone, tail twitching, appalled at what the dog and I had let happen.

I considered calling Ryan, but I realized I was probably overreacting. I did finally manage to fall back asleep, but I still felt tired when I woke up. It was as if part of me had been on alert all night. In the light of day, I felt ridiculous. I'd gotten so worked up over what had probably been a harmless animal.

Once I got dressed and ready for work, I made sure Princess Eloise was happy and fed since I hadn't seen her the night before. She protested loudly, but I picked her up and hugged her before I left. I also gave Rory some breakfast, and I made myself a slice of buttered toast.

I'd packed up the cake the night before in a bakery box, and now I carried it out to the car. I put the cake on the passenger seat and then, almost as an afterthought, I closed the car door and went over to the gate that opened into the backyard. I wanted to see what sort of prints were there. Not that I was all that good at determining animals by their tracks, but I could distinguish between a dog and a cat. And I might be able to tell if the animal that had been lingering on the other side of the fence last night had been a bear.

It crossed my mind that there might have been an injured animal there and that it might still be nearby. I hadn't heard any yips or growls, but it would benefit me to be cautious anyway.

I was looking at the ground as I walked the length of the fence to the gate. I didn't see any tracks of any kind.

In fact, I didn't see anything at all, at least, not until I came upon the cigarette butt.

I didn't smoke. Nor did Mom, Aunt Bess, Jackie, or any of my friends. But I got goose bumps when I realized that whoever had been standing on the other side of my gate last night obviously *did* smoke.

Chapter 13

As I drove to work, I tried to remember who I knew or had met recently who smoked. Did Mr. Dougherty smoke? That would be a much more soothing explanation for me to believe—Mr. Dougherty was enjoying a cigarette while he tested the soil or rocks or whatever he did to see if there were any natural gas reserves beneath our property, and it had been left there before last night. I liked that idea much better than the thought that someone was smoking outside my back gate at two o'clock in the morning.

That had to be it. It had to have been Mr. Dougherty. I'd never seen him smoke . . . hadn't noticed a pack of cigarettes in his shirt pocket . . . and he hadn't smelled of cigarettes, but maybe he only smoked occasionally. Maybe he found testing for natural gas reserves stressful—especially if he wasn't finding any—and having a cigarette calmed his nerves.

There was still the nagging thought in the back of my mind that there could have been a person standing there outside my back gate last night . . . or rather, this morning. But why? Why would anyone simply stand there, especially long enough to smoke a cigarette? Was he—or she—debating on whether or not to try to break in . . . maybe weighing the risks against whatever he hoped to gain by doing so?

I phoned Sarah. She was the only person I told that I'd gone to speak with Walter Jackson. Maybe she could help me put whatever had happened last night into perspective. She'd probably laugh and tell me that my overactive imagination had gotten the best of me. Of course it had been Mr. Dougherty smoking a cigarette on my lawn and what I'd heard last night had been some animal passing through.

My call went to voice mail. Sarah was probably still asleep. I left a message asking her to call me this afternoon if she got time. When I arrived at the café, I parked and texted Sarah to tell her I'd left her a voice mail. Otherwise, she might not check it. Mom always would. My friends—not so much. It must have been a generational thing.

I was still sitting in my car when Luis pulled in beside me. I smiled and waved.

"Good morning," I said. "I'm glad you're here early . . . or that I'm a few minutes late. Whatever the reason, I'm glad I don't have to be here alone this morning."

He drew his dark brows together. "Why? Did something happen?"

I didn't want him to be alarmed. And maybe nothing *had* happened. It could very well be my overactive imagination at work. "It's just weird coming into work alone ever since we found Mr. Landon here in the parking lot. It just makes me feel more comfortable with someone else here, that's all."

He didn't appear to be convinced, but he let the matter go. He nodded to the cake box I carried. "What've you got there?"

"A pistachio pudding cake. Do you like pistachios?"

"I sure do."

"It's really delicious. Have a slice with your lunch."

"I'll do that. Thank you."

Shelly was the next to arrive, since Jackie wasn't scheduled to come in until lunchtime. "Hey, sweeties! How is everybody this morning? Did either of you see that new game show on TV last night? It was so funny! There was this one little old lady, and she was the cutest, spunkiest grandma you ever did see."

I smiled. Normal felt great this morning. "Hi, Shelly. I didn't see the show. Did you, Luis?"

"No. Sounds like it was good, though."

"Oh, it was." She spotted the cake I'd just removed from the box and placed on a cake plate. "Oooh, that looks scrumptious!"

"Yes, it does," Dilly said as she came through the door. "I spotted it even before I walked in here. I see that it's chocolate. Does it have any other flavoring with it?"

I explained that it was a pistachio pudding cake, and she asked me to box her up a piece to take home and have later.

The door opened again, but I didn't know who'd come in until Brendan Carver sauntered up to the counter and asked what everyone was making a fuss over.

"It's this cake Amy made last night," Shelly said. "Doesn't it look delicious?"

Brendan looked at me. "I think it looks real good."

Joey joined Brendan and clapped a hand onto his shoulder. "She does look good. I could go for some of that."

"You and me both. Maybe we can share it sometime." He narrowed his eyes at me. "Sometime real soon."

Their meaning wasn't lost on me. It was, however, lost on Dilly.

"Why would you want to share it? I know you can both afford to have your own."

"I believe you'd better enjoy your breakfast someplace else this morning," I said.

"Why?" Joey asked. "Our money's as good as anybody else's."

"I'm sure it is, but you're making me uncomfortable. I'd appreciate it if you'd leave."

He looked at Brendan and laughed. "Hear that, cousin? We're making her hot under the collar."

"The lady asked you to go," Luis said softly but determinedly.

"Don't get your dander up," Brendan said. "We're going." He winked at me. "But hopefully we've not seen the last of you, Ms. Flowers."

He and Joey left but stood outside the door talking and looking back inside. After a minute, Joey blew me a kiss, and they both laughed as they went and got into Joey's truck.

"Shelly, would you please take care of Dilly's breakfast order?" I asked. "I'll be right back."

I went through the kitchen and stepped out the back door. I left the door open in case Brendan and Joey should for some reason come around here looking for me and I'd need to make a hasty retreat. I took my cell phone from my pocket and called Madelyn.

"Hi, Amy," she answered. "I'm driving back to Winter Garden right now and am about two hours out. Is there anything wrong?"

"Actually, Joey and Brendan have been giving me a really hard time since you've been away." I explained to her about Joey tailgating me and that the police were interested because a truck like her father's had been spotted racing out of town on the night before we'd found Mr. Landon in the parking lot. "I believe the deputy wanted to determine whether the truck had been Joey's or your dad's. The next day, Joey came into the café angry because he thought I'd called the police on him."

"Well, that sounds like Joey. I'll try to smooth things over with him when I get there. Is that all?"

"Not exactly. I . . ." But exactly what *were* they doing that I could tattle on them about to Brendan's big sister? I suddenly felt foolish. "I just feel like they're trying to rattle my cage. Harmless stuff, really, and now I feel silly for calling and bothering you with it. But I'd like them to know I didn't mean Joey any harm."

"I understand."

"It doesn't add up. The way you described Brendan and the Brendan I've met sound like two different people."

"That's because of Joey," Madelyn said with a sigh of resignation in her voice. "When he's around, Brendan apparently feels the need to act like a tough, super-cool guy to impress him."

"I'm terribly sorry I got off on the wrong foot with both of them."

"It's all right, Amy. This has been a stressful time for our family. Maybe when everything calms down, you and Brendan can meet again under better circumstances and you can get to know *my* Brendan instead of Joey's."

"I hope so." I saw that I was getting a call from Sarah. "I'll let you go. Again, I'm sorry to have bothered you with something so trivial."

"No problem. See you soon."

I switched over to Sarah's call. "Hi there."

"How are you? You sounded kinda upset when you left your message."

"I feel silly about the whole thing now. Are you ready to laugh at me? I found a cigarette butt in my yard this morning and became convinced that whatever was driving Rory up the wall at two a.m. was a person." I chuckled. "Then Brendan and Joey Carver came in here making double entendres about my pistachio pudding cake, and I told them to leave. Then I called and told Brendan's sister on them. Which is exactly what she needed from me when she's on her way back to Winter Garden to finalize her father's funeral arrangements."

There was silence on the other end of the conversation.

"Sarah, are you there?" I asked. "You're not laughing."

"That's because I don't think this is funny," she said. "You've convinced yourself that you're overreacting. But given the fact that a man was found with his throat slit in your parking lot a week ago, I don't think you are. Tell me what happened at two a.m."

I told her about waking up to Rory's barking, going outside and not seeing anyone or anything. "There were a couple of thumps against the gate, but had it been a person, he or she could've easily opened the gate and come on inside."

"So either it was an animal or someone was trying to scare you."

"Right. It was probably an animal . . . most likely a cat."

"But then when you went to check it out before going to work, you found a cigarette butt," she said. "Did you save it?"

"You mean, did I bag it and tag it as evidence? You've been watching too many cop shows."

"Maybe so, but when you get home, get a Baggie and a pair of tweezers and save that cigarette butt. If anyone comes and bothers you again, it can be used to prove that they were there previously. It establishes a pattern of stalking."

"You're serious," I said.

"Yes, I am. Label the bag with the date the cigarette butt was found."

"Okay." Sarah was making me feel nervous again.

"Tell me more about Joey and Brendan."

"It wasn't so much what they said but how they said it. I felt threatened by them, and I asked them to leave."

"And did they go peaceably?" she asked.

"Yes, but then they stood outside the door talking and laughing . . . and blowing kisses at me . . . before they got in Joey's truck to leave." I sighed. "I'm probably making mountains out of molehills here."

"Or you might not be. You went with your gut and asked them to leave. I'm proud of you for that. I'm afraid you haven't got enough to ask a judge for a restraining order, though."

"Oh, I know that. They haven't really done anything."

"Eh, that's debatable," said Sarah. "You feel like they've done something, and they're upsetting you, so that's your instincts warning you. They might simply be yanking your chain, or they could actually want to harm you. Either way, be extra careful. Would you like to stay with me for a day or two?"

"No, thanks. I'm fine."

"Are you sure?"

"Positive. Thank you, though."

"I'll call you back after work," she said. "We'll think of something."

When Homer came in at ten a.m., he announced that his hero of the day was Thich Nhat Hanh, the Vietnamese monk and peace activist.

"Seeing you reminds me of one of his quotes. 'Because of your smile, you make life more beautiful.'" He considered me for a moment. "But I see something lying beneath that smile—something that tells me all isn't right with you today. What's going on?"

"It's nothing really."

He flattened his lips. "Amy. You know you'll tell me eventually."

"Okay. Brendan and Joey Carver were in this morning, and I asked them to leave."

"What did they do?"

"Not anything overt exactly," I said. "But I felt threatened by their behavior."

"And did they leave?"

"Yes." I didn't tell him that they blew kisses at me from the door. Obnoxious oafs.

"Have you spoken with Ryan about this?"

I shook my head. "The last time I mentioned Joey to Ryan, Ryan went and talked with him. That resulted in Joey's angry outburst here in the middle of the café and his telling me that 'this isn't over.' I don't want to jab that hornets' nest again."

"Maybe not, but it might be what you have to do to make him stop harassing you."

"True. But it's like my friend Sarah and I were discussing this morning—neither Joey nor Brendan have done anything they can't explain away. If I accuse them of anything, they'll make me look like I'm some sort of hysterical female."

"So?"

"So I don't want to come across that way, Homer. I want to be seen in this community as a strong, competent businesswoman."

"You are." He patted my hand. "I'm sorry these hooligans are giving you grief. If it comes as any comfort at all, Hanh once said, 'Fear keeps us focused on the past or worried about the future. If we can acknowledge our fear, we can realize that right now we're okay.' Right now, you're okay. Hold on to that knowledge and don't let the Carver boys rob you of the present."

"That's good advice."

"I'll also go talk with Phil Poston after I've eaten my sausage biscuit and see if he has any other advice." He shook his head. "Joey is bound to have given Phil's granddaughter trouble after she stopped seeing him, based on the amount of aggravation he's causing you."

"Thanks, Homer. I appreciate that."

He caught my hand before I turned to go make his

biscuit. "One last thought. Hanh also said that hope is important because it makes the present less difficult to bear. I want you to think about how far you've come. I was here with you when you had some of those dark days after Lou Lou Holman's death. You sailed through that hardship and made your dream of owning a café come true."

Tears pricked my eyes. "You're the best friend anyone in Winter Garden could ever have. Breakfast is on me today."

"Nope. I always pay for breakfast. It's my routine."

"Then I'm sending you home with a piece of cake or pie," I said.

"Can you make it two? I'll take one to Phil. He's always more open to chatting if he can do it over something sweet."

Chapter 14

I was happy to see Sarah and her boss, Billy Hancock, come into the café for lunch. At least, I was until they asked me to join them for a moment before Jackie took their order. I could see that whatever they wanted to talk with me about was serious.

Billy removed his black-framed glasses and cleaned the lenses with his napkin. "Sarah says you've been having a little trouble with Joey Carver and his cousin Brendan for the past couple of days."

"A little bit." I looked from Billy's blue eyes to Sarah's warm brown ones.

"They came into the office today," he said. "They wanted to file a civil suit against you for refusing them service here at Down South Café."

My jaw dropped. "Wh-what?"

Sarah nodded. "Of course, Billy refused to take the case—you're our client."

"And even if you weren't, I wouldn't have taken the case," Billy added. "It's a hassle. They don't have a leg to stand on."

"The Civil Rights Act of 1964 prohibits restaurants from refusing service to patrons on the basis of race, color, religion, or natural origins." Sarah raised an index finger. "But in these particular circumstances, Joey had previously come in here yelling at you and issuing veiled threats. And then this morning, he and Brendan had been rowdy and had made you feel uncomfortable. You have witnesses to that."

"I didn't know that, of course—the boys certainly weren't going to tell me—until after they left and I discussed the situation with Sarah," said Billy. "But based on what she told me, you had every right to ask the young men to leave."

"But . . ." I prompted.

"But they might find another attorney who'll take their case." Billy ran a hand through his short, steel gray hair. "If the matter *does* go to court, I'll represent you and I feel confident the matter will be thrown out."

"Don't forget to get that cigarette butt," Sarah reminded me. "In fact, call your mom and see if she can go down and get it now before those idiots think about it—if they are, as we suspect, the ones who left it there—and go get it themselves. You need that piece of evidence in your arsenal."

"Okay, I'll do that right away." I turned to Billy. "Do you really think they'll take this trumped-up mess to another attorney and try to sue me?"

"They might."

"What do they want?"

"Money." He spread his hands. "But you have incidents—and even more importantly, witnesses to these incidents—to attest that these young men behaved inappropriately."

I nodded. "Right." I frowned. "What story did they tell you, Billy?"

"They told me you threw them out for no good reason. I knew better. Then I spoke with Sarah and surmised that this was merely another attempt to get under your skin." He spread his hands. "Hopefully, nothing else will come of it. But if it does, we'll handle it."

"Thank you." I took out a pad and asked for their lunch orders. Billy requested a cheeseburger and fries. Sarah asked for a chef salad. I thanked them again and took the order to Jackie.

I pulled her aside. "Could you please take care of this? I need to step outside and make a phone call."

"All right. Is everything okay?"

"Probably not. I'll explain everything to you as soon as I can."

I went out the back door, glanced around to make sure no one was around to overhear me, and I called Mom.

"Hi there," Mom answered brightly.

For some reason, hearing her cheerful voice made me want to cry. But I couldn't do that. I needed to be strong. "Mom, I need a favor."

"Okay."

"I need you to take a pair of tweezers and a ziplock plastic Baggie and go down to my back gate. About two feet toward the driveway, you'll find a cigarette butt. Pick up the butt with the tweezers, place it in the Baggie, and close it. I'll get it after work."

"You're scaring me," she said.

"There's no need to be afraid. I'll explain everything to you after work." I thought a second. "In fact, would you and Aunt Bess mind if I invite a few people to your house and make dinner for you? That would make it easier to get everyone's input."

"Sure. Do whatever you need to do. I'll go get that cigarette butt right now."

"Thanks, Mom."

"Be careful, all right?"

"Always," I said.

Not long after I returned from calling Mom, Ryan came in for lunch. I gave him my perkiest smile. He saw right through it.

"What's wrong?" he asked.

"Let's discuss it after work," I said softly. "Don't you get off early today?"

"Yeah. I've been putting in a lot of overtime, and I'm getting off at four o'clock."

"Good. I'm going to invite a few people to Mom's house for dinner, if that's okay, and I'd like for you to come."

"Sure. That works for me."

I smiled again—a real one this time, not like the fake one I'd tried to fool him with. "I'll explain everything then. I promise."

"It must be something pretty bad if you've called a family and friends meeting."

"Not as bad as all that." I laughed. "Nothing a piece of chocolate pistachio pudding cake can't fix."

"Well, by all means, bring me one. Along with a chili dog and some homemade chips."

"Coming right up."

* * *

H omer came back to the café just before closing to tell me what Phil Poston had said about Joey Carver.

"I told Phil that Joey was pestering you and that we wondered how we could get rid of him."

"What did he suggest?" I asked.

He shook his head. "He said that getting the ticks off of a junkyard dog was easier than getting rid of Joey Carver."

"That sounds rough. He and his cousin Brendan went to see Billy Hancock today to try to sue me for refusing service to them here at the café."

"Of course, Billy told him to hit the bricks. Didn't he?"

"He did. But that doesn't mean Joey and Brendan won't take their case elsewhere."

"How can I help?" Homer asked.

"I've asked a few people to come to Mom's house for dinner to help me sort things out. I spoke with Sarah just a few minutes ago, and she can't come—she and John have plans. But Jackie, Roger, Ryan, Mom, and Aunt Bess will be there. I'd like for you to join us."

"I'd be honored." He gave me a little bow that reminded me that his hero of the day was a monk, and then he told me he'd see me later this afternoon.

Jackie came up and put her hand on my shoulder. "So what are we making for this war party?"

"It isn't a war party. I prefer to look at it as a planning session."

"Okay. What's it going to be? Shish kebabs?"

"I'm not sure," I said. "I feel like we need two main dishes and plenty of sides to satisfy everyone. I'd like to make something new to see how they go over so I can possibly offer them as specials next week."

"Like what?"

Jackie was one of those people who was reluctant to try new things.

"Like chicken paillard with couscous."

She wrinkled her nose. "What is paillard, and what is couscous?"

"Paillard simply means that the chicken is pounded until it's thin and cooks quickly. And you know what couscous is."

"No, I don't. I've heard of couscous, but I don't have a clue what it actually is."

"It's . . . you know . . . wheat."

"Aha!" She grinned. "You don't know what it is either."

"Couscous is couscous! It's little balls of wheat . . . just wait and see what it is." I made sure the back door was locked and began walking toward the front. "Just promise me you'll try it."

"I'll *try* it. What else are you having in case I hate it?"

"Chicken pot pie made with bacon and cheddar biscuits. And for dessert, a butterscotch cake and a strawberry pie."

She nodded. "That last chicken dish you mentioned sounds way more up my alley."

I stopped and turned to look at her fully.

"But I really will try the other chicken with the coochie-coos." She rolled her eyes, making me laugh.

I was glad she'd waited for us to leave together . . . and that she was going to the store with me. It wasn't like me to be a 'fraidy cat, but Joey and Brendan really had me on edge.

* * *

From the grocery store, Jackie and I went straight up to the big house and began making dinner. Mom joined us in the kitchen.

She took the cigarette butt out of a drawer. "You'd probably better put this in your purse before Aunt Bess sees it and decides to dust it for prints. She's been on a crime show kick lately."

I nodded toward the chair where I'd hung my purse. "Can you drop it in there? I need to get the strawberries sliced for the strawberry pie."

Mom did as I'd asked her and then sat at the table. "Is there anything you'd like to talk about while it's just you, me, and Jackie?"

"No. I don't think there's anything I have to say that I can't discuss in front of Aunt Bess. It just confounds me as to why those two little creeps want to cause me so much trouble."

"It does me too," Jackie said. "I mean, shouldn't Brendan be concerned about who killed his father? Instead, he's giving Amy grief."

"He was a complete shock to me after I met Madelyn, his sister." I topped a strawberry and cut it in half.

"Let me help." Mom got up, retrieved a paring knife, and sat back down. "Why was Brendan such a shock?"

"Well, for one thing, Madelyn is so nice. And she talked about him like he was a sweetheart," I said. "She couldn't say enough good things about him. Then I met him, and he was a jerk to me from the get-go. And I didn't do a thing to him."

"With some people, you don't have to do anything to

them." Jackie put butter into a saucepan and turned on the stove. "They're just jerks."

"True. I even thought at first that maybe the guy was grieving for his dad." I popped the strawberry I'd cut into the strainer. "But he spoke to Madelyn as if he didn't even care that Stu was dead. He said his stepdad had been the only real father he'd ever had."

"If he doesn't care about Stu or helping to find his father's killer, then what's he still doing in Winter Garden?" Mom asked. "Is he waiting for the funeral or the reading of the will to be over? Or is there something else keeping him here?"

"Yeah, and how's he so close with Joey?" Jackie whisked flour into her melted butter. "I thought the Carver kids never visited their dad in Winter Garden."

"According to Madelyn, Stu used to take Joey with him when he went to visit sometimes," I said. "And Joey was a bully to Madelyn. So I don't understand why Stu kept taking him back to Cookeville with him."

"Me either." Mom topped another strawberry, halved it, and tossed it into the strainer. "Unless Madelyn never told him how she felt about Joey."

After we were all seated around the dinner table—I'm happy to report that both chicken dishes were hits, by the way, especially the chicken pot pie—I thanked everyone for coming and then told them why I'd asked them to dinner.

"I mean, besides your wonderful company," I said with a light laugh.

No one else laughed. They were too eager for me to get to the point. So I did.

"As I believe most of you know, this whole thing with Joey Carver began when Ryan and I spotted a truck similar to that of Stu Landon Carver leaving Winter Garden the night before I found Stu." I let *found Stu* suffice instead of going into detail about how I'd found Stu. Everyone already knew that and didn't need a gruesome reminder at the dinner table.

"A few days after that, I went to Sarah's house and was tailgated by a truck similar to the make and model of the one driven by Stu Landon Carver," I continued. "Sarah yelled at the driver before she got into my car, and she told me the truck was being driven by Joey Carver. I informed Ryan of that thinking that it might've been Joey's truck rather than Stu's that he and I saw leaving Winter Garden that night."

"Joey denied that, by the way, so we still aren't sure whose truck we saw," Ryan said.

"After talking with Ryan, Joey stormed into the café and accused me of calling the police on him—which I suppose I technically did—"

"I never gave Joey any indication that I'd learned about the truck from you," Ryan interrupted. "However, I *did* mention that he had been tailgating a yellow Beetle."

"I'm guessing he put two and two together after Sarah yelled at him," said Jackie. "There aren't that many little yellow Bugs in Winter Garden, after all. He probably drove by the café and spotted it."

"Good point," I told Jackie. "After that initial dust-up, Madelyn told me what a vindictive person Joey had been to her. In particular, she told me he'd once slashed her bicycle tires when she threatened to tell on him for something he'd done."

"And Stu didn't tan that boy's hide?" Aunt Bess shook her head in disgust. "Sounds to me like that boy needed a trip to the woodshed. When he came out, he wouldn't have been as eager to tear up someone else's belongings."

I merely nodded and then picked my story back up. "The next morning, Brendan and Joey were driving by my house as I was going to the car. They stopped in the road and talked with me."

Ryan sat up a little straighter. "What? You didn't tell me about that. What did they say?"

"Nothing. It was completely harmless. That's why I didn't mention it to you."

"But you were awfully glad to see me at the café that morning." He arched a brow.

"Of course I was. I'm always happy to see you. Plus, I didn't want to be there alone in case they decided to follow me."

"You know, if that happened more than once, it's stalking," said Homer. "Joey stalked Phil Poston's granddaughter."

"*Did* it happen again, Amy?" Ryan asked.

"I believe someone might've been in my backyard last night." I explained about Rory's barking fit and then finding the cigarette butt this morning. "That's why I asked Mom to gather and preserve the evidence."

"Ha!" Aunt Bess shouted. "We'll get the DNA off that cigarette butt and have somebody thrown in jail." She lowered her voice in a feeble attempt to imitate the voice-over actor from *Law & Order*. "The criminal justice system is represented by . . . a bunch of important people . . . and they're fixing to haul somebody off to the hoosegow! Da DUM da da da DUM!"

Jackie raised her brows at me and then interrupted Aunt Bess before she could continue her . . . whatever it was she was doing. "Shelly told me that Brendan and Joey acted like a couple of pigs this morning. They were throwing innuendo all over the place and even blew kisses at you from outside the café."

"True."

"I wonder how those punks would like to end up on my *People I've Outlived* Pinterest board," said Aunt Bess.

Mom patted her hand. "Now, Aunt Bess, let's not get too excited. I'm sure Ryan has everything under control. Right?"

"Yes, ma'am," he said. "It's like Homer said, what Joey and Brendan are doing could very well be considered stalking. In the state of Virginia, stalking is defined as repeated conduct that makes a person fear for his or her life, of being sexually assaulted, or suffering a bodily injury."

Homer nodded. "The magistrate who issued Phil's granddaughter a stalking protective order against Joey said that the stalker's actions could range from making threats to simply showing up wherever she was and waiting on her every day."

"So Joey has an active stalking protective order issued against him," Ryan said.

"Yes, he does," said Homer.

"Good. That fact alone lends credibility to Amy's assertion that Joey is stalking her."

"What about Brendan?" Roger asked. "Can you find

out if he's ever been arrested for behavior like that? Jackie said he was young, but is he still a minor?"

"I don't think so," I said. "Madelyn said he was in college."

"And even if he was engaged in stalking or assault as a minor, I should be able to find a record of it," Ryan said. "I'll look into it first thing tomorrow morning."

"The thing that bothered me most . . . the thing I asked you all to gather here to help me sort out . . . is the fact that Joey and Brendan went to Billy Hancock's office today to ask him to file a civil suit against me for asking them to leave the café this morning," I said.

For a moment, everyone was silent. Then they all started talking at once. What it all boiled down to, basically, was that any threat of a civil suit could be countered by Amy's and her witnesses' accounts of the cousins' boorish behavior. And if that failed, she could threaten to have the boys charged with stalking.

"But it's not so much that I'm concerned about their winning a lawsuit against me," I said, raising my voice to be heard over the din. "I just can't understand why these boys are targeting me. I didn't do anything to warrant this behavior."

"Some people don't need a reason," said Homer. "They're bullies. And they need to be shown that you won't be intimidated."

Chapter 15

After dinner, Ryan drove me down to my house. It was a balmy night, so his having the top down on the convertible was heavenly.

Neither of us wanted to be inside, so we sat on the porch and listened to the crickets and the frogs.

"They're talkative tonight," Ryan said.

I smiled. "Yes, they are."

He took my hand and apologized again for inadvertently bringing Joey Carver's wrath down on me. "He doesn't want my wrath coming down on him, though, that's for sure. And it certainly will if he does anything else to you."

"He won't." My voice sounded more assured than I truly felt. I changed the subject. "So did you always want to be a police officer?"

"In a way, I guess. I wanted to be a cowboy."

"But your mama didn't want her baby to grow up to be a cowboy?"

"I sometimes think she'd have preferred it to my being a police officer. But on the other hand, she's proud of me. And Dad is too. That means a lot."

"Yes, it does."

"Did you always want to be a chef and an entrepreneur?" he asked.

"Goodness, no. I mean, a chef is *one* of the jobs I wanted to have. But when I was growing up, I wanted to be everything—mainly whatever character I was currently reading about. Nancy Drew was one of my favorites."

"So you wanted to be a detective."

"In a way." I giggled. "Jackie and I were always on the lookout for some mystery to solve. We'd even write them down in our notebooks sometimes. *The Mystery of the Missing Garden Hose* . . . major crimes like that."

"Well, that certainly explains a few things."

"I suppose it does. In the end, though, being a chef won out. I suppose I could've worked in a fancy restaurant in a big city somewhere, but Nana's illness called me home." I paused, thinking about everything that had led me to the Down South Café. "And the gift she left me allowed me to make my dream of owning my own café a reality."

"I don't think you'd have been as happy in a big city."

"I imagine you're right. I enjoy smelling freshly mowed grass and honeysuckle too much when I ride down the road with my windows down."

"Me too," he said. "It's why I have a convertible."

He'd leaned over to kiss me when a vehicle sped past. The driver blared the horn.

Ryan tensed, and I pulled his head back down to mine. "Don't let anyone spoil this moment."

On Friday morning, Jackie and I were getting an update on Dilly's raccoon—who was, by the way, back to normal and "as sassy as ever"—when Madelyn Carver came in.

I smiled at her. "Good morning, Madelyn. Welcome back to Winter Garden."

"I don't feel very welcome," she said. "And neither do my brother and my cousin."

"Madelyn, I explained all of that to you over the phone yesterday. I think Joey, Brendan, and I have really gotten off on the wrong foot, and I'd like to—"

"You told me they were acting up. You didn't tell me you'd kicked the boys out of your café."

"I was here, and Amy didn't kick anybody out of anywhere," said Dilly. "She politely asked the boys to leave. They were being obnoxious and making us all uncomfortable."

"Luis and Shelly could tell you the same thing, but Luis is off today and Shelly won't be in until lunchtime," I said. "I tried to accommodate Brendan and Joey, but they were crude and disruptive."

"Yeah, well, they're considering suing you for denying service to them." Madelyn anchored her hands to her hips.

"They'd better think twice about going that route," Jackie said, stepping out from around the counter. "If they try to sue Amy, she'll have them both charged with stalking. And won't that be Joey's second offense?"

A screech of indignation emerged from the back of Madelyn's throat.

"I don't want anyone to be arrested," I said. "I just want a truce. I prefer not to cause trouble for Joey and Brendan and that they not cause any trouble for me. I'd like us all to be friends."

"I thought we were," Madelyn said. "But I was obviously wrong." She stormed out of the café.

Jackie bit her lip. "Ugh. I'm sorry for bringing up the stalking thing. She made me so angry!"

"That's all right. Maybe it'll keep Brendan and Joey in line . . . and stop them from filing a civil suit against me," I said. "I know I'd win the case, but hiring Billy Hancock would be costly, and having to take off work to deal with a court case would be a major hassle."

"Do you think those goons will try to do something underhanded to get back at you?" Dilly asked.

"I hope not, Dilly. I pray that this matter is behind us."

"I do too," she said.

Roger arrived about an hour and a half later, gave Jackie a kiss hello, and then sauntered over to the counter.

"Hey there, Flowerpot. I bought some security cameras for the outside of your café and for your home too."

I felt my eyes nearly bug out. "You did what?"

"Don't worry. I can return them if it isn't all right with you."

"Roger, this isn't necessary."

"I believe it's absolutely necessary, and I'm sorry I neglected outside security when I renovated the café for you in the first place," he said. "But with everything else on the list and your desire to get the Down South Café open before Independence Day, security monitoring got shoved to the bottom of the to-do list. Now I'm moving it to the top."

"Did Jackie call you?"

"Jackie calls me often. She's my girlfriend, you know. Or if you prefer, significant other, partner, lady love . . ."

I rolled my eyes.

"Yes, I called him," Jackie piped up from behind me. She brushed past me with a coffeepot in her hand. "Be right back. You can yell at me then." She went and refreshed the coffee of two diners sitting at a table on the patio.

"Even if she hadn't, I've had this on my mind since dinner last night," he said. "I really dropped the ball on you with regard to security, and I'm truly sorry for that."

"Roger, you didn't." I lowered my voice to a whisper. "No one could have ever guessed that Stu Landon Carver would end up dead in my parking lot."

"It's not Stu that concerns me at the moment," he said. "Although if you'd had security, it would've deterred the killer from either doing the deed or dumping the body here—whichever one it was. What I'm worried about is that those two jerks will try to get back at you somehow . . . like by setting fire to the café."

I gasped. "You don't really think they'd do something like that . . . do you?"

He looked away from me. "No. But the security cameras will make sure of that. If they try anything, these cameras will catch them. They're as clear as if you were watching them on TV."

Jackie came back with the coffeepot. She put it back on the burner and came to join our conversation. "Did you tell Amy she can check on the café from wherever she's at?"

"No. I was getting to that. The camera feeds are sent off-site. That way, you can use your computer to check on the café remotely." He looked at Jackie for approval. "And if anything *does* happen to the café, no one can destroy the video."

"That's good," I said. "I guess."

"It *is* good. And once I get these installed here at the café, I'm installing cameras outside your house too."

I sighed and looked at Jackie.

"I know you might think we're being overprotective right now," she said. "But we just want to make sure you're safe."

"I'm all for that," Homer said, joining us at the counter and taking his usual seat. "I feel like I missed something, though."

"You did, buddy," said Roger. "I hope I'm getting ready to install some security cameras here at the café and at Amy's house. Want to give me a hand after you have your breakfast?"

"I'll be happy to." Homer beamed, obviously happy to feel included and needed. "It appears I chose an appropriate hero for the day—General George S. Patton."

I gave him a tight smile. I didn't realize General Patton was known for installing security cameras or how the two could possibly be related, but if they were to Homer, I guessed that was fine.

"One of my favorite Patton quotes is, 'If everyone is thinking alike, then somebody isn't thinking.' I'm glad

we weren't thinking alike, Roger, because I hadn't considered security cameras."

Homer was—as Aunt Bess would've said—grinning
like a mule eating briars. I went into the kitchen to prepare
his sausage biscuit.

Jackie passed through the kitchen. "I'll take Homer
his coffee."

"Thanks." I lowered my voice. "Roger has made
his day."

"Hasn't he, though? He's a pretty special guy." She
placed her hand on my shoulder. "I didn't know he was
bringing the security system—honest. I called and told
him what had happened with Madelyn and what Dilly
had said, and Roger told me that he'd see me in a little
bit. I thought that just meant that he had to get back to
work."

I nodded. I knew Roger's heart had been in the right
place, and I realized he was absolutely right about my
needing a security system. I only wished that he'd discussed it with me first. Roger had insinuated himself into
the role of my big brother back when we were still kids,
but even big brothers should respect the fact that their
sisters are grown and fully capable of making their own
decisions. I intended to tell Roger that as soon as I'd taken
Homer his sausage biscuit.

After I'd taken the biscuit to Homer and heard another
of Patton's quotes—this one about success being how
high you bounce when you hit bottom—I asked Jackie to
hold down the fort while I stepped outside for a minute.

She drew her brows together, but I shook my head
slightly. I wasn't defending my position to my cousin. I
was going to have a talk with Roger, and that was that.

Jackie nodded slightly to let me know she'd take care of everything inside the café.

I went outside and found Roger standing on a ladder at the far corner of the café.

"Did you come to hold the ladder until Homer gets finished?"

"No. I want you to come down off the ladder and talk with me," I said.

He paused, cordless screwdriver in hand, and looked down at me. "Now, Amy, you're not going to try to talk me out of this, are you?"

"Come down from there."

"Can I finish installing this camera first, or are you going to make me take it down?" he asked.

"Install it."

He gave me a nod, and I could see him hide a smile.

"And then come down from there and hear me out," I said.

"Yes, ma'am."

I waited not terribly patiently for him to finish installing the camera and climb down from the ladder.

"Spill it," he said when he was standing in front of me.

"I'm not a little girl—or more specifically, your baby sister. When you make decisions that affect me financially or in any other way, you need to consult with me first. Before you ever went out and bought the first"—I waved my arm in the direction of the camera he'd finished installing—"security camera there, you should've come to me and said, 'Amy, I have an idea.' I'd have heard you out. I'd have been reasonable."

"I know that. But you should know me well enough to know that I had the idea, weighed the pros and cons of talking with you about it first, and then I did it," he said. "I figured time was of the essence. I wanted to get everything installed here at the café and at your house before nightfall just in case those punks try anything. As for the financial side, I found the best value for the best quality. If you don't have the money right now, you can pay me back."

"I have the money. That's not the issue, and you know it."

"The issue is that I treated you like I would a sister." He dropped his head. "I'm sorry I cared too much."

I let out a growl and pushed him, making him burst out laughing.

"Do you forgive me?" he asked.

"Yes. But don't do it again."

"I won't. Tell Homer to get a move on, would you?"

Before I could get back inside, I met Homer coming out to help Roger.

"General Patton always said that courage is fear holding on a minute longer," Homer told me.

"All righty." I strode back into the café.

"Everything all right?" Jackie asked as I passed her going back into the kitchen.

"Finer than frog hair split three ways." I was still a little miffed, but I did want those security cameras up before nightfall.

Roger and Homer were finishing up the security cameras outside the café when Mr. Dougherty came in for lunch.

"Wow, what's going on out there?" he asked, hooking a thumb over his right shoulder.

"We're putting up some much-needed security cameras."

"Oh, yeah . . . I heard about your finding that dead guy in the parking lot. It was Mr. Landon, the beekeeper, wasn't it?"

"It was," I said.

"Yeah. I'd talked with him a time or two. He seemed like a nice man."

"He was."

"Would you mind if I push two tables together?" He motioned toward the far right side of the café. "Maybe a couple of those over there?"

"That'll be fine. You must be expecting a larger group than normal today." I smiled. "I hope that means good things are in store for some of the residents of Winter Garden."

"I hope it does too, Ms. Flowers." He went over and pushed together the two tables he'd indicated.

"I'll get Shelly to bring you some menus. How many do you think you'll need?"

He looked up at the ceiling as he counted. "Me, the two boys, the woman, maybe two others. Bring me six to be on the safe side."

He sat down at one table, positioned where he could watch the door.

I wondered who could be joining him. It must be a family. Had he found something promising on their property? He must have, if the entire family was having lunch with him.

I went back to the counter and asked Shelly to take five glasses of water and five menus over to Mr. Dougherty's table.

Just then, Madelyn Carver stomped into the café. With her nose in the air, she went straight to Mr. Dougherty's table.

He stood to greet her. "Hi. I take it you're Madelyn?" He reached out his hand. "I'm Calvin Dougherty."

She shook his hand. "Mr. Dougherty, it's a pleasure to meet you. I've heard nice things about you from Brendan and Joey. However, I'd prefer it if we could have our lunch at the pizza parlor." She glared at me. "My family isn't welcome in this establishment."

"That's—"

Jackie put her hand on my arm. When I looked over at her, she shook her head slightly and mouthed, *Let it go.*

She was right. I'd been going to protest that, of course, Madelyn and her family were welcome at the Down South Café. But did I really want Joey and Brendan there? No, I didn't.

"Um . . . all right," said Mr. Dougherty, moving the tables back the way they'd been when he'd arrived. "The pizza parlor will be fine."

I noticed, however, that he cast a longing glance at the desserts in the display case as he left.

Chapter 16

As Mr. Dougherty and Madelyn left the café, Jackie came over to me and asked, "What do you suppose that means?"

"That Madelyn came in and asked Mr. Dougherty to have the meeting at the pizza parlor?" I asked.

She scoffed. "No. That the entire Carver clan—Joey included—is meeting with Mr. Dougherty."

"I guess it means that either Madelyn changed her mind about allowing testing to be done on the property, or Brendan had it tested while she was away."

"Wait—Madelyn was opposed to the testing?" Jackie asked.

"Well, what she actually told me was that her dad was opposed to the testing because he thought it would disturb the bees. From that, I gathered that she wouldn't want to bother the bees either and that she'd respect her father's wishes." I shrugged. "I suppose I could've been wrong."

Shelly had just finished making a fresh pot of coffee and had overheard our conversation. She stepped between us. "Money is probably going to win out over her dead daddy's wishes . . . and his bees . . . especially where Brendan is concerned."

"Yeah, and I'm thinking he can sway her opinion about anything," I said.

"True." Jackie shook her head. "I think it's odd that Madelyn was all anti-Joey and pro-Amy—even going so far as to give Amy her cell number and asking her to call if she was needed because she didn't entirely trust her brother to do it because he was hanging with Joey—and now she acts like Amy is the most terrible person she's ever met."

"It doesn't surprise me at all," said Shelly. "Of course, I'm older than you girls, but I've seen it time and again. Blood always trumps everything else."

"Where does Joey's family live?" I asked. "Is it close to Stu's property?"

"They adjoin, hon." Shelly waved to a customer who was walking in. "Be with you in a second!" She turned back to me. "Why?"

"Well, Mr. Dougherty must really think he has something in that area. He's been talking with Chad Thomas, whose farm is on one side of Stu's land—"

Shelly interrupted me with a groan. "Dang. I hate to see people that sorry come into a boatload of money like that." Then she pasted on a smile and went to greet our customer.

"She's right," Jackie said. "To think of Chad Thomas and the Carvers becoming filthy rich by having a huge chunk of Winter Garden dug up—"

"And the bees displaced," I added.

"I don't like it much myself."

I wasn't happy about it either. But I didn't want it to sound like I was miffed because there was a possibility of a natural gas reserve under the Carver and Thomas properties when there had been none under ours, so I didn't say anything. I was merely afraid to see what a mining operation would mean to Winter Garden.

Fern Thomas came into the Down South Café at around two o'clock that afternoon. She appeared more timid and out of place than she had the first time I'd met her, waiting by the door, eyes darting left and right.

I went to rescue her. "Hi, Fern. Welcome back."

"Thank you. I want a cake. Or a pie. Whatever you've got. It's for the Carvers."

"Are you guys celebrating together?" I asked with a smile.

She scrunched up her face. "Are we what?"

"Celebrating." My smile faded. "I saw Mr. Dougherty with Madelyn Carver earlier, so I thought maybe there was a natural gas reserve that spanned both your properties."

"Oh. Oh, goodness. Chad won't like that."

"Excuse me?"

"N-nothing," she said. "I've been busy today and haven't had time to make something to take to the Carvers before the wake. Stuart Landon . . . Carver's wake is tonight." She spoke almost mechanically.

"I'm sorry. I didn't realize that." Nor did I mean to appear insensitive. "I should've known."

"Do you have any whole cakes or pies for sale?" Fern asked.

"Yes, we do." I gently propelled her toward the display case. "Take your pick."

"Which would be better for a sad family gathering—cake or pie?"

How should I know? I don't go around asking people if they prefer cake or pie for their sad family gatherings. "It seems to me that a cake would serve more people."

"Then give me a cake—that Bundt cake there with the white icing."

"Good choice."

I boxed up the cake for Fern, she paid for it, and I hurried to hold the door open so she wouldn't drop it on her way out.

After she left, I linked my arm through Jackie's as she was passing by. "Tell me, Jacqueline, do you prefer cake or pie at sad family gatherings?"

"Have you been drinking?"

I laughed. "No. Fern Thomas asked me which would be better at a sad family gathering—cake or pie?"

"What did you tell her?"

"I told her I thought a cake would serve more people," I said. "What would be your choice?"

"At a sad family gathering, I prefer wine." She chuckled. "Poor Fern. Any family gathering she's at is bound to be sad. It's like a little black cloud follows wherever she goes."

"No wonder. Have you met her husband?"

"Yeah, I have. Once again, I'm choosing wine."

That evening, Ryan and I went to dinner and a movie in Bristol. We were almost back to Winter Garden and were laughing about some of the funny scenes in the movie we'd watched when we heard sirens coming upon us. Ryan's eyes flew to the rearview mirror, and then he pulled to the side of the road. Two firetrucks raced past us.

"No, no, no . . ." I started fumbling in my purse for my phone.

"Everything's okay."

"You don't know that. Joey Carver could've set the café on fire . . . or my house. Rory and Princess Eloise might be in the house! Oh, no. *The big house!*"

"Calm down. Joey's at the wake, remember?"

"But he could've slipped out. Or not even gone."

"Let me find out what's going on before you panic."

Ryan retrieved his phone and dialed the Winter Garden police station as I found my phone. I was as afraid to call Mom as I was *not* to call her, but I waited to see what Ryan learned from the dispatcher. If everything was fine at home, I didn't want to scare her half to death.

Only being able to hear Ryan's side of the conversation was torture, but I could tell—or *thought* I could tell—that it wasn't anything as serious as I'd initially believed.

He ended the call. "There's a dilapidated barn on fire out in a field near Winter Garden. It's pretty much in the middle of nowhere."

"Then why are they sending two firetrucks?"

"Because it's been so dry lately. They're afraid the fire will spread."

"Oh. That makes sense." I pulled up Mom's contact on my phone. "I'm still going to check with Mom and make sure everything is okay with her and Aunt Bess."

I phoned Mom, and of course, all was well. Except now Mom was worried about why I'd called out of the blue to see if they were all right. When I told her about

the firetrucks and the dilapidated barn, she said that
was sad.

"Is it the barn near Old Cedar Cove?" she asked.

"I don't know, Mom. I don't think the dispatcher gave
Ryan that much information."

"I just wondered because I know Stu had a couple of
hives out there. I hope they don't get destroyed." She paused.
"Do you think anyone is taking care of his hives now?"

"I'm not sure," I said. "I'll let you know if I find out
anything else. I mainly wanted to make sure you and Aunt
Bess are okay."

"We're perfectly fine. She went to bed a few minutes
ago, so I'm enjoying a little quiet time."

I laughed softly. "Well, go back to enjoying it. I'll talk
with you tomorrow."

"Good night."

When I ended the call, Ryan asked, "What was she
wondering when you said you didn't think the dispatcher
gave me that much information?"

"She wanted to know if the barn was near Old Cedar
Cove because Stu Landon Carver had some hives out
there."

We drove on to Winter Garden. I was relieved to see
that the café also appeared to be fine. My house and the
big house were still in one piece too.

"I have to admit that I'm glad Roger bought those
security cameras," I said. "But I'm not ready to tell *him*
that just yet."

Ryan smiled. "I'm glad too. And you don't have to tell
Roger that either."

We went inside, and I offered Ryan something to drink.
He declined, and we sat down on the sofa.

Both Rory and Princess Eloise came running to see Ryan. Princess Eloise sprang onto his lap.

I laughed. "That's the funniest thing ever. I think that, other than Mom, you're her favorite person."

"What can I say? I'm charming." He stroked the cat's chin. "Right, Princess?"

Her response was a loud purr.

Ryan's cell phone rang. He had to put Princess Eloise on the cushion beside him so he could stand up and check to see who was calling.

"It's the sheriff. I have to take this." He answered. "Hey, Sheriff Billings. What's going on?"

After listening for a few seconds, he replied that he'd be right there. He ended the call and slid the phone back into the holder on his belt.

"I'm sorry, but I have to go."

"Is it about the fire?" I asked.

He nodded. "Sheriff Billings is asking everyone on the force to meet him at the barn. The firefighters found something suspicious."

"Be careful."

"I will." He gave me a quick kiss and left.

I sat down beside Princess Eloise, but she raced over to the table by the window so she could look out and see where Ryan had gone.

Feeling out of sorts, I called Mom.

"Hey, honey. Is anything wrong?"

"I don't know," I said. "Ryan just got a phone call and had to leave. Sheriff Billings has asked everyone on the force to meet him at the barn because the firefighters found something strange."

"And you're scared."

"I wouldn't say scared exactly . . . maybe a little freaked out."

"Would you like to come spend the night with Aunt Bess and me?"

"No. I'm fine. It's a comfort, though, to know that you guys are nearby." I chuckled. "How weird is it that I'm a grown woman and yet when something semi-scary happens, I call my mom?"

"I don't think it's weird at all. That's what families are for," she said. "Did Ryan give you any indication what the *something strange* might be?"

"Actually, his words were *something suspicious*. I'm guessing there was something that made it appear that the fire was arson."

"That makes sense, but I wouldn't think the entire Winter Garden Police Department would be called in to investigate one arson."

"No," I said. "I wouldn't either. It would make more sense if they found bones or something, don't you think?"

"It would. But, you know, we have a lot of coyotes around here. If the firefighters *did* find bones, they are likely the remains of a coyote's prey. They do target live-stock, so that would mean larger bones and could be confusing to the firefighters."

"Sure." We both knew she was merely trying to placate me. If a coyote's prey was large enough for its bones to be confused with those of a human, the coyote wouldn't have been strong enough to carry it off. It would have eaten what it wanted of the animal on-site. Besides, experienced firefighters wouldn't mistake animal bones for those of a human. And Mom and I were speculating. We didn't even know what suspicious thing had been found at the barn.

I told Mom good night and that I'd talk with her sometime tomorrow.

"I'm here if you need me," she said.

"Ditto."

I ended the call and sat on the sofa staring at the opposite wall. So much had happened lately with Brendan
and Joey Carver that I expected them to be involved with
the burning of the barn somehow. It didn't make a lot of
sense, but then there wasn't much that *was* making sense
to me these days.

Mr. Landon Carver was found murdered in my parking lot, although it was believed he was killed elsewhere,
placed in his truck, and driven to the Down South Café
parking lot. Of all places to take the man, why take him
to my café? Whoever had killed him had obviously
wanted him to be found. Had they not, they'd have driven
the truck to his house. I figured that if he'd been there,
his body wouldn't have been found for days.

Walter Jackson said he'd come here to make peace
with Stu. Plus, he didn't appear to be physically able to
kill Stu, put his body in the truck, drive the truck to the
café, move the body to the driver's seat, and then somehow get back to wherever he'd left his vehicle.

That brought up another question in my mind. How
had the killer done all that and then made it back to his
or her vehicle without being spotted? Even if the murder
had taken place in the wee hours of the morning, the
person responsible would have inevitably been covered
in blood and needing to escape after leaving Stu's truck
in the Down South Café parking lot. Had the murderer
had an accomplice?

Rory was snoring softly on the floor at my feet when

Princess Eloise came, pounced onto the sofa, and lay by my side.

I was touched by this unusual display of affection for me by the cat. I stroked her fur, and she purred loudly. Both pets were a comfort to me this evening.

Chapter 17

The next morning, I was on my way to the car when Ryan pulled into the driveway. I walked over to his car. His hair was tousled, his face was dirty, and his eyes were bloodshot.

"You look awful," I said.

"Thanks. You look beautiful."

I blushed. "I'm sorry. I just meant that you look as if you've been up all night."

"I have been. I'm just now going home to get some sleep. Sheriff Billings sent some of the others, including Ivy, home at around midnight. They came back before the rest of us left."

"Would you like some breakfast?"

"No, thanks. I need to get home. I'm afraid I won't be able to hold my eyes open much longer," he said. "But I'll call you when I wake up."

"All right. Be careful."

"I will." He hesitated. "Keep this to yourself, but we believe the barn to be the primary crime scene in the murder of Stu Landon Carver."

I gasped. "But how—"

He shook his head and yawned. "I'll tell you more when I can."

When I arrived at work, Luis was already there waiting and Jackie was parking her car. I quickly maneuvered into my usual spot, hopped out of the Bug, and ran to unlock the door.

"I'm sorry!"

"You're running late this morning, Amy." Jackie winked at Luis. "Was there an early morning rendezvous we should know about?"

"No . . . well, yes . . . but it's not what you're thinking. Ryan came by on his way home from tending to that burning barn last night."

"Is Ryan a volunteer fireman as well as a deputy?" Luis asked.

"Um . . . no." I struggled with what to say that would be the truth but not reveal too much. Not that I actually knew anything, but still. "The sheriff asked some of his people to come in and help investigate. He said the firefighters thought it was suspicious."

"That's weird. Who'd burn down an old barn?"

"I imagine the property owner," said Jackie. "It's an eyesore, and it isn't good for anything. But would it be considered arson if you burned down your own barn?"

"I guess that depends on whether or not you tried to collect any insurance from the damage," I said.

We went inside. Jackie made coffee, Luis restocked the napkin dispensers, and I started the kitchen prep for breakfast.

Dilly came in and called out a hello to all of us.

I stuck my head out of the kitchen to say hi.

"Did y'all know the barn that stood in the middle of that field near Old Cedar Cove burned down last night?" she asked.

"Amy was telling us about it," Jackie said.

"When I drove by, I saw that there's crime scene tape up all over and a lot of official-looking cars and trucks parked around out there. I don't know why," Dilly said, "unless they're afraid the barn is going to fall the rest of the way down and hurt somebody. Is that it? Are they tearing it the rest of the way down?"

I said I didn't know.

"Back about twenty or thirty years ago, there was a rash of barn burnings in Winter Garden and the surrounding area." Dilly came to sit on her favorite stool as she warmed up to her story. "I don't know whether the hooligans responsible were ever caught and punished. But I doubt that old gang would take up barn burning again after all this time . . . unless it's something they thought up in the old folks' home." She laughed at her own joke, and the rest of us joined in.

"Of course, I hope nobody else has got that foolish thought in their heads about burning barns," she continued. "It was awfully troublesome back then, people being afraid that somebody would burn down their barn in the middle of the night."

"Did the barn burners back then set fire to abandoned barns or barns that were in use?" Jackie asked.

"Eh, six of one and half dozen of the other. It didn't seem to make much difference to them either way. Some of the barns were empty, but others had hay or tobacco. They never hurt any animals that I know of." She shook her head, setting her white curls to bouncing. "I never will forget the night Aldus Hawkins's barn burned to the ground and his burley tobacco crop went up in smoke. Gracious sakes, that man was fit to be tied up and dragged."

"I imagine so," said Luis. "That was a lot of money that he lost, unless he had insurance or something."

"I doubt he did back in those days," said Dilly. "I reckon we'll know what happened at the Old Cedar Cove barn in a day or so. In the meantime, I'd like to try one of those quiches Amy has as the special today. Are quiches good for breakfast?"

"They're perfect for breakfast or lunch," I said.

"I've had them for dinner too," Jackie chimed in. "You just can't go wrong with a good quiche."

"Well, then I'll have one. And a biscuit, of course."

Just before nine o'clock that morning, a well-dressed woman who appeared to be in her mid-fifties came into the café. She stood by the door looking uncertain until Jackie asked if she could help her.

"I'm looking for the Winter Garden Funeral Home," the woman said. "Is it far from here?"

"Only about three miles."

"Oh, good. I've got plenty of time to have some coffee and steady my nerves then."

Jackie smiled. "You sure do. What'll you have—dark roast, decaffeinated, or French vanilla?"

"I'd like the French vanilla, please." She sat at the counter.

"Welcome to Winter Garden," I told her. "I'm sorry you're here under sad circumstances."

"Me too. I'm Patricia Vance, by the way. I'm here for Stu Carver's funeral." Her lips curved in a semblance of a smile. "I suppose you knew him as Stu Landon, if you knew him at all."

"We did." I pointed to a jar of the honey still on the shelf. "I sold some of his honey on consignment."

"Stu and his stupid bees," she mused as Jackie sat her coffee in front of her. "Thank you." She added low-calorie sweetener. "I believe Stu liked insects more than he cared for people."

"Some folks are like that, I guess," said Jackie.

"He was. I wasn't married to him all that long, but it was enough time for me to figure that out."

Jackie and I exchanged glances. This was Madelyn and Brendan's mother. Now that she'd told us who she was, I could see the resemblance.

"I can see why this little town appealed to Stu. It's lovely . . . quiet . . . isolated." She sighed. "I've been thinking of going out to the house after the funeral just to see how Stu lived, but I'm not sure if I'll do that or not. Douglas, my current husband, only came with me as far as Abingdon. He said he wouldn't feel comfortable at the funeral."

"I can understand that." Jackie spotted a couple walking in. "Excuse me, please."

"Personally, I think Douglas is being silly," Patricia said. "He says that for me to go to the funeral to support Brendan and Madelyn is one thing, but for him to explain that he's their stepfather is another matter entirely. I don't think so, do you?"

"No. I feel that he'd come across as a concerned parent. But people react to situations differently."

"I know. And I don't know how I'd feel if the situation was reversed. Frankly, I believe Douglas prefers not to think of Stu at all, so I understand his not wanting to see how Stu lived here in Winter Garden or hear what the mourners have to say about him."

"Did he dislike Stu that much?" I asked.

"He did. Douglas thinks of the children as his own—and he was around for them far more than Stu ever was. Stu came around two or three times a year, called occasionally, and sent birthday cards with checks in them." Patricia sipped her coffee. "Douglas was there to teach them to ride a bike, to help with homework, to take photographs before they went to prom. Stu didn't seem to care about any of that. Douglas thinks Stu abandoned them."

I felt like saying that Douglas was pretty much right about that, but I kept my opinion to myself, and she resumed talking.

"Stu claimed he moved here to hide out from members of Callicorp—a company he worked for out in Oklahoma that went belly-up because of Stu—but Douglas said that was a bunch of bunk. He said Stu simply didn't want to be saddled with a family and so he left."

"Do you agree?" I asked softly.

"Yeah. I didn't want to think so initially, but when I realized that was the case, I divorced Stu and gave up the long-distance marriage farce." She looked around the café, and her eyes filled with tears. "Stu could have made a life for all of us here had he chose to. We could've called ourselves Landons and hid out here as a perfect happy family. But it's not what Stu wanted. I lived in denial for a few years hoping he'd come to his senses, but he never did."

"So you think Stu was paranoid—that the Callicorp people were never out to get him?"

"I think there might have been some sort of threat right after we left Oklahoma, but I feel that Stu and his involvement in that ordeal was soon forgotten. Even Walter Jackson came to find Stu because he'd found religion in prison and wanted to apologize for the death threats he'd sent Stu."

"You don't think Mr. Jackson had anything to do with Stu's death?"

"Absolutely not," said Patricia. "I'd like to see the man and find out whether or not he ever got to make his peace with Stu."

"He might be at the funeral. He told me he was staying in town for it."

She raised her brows. "You really are connected around here, aren't you? You must be the one to come to when people need to know what's going on in town."

I let her comment pass without expressing an opinion either way.

"I'm glad Walt will be at the funeral. I'm looking forward to talking with him," Patricia said. "I want him to know I forgive him. Everything that happened with Walt, Callicorp, Stu, and all the rest was such a long time ago. I have a happy life now, and I probably owe some of that happiness to Walt in a strange way. What he did was very wrong, but he gave Stu the excuse he needed to leave us behind and let us find a better life."

I mentioned that my orders were going to start piling up and that I'd better get back to the kitchen. Then I wished her well, gave her detailed directions to the Winter Garden Funeral Home, and headed for the grill.

M r. Dougherty came in for lunch.
"Hi there, Mr. Dougherty," I said. "I'm glad you came back to the Down South Café. I was afraid you might not after yesterday."

He huffed. "In my line of work, you don't let other people's squabbles concern you."

"That's a wonderful philosophy."

"Yes, ma'am, and it serves me well. I missed out on your fabulous desserts yesterday. I won't be doing that today." He took a corner table.

"How many will be joining you?" I asked.

"It's just me today. Flying solo."

His phone must have buzzed because he took it out and began speaking into it. He started out talking with a booming voice, but then his voice became quieter and quieter until it was practically nothing more than a hiss.

I unobtrusively put a menu on his table and went back to the kitchen.

"What do you think is going on with the Ives Oil and Gas guy?" Jackie asked me when she joined me a minute or two later.

"Mr. Dougherty?" I glanced over at his table. "He was fine when he came in, but then he got a phone call that seemed to bother him."

"It's apparently still bothering him. He's talking with someone, and he looks majorly ticked off. I went to take his order, and he waved me away. I'll go back when he's finished."

"Maybe Mrs. Dougherty doesn't like him working weekends," I said.

"Is there a Mrs. Dougherty?"

I shrugged.

Luis came into the kitchen with a tub full of dishes. "Are you guys talking about the angry dude?"

"Yeah," said Jackie. "Amy thinks he's getting fussed at for working weekends, but I feel like that wouldn't make him angry—he'd be more apologetic in that case."

He nodded. "Makes sense to me. Besides, when I walked past him, I heard him say something like, 'These people out here will kill me . . .' I guess it could still be personal. He could be saying that the people here would kill him if he didn't work on Saturdays. Who knows?"

Jackie waited until he ended his call, and then she went and took his order. He asked for a bacon cheeseburger with a side of potato salad.

When I had Mr. Dougherty's order ready, I took it out to him myself.

"Here you go," I said. "Do you need a refill on that tea? And how about dessert? Have you decided which one you want yet?"

"Not yet."

I put my fist on my hip. "All right, mister. You were in a chipper mood when you first came in here. What happened?"

He shook his head. "I'd better not say."

"You can trust me. Besides, I might be able to help."

"I doubt you can help this, Ms. Flowers. Ives Oil and

Gas is wanting me to pull out of Winter Garden without doing any further testing."

"Are you serious? But I thought you'd found some promising leads."

"I have. It's political. The local lawmakers want us out."

"I'm sorry. Would it help if your dessert is on the house?"

He grinned. "That always makes things better. And in the meantime, I've bought a little time. So maybe the powers that be at Ives can get the lawmakers to change their minds."

"I hope so." I really preferred that the oil and gas developers stay out of Winter Garden for the sake of preserving our quiet community, but I hated to see Mr. Dougherty—and people who might benefit from the development—disappointed.

He glanced around to make sure that the other diners were too busy talking among themselves to pay any attention to us. "If you don't mind, could you sorta keep this under your hat? I'd hate for the Carvers or Thomases to hear something negative when Ives might still be able to turn this thing around."

"Your secret's safe with me." And Ryan. I'd have to tell Ryan. And maybe Jackie. But that's all. Neither of them would tell the Thomases or the Carvers.

Chapter 18

&W e were getting ready to close up shop that afternoon when Sarah came into the café.

"Hi there. I hope I'm not too late to buy a cake," she said. "John is coming over for dinner this evening, and I want a good dessert to go with our meal."

"Then you've certainly come to the right place at the right time," I said. "Luis, Jackie, and I were just getting ready to divvy up the desserts left in the display case."

"Are you serious?"

"Completely. We always do on Saturday because we know the desserts won't remain fresh over the weekend."

"So we have to eat them," said Luis. "My family is thrilled that I have this job."

Luis actually had this job to pay for school, though he was now out for the summer. I knew his parents were extremely proud of him for working so hard. And his younger brothers and sister really were delighted with the desserts he brought home on Saturday. They especially liked cookies. If we didn't have many on Saturday morning, I'd make a fresh batch for Luis to take home to them.

From what we had left in the display case, Sarah chose a chocolate brownie pie. She took her phone from her pocket, glanced at the screen, and said, "I have to take this. Amy, could you please box up that pie and bring it outside to me?"

"Sure."

I knew Sarah well enough to know that she simply wanted to speak with me privately. I took the pie from the refrigerated display case, put it into a pastry box, and took it outside. Sarah had turned her car engine on and was sitting in the driver's seat. She motioned for me to come around to the passenger side.

I slid into the car. "Ahhh, you have an amazing air conditioner."

"Thanks. I wanted to talk with you alone, but I didn't want my pie to get gunky. I didn't have a call, by the way."

"I never thought you did."

She grinned. "You know me too well. I wouldn't have really cared to have discussed this in front of Jackie, but I don't know Luis very well. I don't believe he'd go around spreading rumors, but I wouldn't want Billy to know that I'd mentioned this."

Now I was intrigued.

"Chad Thomas came into our office yesterday," she continued. "He was asking Billy who he needed to talk with to make the Carvers a fair offer on their father's property. Billy told him to see the tax assessor to get the property value. When he left, I think he was going to the county tax office."

"Hmm. Now what Fern, Chad's wife, said yesterday about Chad not being happy with the thought of the Carvers meeting with Mr. Dougherty makes a little more sense. She came in to buy a cake. I jokingly asked if she and the Carvers were celebrating together since Mr. Dougherty was meeting with the Carvers earlier in the day. I had no idea then that she was buying the cake for Stu's wake."

Sarah nodded. "I see what you're saying, though. If Fern went home and told Chad that the Carvers had met with Mr. Dougherty, then he'd know there was a chance their property had also tested favorably for the presence of natural gas."

"Right. So the odds of them selling the property to him likely went right down the drain."

"Yeah, especially at a *fair* price."

"And since Mr. Dougherty met with Chad Thomas, Madelyn, Brendan, *and* Joey Carver—whose land also adjoins to Stu's property, then those three plots could be sitting atop an extremely profitable reserve," I said. "Would Chad Thomas really be so selfish as to want it all for himself?"

Sarah and I smiled at each other. Of course he would.

J ackie and I chose half a boysenberry pie and half a peanut butter pie to take to the big house to serve with lunch tomorrow. We were serving fried chicken, potato salad, and Mexican corn, so either pie would work with the meal.

I was making dinner for Ryan this evening. I planned to make barbecued pork chops, baked potatoes, and cole slaw. I picked the key lime pie for dessert. I took the pies home—mine and the two halves we were serving with lunch tomorrow—and put them in the refrigerator before I went to the grocery store to get what I'd need to prepare this evening's meal. Prior to heading back out, I called Mom to see if there was anything she and Aunt Bess needed.

Mom told me to hold on while she checked with Aunt Bess. Within a few seconds, she gave me the answer.

"Aunt Bess needs raisin bran and skim milk, and I could use some hazelnut creamer. I'm about out."

"Is there any particular brand of raisin bran that Aunt Bess prefers?"

"She likes the cheaper brand but not the cheapest brand," Mom said. "It's like a step up from the store brand but not as expensive as the bigger name brand."

"This should be fun." I told Mom I'd be there in a little while with the items they'd requested.

I drove to the store half wishing that my air conditioner was as good as Sarah's. Mine did all right, but it was pretty sluggish compared to the one in Sarah's newer car. But I wasn't ready to get a newer car and part with my little Bug yet, so I'd make do and not complain.

I strode into the grocery store and quickly gathered what I needed. I started with the items Mom and Aunt Bess had wanted because I was afraid I'd forget them otherwise. I went to the cereal aisle and chose three different brands of raisin bran. One of them was bound to be the brand preferred by Aunt Bess. I then got the creamer, baking potatoes, cabbage, carrots, pork chops, and milk.

I hurried to the checkout lane, delighted by how

quickly I was making it through the grocery store. Usually this place was swamped on Saturday afternoons with cart-to-cart traffic and clusters of people blocking the aisles while they chatted with people they seldom saw anywhere other than at the grocery store. But today hadn't seemed that bad.

I was standing in line behind one other customer . . . and this customer had only about twenty items. I was sure to finish up the checkout process soon, be back in my car, and on my way to the big house. I was beginning to wonder what I'd wear when Ryan came over when I realized my optimistic thoughts had set me up for a disappointment. One of the twenty items the customer ahead of me had in his cart needed a price check.

I stifled a groan and turned to glance behind me. Someone had come up behind me in the line. She seemed familiar, but she had her face down and was staring into her purse.

I nonchalantly perused the tabloid headlines. I saw a small, thick comic book on the stand and smiled because the kids from Riverdale were still popular. I turned to comment on that fact to the woman behind me who'd seemed familiar.

When I turned this time, she tried to lower her head again, but I could see that it was Fern Thomas.

"Fern, hi! How are you?"

"Fine."

I could see her face much better now, and there was an ugly bruise on her left cheek. "Oh, my goodness, what happened?"

"Oh . . . yeah." She tried to cover the bruise with her hair. "I've been trying to hide it because it's so embarrassing. I'm as clumsy as can be." She shook her head. "Fell while carrying a load of laundry *up* the basement stairs. Can you believe that? Most people fall down stairs—I fall up them."

"I hope you feel better soon." Her scenario *was* hard to believe. Was she covering for Chad? Had he hit her?

"I'll be fine. I'm just glad it wasn't worse."

The cashier finally found the price of the item in question and finished checking out the customer ahead of me. I moved ahead and quickly completed the checkout process.

I turned and told Fern good-bye before leaving.

"See you." She resumed placing her groceries on the conveyor belt.

When I went into the big house to take Mom and Aunt Bess their groceries, I left the car running to keep my stuff cool.

Aunt Bess was on her Pinterest boards when I walked in. She was posting a photo of a man with facial hair arranged to look like a giant spider on her *Lord, Have Mercy* board.

"I've done been checking out the dating sites today," she said. "And there's not a new soul on there . . . just the same sad people who were there the last time I looked. I was out of all their leagues."

"I'm sure you were, Aunt Bess. Come and see this cereal I've brought you. I didn't know which one you'd want, so I got three different kinds."

"Three kinds. Well, ain't you the berries? Thank you." She got up and came into the kitchen, where Mom showed her each box.

She picked up one. "Now these here are my favorites. I'm not too awful fond of them there in the white box—

they're a tad bland—but I can mix them with that other box that's too sweet and they'll be all right."

"Well, if you just want your favorites, I can take the other two boxes back," I said. "Or you can use them to feed the birds or the squirrels or something."

"I'm not wasting good raisin bran. And I'm not Dilly Boyd. I don't make it my mission in life to feed wild animals. I figure God's got that taken care of." She held up an index finger. "Mark my words, that raccoon is going to attack Dilly one of these days, and she'll wind up with rabies. She might have to get them shots in her belly and everything. They say that's awfully painful."

"I hope that never happens."

"Me too," said Aunt Bess. "But I'm betting it will. That raccoon might be the very thing that puts Dilly on my *People I've Outlived* board."

"Maybe so." I looked at Mom, and Mom just shook her head.

Aunt Bess went back to her computer to see what other strange things she could find for her *Lord, Have Mercy* board.

"Come outside with me a second," I said. "I want you to see if you think my air-conditioning is working okay in the car."

She frowned. "Honey, I don't—" Realization flooded her face. "Aunt Bess, I'll be right back inside. Amy wants me to help her with something."

We stepped out and got into the Bug.

Mom closed her eyes and rested her head against the back of the seat. "Feels good to me. What'd you want to talk about?"

"I ran into Fern Thomas in the grocery store, and she had a bad bruise on her face."

"Fern Thomas . . . I don't know her."

"She's Chad Thomas's wife," I said.

"I'm afraid I don't know him either. Should I?"

"Probably not, except he's the farmer whose pesticides Stu Landon Carver thought were killing his bees."

Oh, yeah, that's right. I remember now."

"Roger said that Chad had a bad temper, and now his wife comes to the grocery store looking as if someone hit her."

Mom placed her hand over mine. "Don't jump to conclusions, Amy. Did you ask Fern about the bruise?"

"Yes, and she told me she fell up the stairs while carrying a load of laundry."

"That makes sense. I mean, if it was a made-up story, wouldn't she have said she fell *down* the stairs?"

"She said that too," I said. "Not that thing about it being a made-up story, but she said that most people fall down stairs but that she was so clumsy, she fell up them."

"What makes you think her husband hit her?"

"Fern was in the café yesterday buying a cake. It was for Stu Landon Carver's wake, but I didn't know it at the time and foolishly asked Fern if they and the Carvers were celebrating Ives Oil and Gas discovering the possibility of natural gas below their properties. And Fern said Chad wouldn't like that."

"Wouldn't like what—your joke?"

"No. I took it to mean that Chad wouldn't like the fact that Mr. Dougherty and the Carvers must believe that there's natural gas on their property. Sarah spoke with

me earlier today and said that Chad Thomas was trying
to buy the land off the Carvers."

"And he was angry because now it was unlikely that
they'd sell."

"Exactly," I said.

"Still, would that make him angry enough to hit his
wife?"

"Maybe. What if when she told him, it made him so
mad that he felt like he *had* to strike out at something,
and that something was her? Maybe she was the only
person around at the time for him to take his wrath
out on."

"Or maybe she fell walking up the steps with a load
of laundry," Mom said gently. "I did something similar
to that once. Remember?"

"Yeah, but you weren't living with a man known to
have a terrible temper at the time."

"True. But I fell, and it was an accident, and I looked
like a battered woman for a month."

I sighed. "I know."

"Hopefully, if Chad did hit her, she'll go to the authorities."

"I hope so. But somehow, I doubt she would."

"I'd better get back in there to Aunt Bess before she
decides to date someone she's adding to her *Lord, Have
Mercy* board," she said. "If old Spider Face ever showed
up at the front door, I might have a heart attack."

By the time Ryan arrived for dinner, I had everything
almost ready. As he walked through the front door,
he stopped, closed his eyes, and inhaled.

"Wow. Dinner smells fantastic."

I smiled. "Hopefully, it'll taste every bit as good."

We went into the kitchen. I told him to have a seat while I went and got the pork chops and corn off the grill. When I brought the food back, he'd poured us both a glass of tea.

"Thank you."

"Thank *you*." His stomach growled.

We both laughed.

"We'd better get to it." I went to the refrigerator and took out the cole slaw and the key lime pie.

"What did I do to deserve all this?" Ryan asked.

"You're dating a chef," I said. "Plus, you had to work hard last night."

"That's true." He took a pork chop and an ear of corn and put them on his plate. "Between us, there was a hunting knife found in the barn just beyond the worst of the blaze. The firefighters found it after they extinguished the fire and were suspicious because it had the letters *S* and *L* engraved in the hilt."

"So the knife belonged to Stu Landon Carver?"

"We're not a hundred percent sure yet, but there's a good chance it did. Plus, we believe it to be the murder weapon."

"Poor Stu . . . killed with his own knife."

"That's what we're thinking," Ryan said. "Again, it's not definite yet, but we believe Stu Landon Carver's attacker followed him to the hive, the two of them argued, and Stu was murdered there."

"But how did the attacker get Stu from the hive to the barn? Were the hive and the barn that close?"

"They were fairly close. We're just speculating, but we

believe that the killer might've knocked Stu unconscious and then dragged or carried him into the barn to finish him off."

My mouth had suddenly gone dry, so I took a drink of my tea. "Who owns the property where the barn was located?"

"Andrew and Ellen Hart. They currently live in Florida and only check on the property when they visit relatives."

"If they live in Florida, why are they hanging on to pastureland in Winter Garden?" I asked.

He shrugged. "I couldn't say."

"Do they have someone managing the property?"

Ryan shook his head. "As far as we can tell, they allowed Stu to keep two hives on the property, and they let Chad Thomas mow the fields for the hay. He then feeds the hay to his cattle."

"And you think Stu's attacker followed him to the hive? How would he know where Stu was going? Did he know where the hives were?"

"I believe lots of people knew the location—or had a general idea—of where the hives were kept. Stu wasn't secretive about them. In fact, one of the deputies noted that there was a map on Stu's refrigerator detailing where all the hives were located in case something should happen to him."

"He really cared about those bees," I mused. "And he was really paranoid."

"I'm not so sure he was as paranoid as all that."

"You're right. He thought someone was out to get him, and someone did."

He chuckled. "That's not what I meant. I think he was

just super careful to make as many provisions for his hives as he could . . . just in case. But I don't think he was as concerned about Callicorp as he let his family believe."

"You agree with his ex-wife that he wanted an excuse to live alone."

"I do. He was a solitary guy." Ryan cut into his pork chop. "But answer me this. The police department believes Stu Landon Carver was murdered in an abandoned barn in Old Cedar Grove, put into his truck, and driven to the Down South Café. So how did the killer get back to whatever vehicle he'd used to follow Stu to Old Cedar Grove?"

"He had to have had an accomplice."

"I'd just been thinking the same thing myself," I said.

Chapter 19

At Sunday lunch, the main topic of conversation was what the Carvers were planning to do now.

Actually, Aunt Bess brought it up. And the way she brought it up was, "What's that clan of Carvers planning on doing now that they've buried Stu?"

"What do you mean?" I asked.

"Well, I saw in Friday's paper that the funeral was yesterday morning," she said. "So are they going to sell the house and go back to wherever they came from? Or do you think they might put down roots here?"

"When Madelyn first arrived—back when she liked me and would talk with me—she told me she might stay on in Winter Garden, keep up her dad's beehives, and make a life for herself here," I said. "She did say that it would depend on what her brother, Brendan, wanted to do."

"True," Jackie chimed in. "But that was before they knew there might be a natural gas reserve beneath their property."

Mom spooned some potato salad onto her plate. "If they think they can make a fortune by holding on to Stu's land, then I'm guessing that's what they'll do."

"Greedy so-and-sos." Aunt Bess shook her head and took a drink of her tea. "They'll be wishing they had sold that land when they're all blown to Kingdom Come over there."

"If it's true that there's a natural gas reserve under the Carvers' land, wouldn't Ives Oil and Gas pay them for the property, raze the home, and then give the family a small royalty off any gas extracted from the land?"

"I believe so," said Jackie.

"That's why Stu didn't want that man from Ives poking around his land," said Aunt Bess. "Stu was some kind of scientist or something himself, wasn't he? He probably knew whether or not there was gas underneath his land. But he'd rather have the land, his home, and his bees than the money they'd give him to tear it all up."

"I believe Stu's ex-wife would agree with you, Aunt Bess. She came into the café yesterday." I bit into my chicken leg.

"What? You got to meet Stu's ex-wife?" Aunt Bess placed her hand on her chest. "And you're just now telling us about it? What's the matter with you?"

I shrugged, my mouth still full of chicken.

"Hurry up and swallow, and tell us about Stu's wife," she demanded.

I swallowed, took a drink of tea, and then told them about Patricia Vance. "She was nice. She came in because she needed directions to the funeral home, stayed for a cup of coffee, and—it must have been her nerves talking— told me all about Stu."

Aunt Bess leaned across the table. "What did she say about him?"

"She said she could see why he'd enjoyed Winter Garden so much. It was somewhere he could live a quiet life. She said that's the kind of life he wanted—a simple, solitary life."

"Then did she say something like, 'I got to thinking about him leaving me and our children to raise on my own, it made me furious, and I came up here and killed his sorry butt'?" she asked, pushing her glasses up on her nose.

"No," I said. "She seemed thankful that Stu had left so that she and her children could have Douglas, their stepfather."

"That Brendan is one of those hooligans who was being mean to you," she mused. "Maybe the stepdad came up here and killed Stu because he was so aggravated at having to raise Stu's bratty young'uns."

"Could be," I said.

"Or it's possible that neither of the Vances had anything to do with Stu's murder," Mom said.

"I'm just throwing out possibilities," said Aunt Bess. "By the way, Amy, are those jackals still bothering you?"

"They haven't been since Roger installed the security cameras. They were an excellent deterrent."

Jackie shot me a triumphant grin. "I'll let him know how grateful you are."

I glared at her. "Don't you dare."

I spent the rest of Sunday afternoon lazily and peacefully watching cooking shows on television. I enjoyed some of the shows, and I critiqued the others to Rory. And I got a few ideas for new dishes to test at the café.

Monday morning came just a wee bit too early, but I managed to get up, shower, dress, and make it to the café a good ten minutes before anyone else. I'd already made the coffee and started the kitchen prep when Shelly and Luis got there.

I heard someone else come into the café and figured it was Dilly. I stepped out of the kitchen to say hello and found that it wasn't Dilly—it was Walter Jackson.

"Mr. Jackson . . . good morning."

"Hello, Amy. How are you?"

"I'm fine. And you?"

"I'm well. I came by for one more of your delicious meals before I leave Winter Garden."

"Oh. You're leaving today?"

He nodded. "I said I'd stay for Stu's funeral, and that was Saturday. I took in some of the sights yesterday, and now I'm ready to head home."

"I hope you've enjoyed your stay," I said. "Before it slips my mind, did Ms. Vance speak with you at the funeral? She told me she hoped to see you and ask if you'd made your peace with Stu."

"I did see her," he said with a sad smile. "Stu was a fool to treat her and his children the way he did." The smile was replaced by a slight frown. "I did hear an interesting conversation between Stu's son, Brendan, and his stepfather after the funeral. What's the stepfather's name—Douglas?"

"I believe so." I thought it strange that Douglas had apparently changed his mind about the funeral after telling his wife that he thought it would be awkward for him to be there, but I didn't want to interrupt Mr. Jackson's story.

"It struck me odd that Douglas said he'd missed Brendan and wasn't a month in Winter Garden long enough."

My jaw dropped. "A month?"

"Yeah, and Brendan said he hopes a big deal will be coming through in a few more days that will allow him to torch the old man's house and come back to Cookeville a rich man," said Mr. Jackson. "Then they laughed and hugged. I thought it was disrespectful for Brendan to speak of burning his father's house down at his funeral. Don't you?"

"I sure do, Mr. Jackson."

He shook his shoulders as if making a concerted effort to shake off his melancholy. "I'd better order and eat up, so I can go by the police station before leaving town. The sheriff asked me to tell him, you know."

"Right." I wondered if I should suggest to Mr. Jackson that he relay the conversation he overheard between Brendan and Douglas to the sheriff. It wasn't as if Brendan was confessing to anything. But why had he been in Winter Garden for a month? And why didn't Madelyn seem to know that?

Mr. Jackson gave me his order, and I had to snap out of my woolgathering to make his breakfast.

The first chance I got, I called Ryan. I told him about Mr. Jackson's visit to the café and about the conversation he'd overheard between Brendan Carver and his stepdad, Douglas Vance.

"So what do you think about that—about Brendan being in Winter Garden for a month?" I asked. "And why didn't Madelyn know? Where did she think he was during that time?"

"Mr. Jackson shared that same story with Sheriff Billings before he left here. I have to wonder if he was testing it out on you before telling it to the sheriff."

"Wait, you think Mr. Jackson was lying about that?"

"Something you find out early on as a police officer is that people tell you what they want you to know," Ryan said. "Now, the story might have been true. Or it might have been a way to deflect suspicion from himself onto Brendan Carver . . . especially since Brendan has made it clear that there's no love lost between him and his dad."

"Oh. That makes me feel gullible."

"Not necessarily. I'm not saying Mr. Jackson's story isn't true. We simply need to verify it first."

"Okay," I said. "That makes me feel a teensy bit better. So did Mr. Jackson leave Winter Garden?"

"As far as we know. We had no evidence to hold him."

After speaking with Ryan, I called Madelyn. I knew there was a good chance she wouldn't take my call, but she did. Granted, she had an attitude, but she answered the call.

"What do you want?" was her greeting.

"I hate that our misunderstanding about Joey and Brendan cost us our friendship," I said. "Why don't you come by the café today for lunch . . . on me?"

"I'm busy today."

"I . . . I need to ask you something." I might not get the opportunity to talk with Madelyn again, so I bit the bullet and asked. "Where was Brendan for this past month—before your father's death?"

"At school in Radford. Why?"

"Are you sure?"

She huffed. "You're a real piece of work, you know that? Where do *you* think my brother has been?"

"Walter Jackson came into the café for breakfast and said he overheard Brendan talking with Douglas. He said Douglas told Brendan he missed him and that being in Winter Garden for a month was long enough."

"That's ridiculous. Maybe he said it *seemed* like Brendan had been here a month. He and Douglas are tight."

"Okay. I guess I was hoping that Brendan had come to see his dad," I said. "I get the impression they didn't get along very well, and I was hoping that had been resolved before Stu died."

"Yeah. Whatever. Just mind your own business, all right?"

"I—"

Madelyn ended the call.

"I will," I finished lamely.

I thought the matter with Madelyn was over until I saw her walk into the café about an hour and a half after we'd spoken. She looked as if she'd been crying.

I hurried over. "Madelyn, are you all right?"

"No. Is that offer for a free lunch still good?"

"Of course it is. I'll get you a menu." I got her a menu and a glass of water. "Just look this over and order whatever you want. I'll make sure Jackie knows there's no charge."

"Aren't you going to ask?"

"Ask what?"

"About Brendan," she said.

"No. If you're willing to take a chance on being friends with me again, I'm not going to ruin it by putting my nose where it doesn't belong," I said.

She smiled slightly. "As much as I appreciate that sentiment . . ." She nodded to the chair across from her. "Can you sit a minute?"

"Sure." We weren't terribly busy at the moment and I gave Jackie a tiny wave, letting her know to come and get me if she needed me. I sat down opposite Madelyn.

"Brendan wasn't at school this past month. I'd thought he was because he was on academic probation, and I believed he was taking summer classes to get straightened out."

"But he decided to take the summer off?"

She rolled her eyes. "He's decided to take *forever* off apparently. He says he's not going back to school. He's been staying with Joey all this time so Mom wouldn't know."

"So Douglas knew but your mom didn't? That doesn't seem right—Douglas keeping secrets that big from her."

"Tell me about it. But I told you Brendan and Douglas are tight. They tell each other everything." She ran a hand through her hair. "I can understand them not wanting to worry Mom. And maybe Douglas hoped he could change Brendan's mind or else help him come up with a plan for his future before talking with Mom about it."

"What about your dad? Did Brendan spend any time with him while he was here?"

"He says he didn't."

"That's odd," I said. "Winter Garden is such a small town. You typically can't get away from anyone. It seems to me that whenever I go to the grocery store, half of Winter Garden is there no matter what time it is."

She nodded. "He was so evasive about having talked with Dad that I'm guessing he's bound to have run into him somewhere. Or maybe he just flat out went to see him. But if he did, the encounter did nothing to ease their relationship."

"I'm sorry. Although I doubt Brendan would admit it, I believe that fact makes Stu's death even harder for him."

"I think you're right, Amy. I just wish I could get him away from Joey. Joey is a bad influence. He always has been. Even though Brendan is the older one, and you'd think it would be the other way around, Brendan is so easily swayed by Joey."

"Have you thought any more about what you're going to do?" I asked. "You mentioned when you first arrived in Winter Garden that you were considering keeping your dad's house and maintaining his hives."

She smirked. "I'm sure you realize from seeing me with Mr. Dougherty the other day that there's a possibility of a natural gas reserve being below the property that encompasses Dad's land, Joey's parents' land, and the Thomas land. I guess whatever I decide will depend on what Mr. Dougherty's company finds."

"That's exciting."

"Maybe. I've never been one to count my chickens before they hatch, though. They'll have to show me solid proof of a natural gas reserve before I sign any paperwork with Ives Oil and Gas."

Chapter 20

&N ot long after Madelyn left, Mr. Dougherty came in for lunch. He asked Shelly to let me know he was there, and she came into the kitchen and got me. She took over my lettuce shredding, so I could talk with our customer.

I went into the dining room and spotted Mr. Dougherty sitting at a table to the right of the door.

"Hi there," I said. "Shelly told me you wanted to talk with me."

"Yeah. I thought I'd let you know that I'll be leaving Winter Garden later today. But I'll certainly stop back in at the Down South Café whenever I'm passing through."

"So where are you off to?"

"Kentucky. The lawmakers here won out, so I'm taking my testing materials a few hours up the road." He bobbed his head. "Got the call this morning."

"I'm sorry you'll be leaving us. I'll make you up a package of cookies for the road."

He grinned. "I'd appreciate that."

I was getting ready to ask what assortment he'd like when Chad Thomas burst through the door. I took a step back as he stormed over to the table.

"Fern told me you're leaving town. I demand an explanation, and I want it now!"

Mr. Dougherty stood and also took a step away from Mr. Thomas. He held up his hands. "The local lawmakers have pulled the plug on Ives Oil and Gas continuing our research in this area."

"That's a load of crap, and you know it!"

"It's not," said Mr. Dougherty. "If you don't believe me, call your mayor and ask him."

Mr. Thomas turned the table over, breaking the glass and spilling the water Shelly had already given Mr. Dougherty.

I turned and shot a look at Shelly.

She nodded, phone in hand. "I'm calling the police!"

Mr. Thomas advanced toward Mr. Dougherty, and poor Mr. Dougherty backed up until he hit the wall.

I didn't know what to do. Did I step in and risk being hurt myself? Or did I let Mr. Dougherty fend for himself?

Luckily, I didn't have to wonder for long. Ryan strode through the door, assessed the situation, and stepped between the two men. He raised his arms, making the men keep their distance from each other. I didn't think that was a problem for Mr. Dougherty, but Mr. Thomas looked as if he was considering taking them both on.

"What's going on here?" Ryan asked.

"That smarmy snake oil salesman came around here

promising us the moon, and now he's taking off on us!" Mr. Thomas shouted. "He's leaving us with nothing!"

"I've been reassigned," Mr. Dougherty explained to Ryan. "I didn't take anything from these people, and it isn't my fault that your local lawmakers don't want Ives Oil and Gas researching possible natural gas reserves in the area."

"You heard the man," Ryan said to Mr. Thomas. "I think you need to apologize and take your lunch order somewhere else for today before this—"

Mr. Thomas threw a punch at Ryan. Ryan ducked it. Then he wove around behind Mr. Thomas and pulled one arm behind Mr. Thomas's back. The big man wasn't going to be that easy to take down, though. He whirled and spun out of Ryan's grasp.

Mr. Dougherty stepped in and grabbed Mr. Thomas's right arm as Ryan grabbed the left and pivoted behind Mr. Thomas and managed to secure both the man's wrists in handcuffs.

Ryan nodded a thank-you to Mr. Dougherty and began reciting Mr. Thomas's rights as he walked him out of the café.

"This ain't over!" Mr. Thomas yelled.

"Don't make me Taser you." Ryan walked him to his squad car, opened the back door, and ushered him inside.

"Wow." I realized I was trembling as I moved away from the window, so I sank into a chair.

"That was intense," said Mr. Dougherty, sitting in the chair beside the one I sat on.

"It was."

Shelly brought me a glass of water and put her hand on my shoulder. "Do you need me to drive you home?"

I shook my head. "No. I appreciate your concern, but I'll be fine. It was Mr. Dougherty and Deputy Hall who were in the thick of things." I passed my water glass to Mr. Dougherty. "Are you all right?"

"Yeah. I've just never had anybody get that worked up on me before. I mean, I realized the man had a quick temper, but I didn't know it was *that* bad." He drank the water. "And there wasn't any sort of guarantee that he had a reserve on his property. We were simply going to do more testing to see."

Shelly scurried back to the kitchen and got a glass of water for me. I gratefully accepted it. It was sweet that she'd thought of me over our customer. I understood that she was as shaken as the rest of us and encouraged her to have a seat. Fortunately, there were no other customers in the café at the time.

Luis came from the back and asked what was going on. In bits and pieces, each of us related what he missed, as he picked up the overturned table. Then he went back to the closet for the broom and dustpan to clean up the glass.

"I'm really sorry you had to go through this," I told Mr. Dougherty. "Whatever you want for lunch is on the house."

"I couldn't do that. It wasn't your fault that Mr. Thomas came barging in here like a maniac. In fact, I was glad when I called the Thomas house this morning and got Fern. I knew she'd be the more reasonable of the two," he said. "I hated breaking the news to any of the Ives prospects, but I didn't want to simply disappear on them, making them wonder what had happened. Some people in my business do that, but I think it's unfair."

"Madelyn Carver was in earlier, and she didn't seem to know anything about your leaving," I said.

"I didn't have Ms. Carver's cell number, so I called Joey's mother. She seemed fine with it and said she'd pass the information along." He raised his brows. "Based on Mr. Thomas's reaction, I hope to be out of town before Brendan and Joey find out. I've pretty much lost my appetite, but I'll take those cookies if the offer still stands."

I assured him it did, and we walked over to the counter so Mr. Dougherty could select his cookies. After making sure he was okay to drive, I wished him safe travels, and he quickly left.

After Ryan got Chad Thomas squared away at the jail, he returned to the café.

Even though there were a few customers in the dining room when he came through the door, I came out from behind the counter and gave him a quick hug. "I don't know how you got here so quickly, but I'm so glad you did."

He grinned. "I was just coming for lunch. Talk about being in the right place at the right time."

"I'll say. I imagine you're really ready for that lunch now."

"I am. I'll have a hot dog and potato wedges, please."

"All right. And for dessert, how about a warm fudge brownie à la mode?" I asked.

"Well, if you'd make it, I certainly wouldn't let it go to waste."

I went into the kitchen and began making Ryan's lunch.

When Shelly brought up another order, I quietly asked her not to accept payment for Ryan's meal.

"I don't know what Chad Thomas might've done had he not been here," I said.

"Oh, hon, I agree a hundred percent. That was downright scary."

Luis was at the sink washing dishes. "I'd have saved us all."

"We know," I said. "But still . . ."

"Yeah," Shelly agreed with a wink. "Still."

By the time Ryan had finished his lunch, it was just about closing time.

"Why don't you go ahead and take off?" Shelly suggested. "Luis and I can handle cleanup today."

"Are you sure?"

"Positive." She lowered her voice. "Go snuggle with that handsome man for a few minutes before he has to go back to fighting crime and saving lives and all that good stuff."

I laughed. "All right. If you need me to come back, all you have to do is call."

"Go."

"Shelly's running me off," I said to Ryan. "Can you come over to my house for a little while?"

"As a matter of fact, I can. Sheriff Billings said that since I'd worked through lunch, I could take the rest of the day."

"Then I'd almost say that altercation with Chad Thomas was worth it." I reconsidered. "No, I wouldn't."

"If you don't mind, I'm going to go home, change out of this uniform, and get cleaned up before coming back to your place."

"I don't mind in the least." It would give me a chance to do the same.

It was a mild day, so when Ryan returned, we sat on the front porch and chatted while drinking lemonade.

"How much time will Mr. Thomas have to serve for the stunt he pulled at the café today?" I asked.

"Not any. He was awaiting bail when I left. He'll pay a fine and maybe get probation."

"I guess that's okay. He didn't do any real damage. But I'm afraid to imagine what he might've done had you not got there when you did."

Ryan raised my hand to his lips. "I'm glad I did." He kissed my hand and then lowered it again. "The entire way to the police station, Thomas raved about having been cheated. He said Dougherty was nothing more than a two-bit swindler. I finally asked him what he'd lost. You know what he said?"

I shook my head.

"He said, 'Millions of dollars.' I said, 'You didn't lose millions of dollars—you never had it.'"

"I can guess how well that went over."

Ryan laughed. "Oh, yeah. He raged even more that Dougherty had cheated him out of his fortune, as well as his future children's fortune."

"Hmm. Roger told us that the Thomas brothers had terrible tempers. One of them certainly proved him right today."

"Did Thomas do any damage to the café?"

"No. The table was fine. Luis cleaned up the broken glass and then mopped up the water."

"He's a good kid."

"He is." I smiled. "He told Shelly and me that he'd have saved us all if you hadn't shown up."

"I have no doubt he would have . . . despite the fact that he was nowhere to be found when all the drama was going down."

I laughed and squeezed Ryan's hand. We sat in silence for a few minutes, watching a blue jay flit from pine tree to pine tree.

There was no trace of my frivolity left when I said, "It's beginning to look like Stu Landon Carver's killer is going to get away with his—or her—crime. Walter Jackson has left town, and there aren't any new leads."

"You're forgetting about the knife. We're hoping Ivy can get some DNA off that."

"What do you think the killer's motive was for burning the barn—and for burning it the night of Stu's wake?"

"The motive was fairly obvious—to destroy any evidence that might still be discovered. It was just pure dumb luck that we found the knife. It was well hidden, and I imagine the killer thought it had been ruined, at least as far as evidence gathering was concerned. As for the timing . . . the killer might've run a bigger risk of getting caught if he'd burned the barn on the night he murdered Stu." Ryan leaned forward and began talking more like a lawyer than a police officer. "We've already determined that it was a busy night for our perpetrator. He—or she, as you've pointed out—murdered Stu Landon Carver in the barn at Old Cedar Cove, leaving behind what we believe to be the murder weapon. Then he and, likely, an accomplice put Carver's body into his own truck and drove it to the Down South Café parking lot."

"Or since we believe there to be an accomplice, they could've taken the body in their vehicle and then transferred Stu to the truck when they arrived at the café."

"Fair enough. But then the killer had to make a getaway, clean up whatever vehicle he'd arrived in because he was bound to have been covered in blood, ditch his clothing and clean himself up, and get back safely to wherever an alibi awaited. Who has time to burn a barn when you've got all that going on?"

"True. But why burn the barn on the night of Stu's wake specifically?" I asked. "Do you think it was some sort of sick revenge thing?"

"No. I believe it was the best possible time for the killer to burn the barn. There were only two people who had any legitimate reason to be around that old run-down barn—Stuart Landon Carver and Chad Thomas. And Thomas only mows the pastureland twice a year, three at the most. With Carver dead, there was a remote possibility someone would come to check the hives."

"And with just about all of Stu's friends and family at the wake, the murderer knew he—or she—wasn't likely to be disturbed. That makes sense. But what if someone had checked the hives prior to the barn being destroyed?"

"I'm guessing our perp was just hoping that if anyone did, they wouldn't venture into the barn," Ryan said.

"But what about the Down South Café? Why leave poor Stu in his truck there? Why not the grocery store or a gas station?"

"I'm not entirely certain, but my bet would be on our killer wanting Carver to be found as soon as possible. This person might've known that you were selling Carver's honey on consignment, so you'd know who he was, and thought he'd be discovered more quickly at the café than at some other location."

"Maybe. I mean, I suppose people at the grocery store or gas station might simply pass him by thinking an old man was napping in his truck. But don't most murderers want to *hide* their victims?"

"Not if the victim had something the killer wanted. If Carver wasn't found, he wouldn't be declared dead, and his estate wouldn't be handed over to his survivors."

I gasped. "The natural gas reserve! Whoever killed Stu believed there was gas on that land. And now that the lawmakers have shut down the Ives Oil and Gas prospecting, his death was completely pointless."

Chapter 21

When Homer came in for breakfast on Tuesday morning, he told me his hero was Robert Wyatt. I'd never heard of the man.

"He's an English musician. One of his quotes that resonated with me was this: 'I know people who grow old and bitter. I want to keep making a fresh start.' I like it. I feel that I kinda make a fresh start every morning when I choose my hero of the day."

"That's a good philosophy," I said.

"And I believe Winter Garden is ready for a fresh start too. All the excitement, disappointment, and general upheaval brought on by the arrival of Ives Oil and Gas can go back to normal now that Mr. Dougherty has left us." He sipped his coffee. "Don't you agree?"

I nodded.

"We wake up to a clean slate every morning—a new beginning," Homer continued.

"It's not always that easy, Homer," said Jackie. "There are some things you simply can't forget about or leave behind."

I knew she was talking about her mother, who'd recently gone into a rehab facility. Aunt Renee had left Jackie with Aunt Bess when Jackie was only sixteen. She'd faded in and out of both their lives since then, and Jackie had a lot of resentment over it. During her last visit to Winter Garden, Jackie had talked her into entering rehab.

"True," said Homer, "but perhaps you can change your outlook. Something that seems like a negative could become a positive. Right?"

"Yeah, maybe." Jackie picked up a coffeepot and went to check on some of her other customers.

"Let me get that sausage biscuit for you," I told Homer.

As I went into the kitchen, I thought about what he'd said about Winter Garden basically getting back to normal now that Ives Oil and Gas had stopped their prospecting endeavors. But I didn't see how our town could regain any sense of normalcy if Stu Landon Carver's killer was never caught. And that's how it was really beginning to look to me.

Sure, the knife might hold some evidence. But if any DNA or fingerprints had been found in or on the truck, there hadn't been anything conclusive enough to arrest a suspect. If the killer had been careful enough to keep from leaving any evidence in a truck, didn't it stand to reason that there wouldn't be any found on the murder weapon?

I wished the quiet, peaceful life *would* return to Winter Garden. I just didn't see how it could with all of us looking over our shoulder for a killer.

* * *

It wasn't too long after Homer left that Madelyn Carver shuffled into the café and slumped onto the nearest stool.

"Coffee and one of those chocolate doughnuts with the white frosting, please," she said.

"Are you okay?" Given her demeanor, that was probably the stupidest question I could ask, but I didn't know what else to say.

"My nerves are shot. I called an attorney friend this morning to see if our family has any legal recourse against Ives Oil and Gas for discontinuing the testing. He told us that we don't."

I poured her coffee and then returned the carafe to its base.

"First off," she continued, "Ives never declared definitively that there is a natural gas reserve located beneath my father's property. They only found promising circumstances for there to be, and further testing was needed to determine whether or not the land was worth mining." She sighed. "Even if we were sure there *is* natural gas on our property, there's nothing we can do about it. We can't mine it ourselves, of course. And we can't bring another gas company in to mine it for us because of the lawmakers' block."

"That's too bad," I said, putting her doughnut on a plate and giving her a fork, knife, and napkin.

"The worst part is that I absolutely can't get that through Brendan's head—or Joey's either, for that matter. They're angry and feel that they're entitled to . . ." She shook her head. "Something. I'm not quite sure what.

Money, I'm sure. Yes, wouldn't it have been fabulous if Ives had found a huge natural gas reserve under dear old daddy's property, and his children would have wound up millionaires? But life seldom works that way, does it?"

"I'm afraid not." At this point, I could do little but nod and murmur my agreement while she continued to rant.

Madelyn used the knife and fork to daintily take a bite of her doughnut. Given her state of mind, I half expected her to just pick it up and shove it into her mouth. That's probably what I'd have done.

"I didn't even know Brendan had left college and had been hiding out here with Joey for a month until you told me," she said. "That's ridiculous. Douglas has always babied Brendan and let him slide about things he'd have never let me get away with. I don't know whether it was because I was the oldest or because I was a girl, but I had a narrow line to toe."

I watched her take another bite of her food. I really needed to get into the kitchen and finish lunch prep, but I couldn't simply walk away. It was obvious she needed to talk.

I got the coffeepot and topped off her barely touched coffee.

"But letting Brendan completely slack off like this and bum around with Joey? What is Douglas thinking? This is Brendan's future we're talking about! We can't just stand by and watch him blow it."

"Playing devil's advocate here, what can you really do?" I asked. "I'm guessing Douglas is trying not to alienate Brendan while hoping he comes to his senses. Brendan's decisions are his to make at this point—you can't force him to return to school. Even if you do, he won't succeed unless his heart is in it."

"I know." She blinked back tears. "Mom had such a hard time raising us on her own . . . until she found Douglas, I mean. I tried to help. I always felt like a second mother to Brendan."

"Oh, Madelyn, that must've been so hard for you. You're only a year or two older than Brendan, aren't you?"

"I'm three years older. I carried a lot of resentment around for Stu until I realized he was merely living his life the best way he knew how." She gave a mirthless chuckle. "I think I came to that epiphany in some college psych class. Anyway, despite my enlightened view of my father, I still sometimes became so angry at the way he treated us and our mother—Mom, especially, because he took her from the only home she'd ever known and then abandoned her. No wonder Brendan hated him. Sometimes, I did too."

"I understand."

"I don't see how you could. You look like you've never seen any heartache in your life."

"I have. We all have. In fact, my dad left when I was only four years old. He didn't wander in and out of our lives like Stu did yours—he just left. We don't even know where he's at."

"Did your mom remarry?"

"Nope, she never did. She dated now and then—still does—but it's never anything serious. I don't know if that's because she still pines for my dad or because she simply refuses to have her heart broken again."

"I'm sorry."

"It's not a big deal," I said. "In fact, I think his making a clean break made it easier for us than it was for you and your family. Every time Stu came back into your lives and then left again, the wound was reopened."

"Yeah." She looked at the display case. "Could I get a half dozen of these doughnuts to go, please? Not all for me—I thought Brendan and Joey might like some."

"Of course." I put the doughnuts into a bakery bag.

The lunch rush was just picking up when Jackie came back to the kitchen and told me a woman was asking for me. I had her watch the grill—and the stove and the oven—while I went to see what the woman wanted.

I stepped over to the far end of the counter where the woman was perched on a stool waiting. She was wearing a navy blue baseball cap and black sunglasses, and I didn't recognize her at first.

That's when she told me, "Hey, Amy. It's me, Fern."

"Hi, Fern."

"I need my meal to go. And could you please not mention to Chad if you see him that I came in here? He's declared the Down South Café off-limits since y'all got him in trouble with the police."

I felt like my eyebrows shot up so high, they were nearly on top of my head. "We did not get him into trouble. His temper got him into trouble."

"Still, ain't there some way you could drop the charges or something?"

"I didn't file charges. Deputy Hall was here and arrested your husband after breaking up the fight. Why was Chad so angry with Mr. Dougherty in the first place—he wanted to develop the reserves as much as the property owners did?"

"I don't know about that," said Fern. "It might've been a feather in Mr. Dougherty's cap to find gas for the company or whatever, but that money sure could've changed the lives of a lot of Winter Garden residents, especially Chad. Heck, it could've helped you too, Amy—it would've brought more people to the area."

"I'm not sure that's always a good thing."

"Yeah . . . well . . . I came for a fried chicken breast, some cole slaw, and some potato salad. How long would it take for you to get that together for me?" She looked all around the dining room, and I realized she was looking out all the windows. "I hope Chad doesn't drive by and see my car here. I just wanted a good lunch today, and I didn't feel like making it myself."

"I understand."

"And how about a biscuit? Can I get a biscuit with my meal?"

"Of course. I'll have it out here to you as soon as I can."

"Thanks." She continued watching the windows.

After work, I went by the grocery store. I'd come across a recipe for chicken curry that I wanted to let patrons sample. I wasn't sure there were many residents of Winter Garden who were up for Indian cuisine—the dish might not go over any better than the sushi did—but I wanted to give it a shot. I needed some cumin, ginger, and cardamom.

I was in the spice aisle when I spotted a familiar-looking figure from the corner of my eye. I turned my head to get a better look and realized Walter Jackson was walking by.

"Mr. Jackson?" I hurried after the man. What was he doing here? I thought he'd left Winter Garden.

He was headed for the door.

I quickened my steps. "Mr. Jackson!"

He went on out the door and into the parking lot.

I abandoned my spices on a nearby shelf so I could run outside and talk with him. But even though I stood at the door and looked out over the parking lot at least twice, I couldn't see where Mr. Jackson had gone.

I went back into the store, retrieved my spices, and took them up to the checkout line. As I was paying for my items, I was still looking through the glass storefront to see if I could spot Mr. Jackson.

"Is everything all right?" the cashier asked.

"Yeah. It's fine. I thought I saw someone I knew."

"That happens to me all the time."

I nodded, took my groceries, and headed for the car. Once inside, I called Ryan.

"Hi, beautiful."

"Hey there. Guess who I just now saw at the grocery store?"

"Elvis? An alien? Brad Pitt?"

"Okay, please stop guessing," I said. "It was Walter Jackson. I thought he left Winter Garden."

"He did. Or at least he told us he was on his way out of town yesterday morning. We assumed he left. What reason could he possibly have for hanging around?"

"I don't know. But it was him. I called out to him and tried to get him to stop, but he left the store and I lost sight of him."

"Are you *sure* it was Walter Jackson?" Ryan asked. "It could've simply been someone who resembled him. The website NOLO has an entire page dedicated to eyewitness identification, and there are a lot of factors to take into consideration."

I interrupted so he'd get out of super-cop mode. "Okay, sure, it could've been someone who merely looked like Walter Jackson. Like you said, what possible reason could Mr. Jackson have for remaining in Winter Garden?"

"Other than the fabulous food at the Down South Café."

Now he was just trying to humor me. "There's something else I want to talk with you about. Consider this a concerned citizen simply pointing out suspicious behavior."

"All right. Let's hear it."

"I'm afraid Chad Thomas is abusive toward his wife." I told him about seeing Fern with the bruise on her face—and I added that Mom suggested that Fern really could have had an accident so I tried to let it go. And then I told him about her wearing the ball cap and sunglasses and watching over her shoulder to make sure she wasn't being caught at the café today. "She never took those glasses off, Ryan, and she appeared to be terrified that he'd catch her."

"I wouldn't be surprised—given what I've seen of Chad Thomas lately—to learn that he is abusing his wife. That said, he could be beating her every day of the week and twice on Sunday and there's nothing we could do about it until she presses charges against him. And even if she did, she might drop them later."

"Because she's that afraid of him?" I asked.

"That, or because he's convinced her he's changed and it'll never happen again. We see it all the time. She has to let us help her before we can."

I must've been quiet just a second too long.

"Amy, don't go putting your nose into a situation you know nothing about," he warned. "If Fern Thomas wants help, she'll ask for it. And then you can direct her to the authorities. But stay out of that couple's business. I don't want you to wind up getting hurt."

Chapter 22

He omer came in on Wednesday morning whistling a little tune. He plopped down on his stool and announced, "There is a value in taking a stand whether or not anybody may be noticing it and whether or not it is a risky thing to do. That's a quote from my hero of the day, businesswoman and philanthropist Teresa Heinz Kerry."

"So you're all about risk taking today, huh?" I smiled. "I'm glad. I'm making chicken curry for people to sample today and I hope you'll try it."

"I'm not sure how well that dish would go with a sausage biscuit."

"That's all right. It isn't ready yet."

He breathed a sigh of relief. "Well, then, if it's done before I leave, then I'll give it a try. If not . . . maybe next time."

I waved and called good-bye to a patron who was leaving. Then I turned back to Homer. "Speaking of risk taking, what if you thought someone was being abused? Would you stay out of it? Or would you take a risk of making someone angry or of possibly getting yourself in trouble?"

"Would this trouble be danger?"

I nodded.

"You'd better be more specific."

I explained to Homer that I suspected Fern Thomas was being abused by her husband. I told him what had prompted my suspicions and that I'd spoken about them to Ryan. "Ryan says that even if Fern is being abused, there's nothing the police can do about it unless she presses charges against Chad. I'm really concerned about Fern, and I'd like to help her."

"You do realize that she might not want or need your help, don't you?"

"Of course I do. But surely you can understand my concern."

He mulled this over and sipped his coffee. "Maybe you could, in a roundabout way, ask Fern if she's being abused and urge her to seek help if she is."

"I suppose I could call Fern and invite her to my house for some tea or lemonade," I said. "I could say I'd like to get to know her better."

"Good idea." He looked at his watch.

"I'm on it." I went into the kitchen and started making his sausage biscuit.

H omer left before the chicken curry was finished, but other patrons coming in for lunch tried it. Most seemed to enjoy it.

"That Indian dish seems to be going over fairly well," Jackie said as she brought an order up to the window. "Are you going to offer it as a special next week?"

"I'm considering it. I'll see how well it goes. Are people talking like they'd order it if I did have it as the special of the day?"

"I'll ask. I've just been asking if they'd like a sample. The ones who've accepted samples have appeared to like it."

"Wait," I said as she started to dart back into the dining room. "Could you come in here for a second?"

Jackie came into the kitchen and I confided to her that I planned to call Fern after work. "I'm going to offer her a friendly ear. If she confirms my suspicions that Chad is abusing her, I'll encourage her to seek help."

"Be awfully careful in how you approach Fern. Remember, she loves Chad—or at least, she did once."

"Of course I'll be sensitive. I'm not going to come right out and ask the woman if her husband beats her."

"I know. Just be . . . delicate."

During a lull in the afternoon, I looked up Fern's phone number using the white pages on my phone. I made the call.

"Hi, Fern. It's Amy Flowers from the Down South Café."

"What do you want?"

"I called to ask if you'd like to come over to my house for tea and lemon bars this afternoon at around four thirty."

"Why?"

"I thought you and I could chat and get to know each other better."

"Well . . . I guess I could come by for a few minutes. What's your address?"

I gave Fern my address and then got back to work.

After work, I went home and prepared for my meeting with Fern. I thought I should do a little research first to see how I might approach the topic. As Jackie pointed out, I needed to be delicate.

I did an Internet search and found a website detailing how one should talk with someone suspected of suffering abuse. I clicked on the link and went onto the site. The first thing I noticed was that there was a bar along the top of the page that said, *Safety Alert! To Exit Site, Click Here!* I clicked the bar to see what would happen and was taken to the Google homepage. I thought that was really clever. If a person was browsing this site and his or her abuser walked in, a quick click could take them to an innocuous site.

I went back to the original page and read that I should speak with the victim about her experience without judgment or agenda. I should express concern, show support, and urge Fern to seek help. I shut off the laptop and told Rory I believed I was ready. He woofed to indicate that he was too.

Princess Eloise came meowing and winding around my ankles to remind me that I'd been home for several minutes and had not yet put food in Her Majesty's dish. I fed the pets, then I got washed up and took the lemon bars I'd brought home from the café and arranged them on a decorative plate.

I put the bars, a small pitcher of iced tea, and two

tumblers filled with ice on a serving tray. I carried the tray out to the front porch and placed it on the white wicker table between the matching rockers. I sat on one of the rockers and waited for Fern to arrive.

As I was sitting there, a hummingbird—looking and sounding like a colorful, overgrown bumblebee—darted forward and back.

"You're in the wrong place," I said. "The hummingbird feeders are at the big house on the left side of the wrap-around porch."

Almost as if it understood my words, the bird flew away.

Moments later, Fern pulled into my driveway. She got out of her compact car and came around to the front porch. She stood there assessing me.

"Come on up and have a seat," I said.

She slowly walked up the stairs and sat on the available rocker. "What do you want? Why did you ask me to come here?"

"I'm interested in making friends with you, that's all."

"You don't think I have any friends?"

"I didn't say that. I'm sure you have plenty of friends, but we can always use another. Don't you agree?"

"I don't know."

"If you don't want to be friends, then why did you agree to come?"

"I wanted to see what you were up to—why you'd invite me to your house."

I decided to level with her. "Look, after seeing the bruise on your face at the grocery store and then watching how nervous you were at the café yesterday, I became concerned that Chad was abusing you. Is he?"

"That's crazy! Chad is a wonderful man. I couldn't ask for a harder-working husband or a better provider."

"That's wonderful. I'm glad I was wrong."

"You *are* wrong! Here I thought you might really want to be my friend, but all you want to do is tear down my husband."

"I do want to be your friend, Fern. And I'm not trying to tear down Chad—I don't even know Chad—I was only looking out for you. I wasn't making any accusations— merely asking a question."

"You went off to that big-city chef school and came back here to Winter Garden thinking you're better than everybody else."

"No, I—"

"You're no better than that Calvin Dougherty or Stu Landon! They thought they were better than everybody else in Winter Garden too. Landon even tried to hide who he really was, but Chad knew. Chad's smart. He always said, 'That beekeeper is in too deep with the Carvers not to be one of them.'"

"What difference does it make?"

"The man was a liar—that's what difference it makes. He'd have the whole town up in arms against Chad just because Chad had to spray his crops. Didn't that stupid beekeeper want my husband to make a living? Did he want Chad to just let the bugs eat up our crops?"

I thought Chad could've certainly been more responsible in his spraying, but I wasn't about to say so.

"And that Calvin Dougherty was another liar. He told us that if there was a natural gas reserve beneath our land, we could have a life of leisure," Fern ranted. "Chad works so hard. Did you know that in addition to running the farm, he works at the steel mill in Meadowview, cuts down trees, and mows people's fields? Did you know he did all that?"

I shook my head.

"No, you didn't know. You don't even care. I was glad Chad was finally going to have an easier time of things for the first time in his life. Did you know that Chad had to start helping his daddy on that farm when he was only ten years old?"

"I didn't know that, Fern. And I'm sorry for any mis-understanding. I certainly didn't intend to upset you. It's clear that I misread the situation." I stood. "Thanks for stopping by, but I really need to go inside and get dinner started. I suppose you need to do the same."

"So that's it?" Fern demanded. "You want me to leave now?"

"You've been angry from the moment you arrived. Why would you *want* to stay?"

Fern stood. "I don't want to stay. I—"

A truck roared by, slammed on its brakes, and then backed up. We looked over and saw that it was Chad Thomas. He gave Fern a hard look before driving on.

Fern stomped her foot and gave a growl of frustration. "Well, thanks a lot for getting me in trouble!" She jumped down from the porch, bypassing the steps altogether, got into her car, and sped off.

Feeling completely bewildered, I called Jackie. "Are you ready to say 'I told you so'?"

"Always. It blew up in your face, didn't it?"

"You ain't just whistling *Dixie*, it did. Do you and Roger have plans tonight?"

"No. He's working over trying to get this latest project done."

"Want to come over for dinner?" I asked.

"Can we have something simple—like pimiento cheese sandwiches?"

"Sure. I'll make a salad and some Parmesan garlic tortilla chips to go with them. And, of course, we have lemon bars."

When Jackie got to my house, we ate at the kitchen table. I told her about the Fern visit from beginning to end.

"Then Chad drove up, gave Fern a look, she accused me of getting her in trouble, and then she stormed off."

"Maybe she has that Munchausen syndrome," said Jackie.

I frowned. "You think Fern is injuring herself to make people think Chad is beating her?"

"No, no, no. I meant that thing where people fall in love with their attacker. What's that called?"

"Stockholm syndrome? I'm not sure—I'll have to look it up later."

"You do that, Ms. Freud."

"At least I know the difference between Munchausen and Stockholm," I teased.

"Okay, then, smarty pants. What *is* Munchausen syndrome?"

"Munchausen is where someone intentionally fakes being sick or gives herself an injury in order to be treated like a victim."

"Huh. Maybe I was right then. Maybe that's what Fern has."

Later that night after Jackie had left, I got to thinking

about Fern and wondering if she *could* have Munchausen syndrome. I went into the fancy room, got out my laptop, and sprawled onto the fainting couch.

My investigation of Munchausen syndrome led me to histrionic personality disorder. I looked into that a bit more and discovered that the disorder, more common in women than in men, makes the sufferer excessively sensitive to criticism or disapproval. *That certainly fits. I found that out this afternoon.*

The article I was reading suggested that histrionic personality disorder is characterized by a long-standing pattern of attention-seeking behavior and extreme emotionality. The sufferer might not think before acting. She might make rash decisions.

"A person with histrionic personality disorder will often act out a role, such as princess or victim."

Role of victim, huh? That could certainly apply to Fern. Maybe Chad didn't beat her, but she wanted people to think he did so that she could get attention. On the other hand, maybe he did beat her and she had Stockholm syndrome.

And I could be completely grasping at straws simply because I wanted to understand what had taken place on my porch this afternoon. I shut off the laptop, deciding it was best from now on to give both Fern and Chad Thomas a wide berth and to let them live their lives as they saw fit.

I went into the living room and watched TV for a little while, but my mind kept returning to Fern. Here I'd been thinking that Fern had been trying to cover up the fact that she was being abused by Chad, but today she'd seemed completely off her rocker. Although I'd seen ample evidence of Chad's explosive temper, that didn't mean he was abusive to Fern. What if all along he'd been trying to hide how disturbed she was from the rest of the world? Was that why he hadn't wanted her with him while he conducted business? I'd thought it was because he was being controlling, but maybe he simply didn't want her to go off on one of her tirades.

Deciding to shut off the television and do a little more research about what kind of wackadoo codependent relationship the Thomases might have, I went back to the fancy room to retrieve my laptop. Although I wanted to know for my own enlightenment only, I began to wonder as I walked through the house just *how* disturbed the couple might be. Could they be responsible for Stu Landon Carver's murder? It had been firmly established that the killer had an accomplice. And it had seemed to me this afternoon that Fern would do anything Chad wanted her to . . . even help him move a body.

Just before I stepped into the fancy room, Rory began barking. Not turning on the light, I went over to the window and peeped out to see what had drawn the dog's attention. I saw the silhouette of a slight figure and the glow of a burning cigarette.

Darn those Carver boys! I was not going to put up with their aggravation. And what about that security system? If there was someone lingering in my yard, shouldn't the company have sent someone to check it out by now?

I raced back to the living room to get my phone. I snatched it up off the coffee table, called 9-1-1, and hurried back to the fancy room. As I was telling the dispatcher what was going on, I saw the silhouette move to the gate.

"The person is coming through my back gate!" I shouted into the phone. "Get somebody here now!"

"Ms. Flowers, please remain on the line until—"

"I can't! I'm afraid they'll hurt my dog!"

The dispatcher was saying something, but I ignored it. I left the line open and slid the phone into my pants pocket as I went to the back door.

At first, I tried calling Rory to come to me through the door. He wouldn't. He steadfastly barked at the intruder. I grabbed the cleaver out of the knife block and cracked open the door.

"You'd better get out of here!" I yelled. "The police are on their way, and I have a weapon!"

"I don't care about your weapon. And I don't care about your dog."

"Fern?"

She stepped closer to the door. "Tell this mutt to shut up."

"What are you doing here?"

"I thought about what you said today," she said sweetly. "Can I come in and talk with you?"

Radically shifting emotions.

"No," I said. "We'll talk tomorrow. Rory, come on inside."

Rory listened to me this time and ran onto the porch. I opened the door enough for Rory to get inside, and Fern tried to rush the door.

I slammed the door shut and locked it.

"Please, Amy! Let me come inside. Chad is on his way here. He'll hurt us both."

"Just stay where you are then. The police will be here any minute."

"It'll be too late. He'll kill us . . . just like he did the beekeeper."

I hesitated. What if I didn't let her in and Chad *did* kill her? I'd never forgive myself. And yet I'd already decided that Fern was unbalanced. And the police really would be here soon. It might seem like it was taking forever, but it had been only about three minutes since I made the call.

"Get in your car and lock the door," I told her. "You'll be fine until the police get here. You can have them arrest Chad then."

I jumped back when I heard a loud thump against the door. The voice that spoke next was Fern's but it was gravelly and menacing. "You let me in that house right now, or I'll slit your throat just like I did Stu Landon's. Do you have any idea how warm a man's blood is when it courses from his body? It—"

She gave a strangled cry, and then I heard a thud.

Was it Chad? Had he killed her?

"Amy! Let me in!"

"Mom?" I threw open the door. There stood Mom on the stoop with a baseball bat. I quickly pulled her inside, shut the door, and locked it again. "What are you doing?"

"I think I knocked out that freak who was trying to get into your house."

We were both breathing as if we'd been running a marathon. Mom's eyes were as wide as saucers, and I imagined mine were too.

"I'm not taking any chances, though. Call the police."

I took the phone from my pocket. "They're on the way." I held the phone to my ear. "Are you still there?"

"Yes, ma'am."

"You might need to send an ambulance too," I said. "My mom hit the intruder with a baseball bat."

"Softball, dear."

"Softball," I repeated to the dispatcher. I didn't know what difference it made, but apparently it did to Mom.

Mom and I were still huddled with Rory, the cleaver, and the baseball bat at the back door when Sheriff Billings and Ryan arrived. Fortunately, the ambulance came to take Fern to the hospital a couple of minutes later. She was all right, other than a mild concussion.

Chad Thomas got to the house before the ambulance pulled away. He'd wanted to go to the hospital with Fern, but Sheriff Billings detained him until he'd answered some questions. I'd already told the sheriff that Fern had confessed to killing Stu Landon Carver, and Mom confirmed that she'd heard the confession too.

Torn between admitting to committing a crime and getting to the hospital to be with his wife, Chad had finally asked the sheriff, "If I tell you everything, will you let me go check on my wife and I promise to come right back to the police station afterward?"

"Yes," the sheriff said. "I'll send Deputy Hall with you, and he can bring you back."

"All right."

And then the twisted tale unfolded.

Fern had always thought Chad should have Stu's farm. The land adjoined, and it would make a huge, profitable farm for the Thomases. And she'd always hated the fact that Stu tried to tell Chad when he could and when he couldn't spray the plants. They were Chad's plants. He could do with them as he liked.

Chad had tried to hide it from Fern that he also wanted

Stu's land, but she overheard him talking with Calvin Dougherty about it.

"Why had you tried to hide the fact from her?" Sheriff Billings asked.

"Because I've seen how she can get sometimes. She gets obsessed with things . . . with people." He looked at me. "I tried to make her quit coming around your café, but she was already obsessed with you. She'd come around here at night and just watch your house."

"Why?" I asked.

My interruption got me a sharp look from Sheriff Billings, but then he repeated the question to Chad.

Chad shrugged. "I don't know. She thought Amy had a happy life . . . and I guess she wanted it."

"Okay, now go back to discussing the farm," said Sheriff Billings. "Are you telling me that your wife, Fern Thomas, killed Stu to get his land?"

"I'd been fussing with Stu," Chad said. "He came over here and said my pesticides were killing his bees. But I couldn't spray my fields when he wanted me to because I have another job. I told him he was more than welcome to spray my crops himself, and he said that suited him. I was mad, he was mad; but he left, and when I'd had time to think about it a little more, I thought that if he wanted to spray my crops, that was fine. It would save me some work. So I went to talk with him."

"And did you find him at home?" the sheriff asked.

"No. So I figured he'd gone to check on his other hives. I went out to the Old Cedar Cove hive first, and sure enough, he was there. But Fern's car was there too." Chad ran his hand through his hair. "I hadn't realized it because I'd gotten back on the lawn mower and was working on the backyard, but Fern had followed Stu to the hive when he left our house."

"What happened when you arrived at the hive?"

"I went up there, but there was no sign of either of them. I thought they must be in the barn." He lowered his head. "They were."

"And what did you see, Mr. Thomas?"

"She'd killed him. She told me she'd pretended to flirt with him. When he turned to walk away from her, she'd taken his knife and cut his throat. He was lying there in the dirt." His voice broke. "I tried to save him. I swear I did. But there was nothing I could do . . . nothing anyone could do."

"What happened next?"

"She told me that now I could spray whenever I wanted and that I could buy Stu's land and have all the gas reserves."

"And then?" the sheriff prompted.

"I didn't want her to go to prison. I helped her. I wrapped Stu's body in an old sheet I had in the backseat of my truck, and we drove to the café. We figured he'd be found there, and that the town would put his assets up for auction. We didn't realize he had any family."

"All right. Mr. Thomas, Deputy Hall and I are going to take you to see your wife. And then both of you will be charged—her with murder, and you with accessory to murder. Do you understand?"

"Yes, sir."

After they left, Mom and I sat on the sofa in the living room. I took her hand.

"Thank you for being here. How did you know to come?"

She smiled softly. "I've been keeping a watch on this house off and on pretty much since you had me come get that cigarette butt. Tell Roger the security cameras are nice, but they're not in the same league as a mom with a softball bat."

"Amen to that."

Chapter 23

A week later, things were pretty much back to normal in Winter Garden and at the Down South Café. My first customer that morning—even before Dilly—was Walter Jackson.

"Good morning, Mr. Jackson!"

"I imagine you're surprised to see me."

"I'd thought you were returning to Oklahoma soon, but I'm glad you've decided to extend your stay."

He nodded. "Actually, I've decided to stay on here in Winter Garden. I'd already realized I had nothing and no one to return to in Oklahoma, so I'm looking for a place here. My landlord is going to send my belongings to me." He chuckled. "I'm glad of that. I'm too old to go all the way across the country for some clothes and a few books."

I smiled. "You know, I thought I saw you in the grocery store shortly after Stu Landon Carver's funeral. I called to you, but you didn't seem to hear me."

"I did hear you, and I apologize for being so rude. It's just that at the time, I believed everyone in Winter Garden thought I was involved in Stu's death and that I was up to no good." He looked down at the floor. "But then I ran into Dilly at the bookstore a couple of days later. She's actually the one who convinced me that if I gave Winter Garden half a chance, they'd give me one too."

"That certainly is true."

I'd barely gotten the words out of my mouth when Dilly came into the café.

"Good morning! There's my handsome breakfast date."

My eyes widened. Dilly and Mr. Jackson were dating? A flurry of thoughts went through my mind: *Good for Dilly. Wait—she hardly knows this man. All any of us know about him is what he's told us. But she looks so happy. And so does he. Oooh, Aunt Bess is going to be jealous.*

M adelyn Carver came in for lunch. She, too, had plans to stay in Winter Garden—for a while, at least. She'd told me earlier that she was planning to hang around until after Fern and Chad's trials. She wanted to see her father get the justice he deserved.

Jackie popped her head into the kitchen. "Madelyn wants to talk with you."

My lips tightened. It wasn't that I didn't want to go chat with Madelyn. I just had so much to do. We were slammed.

"I'll take over for you for a minute," she continued. "Let me finish preparing this chef salad while you talk with our guest."

"All right. Thanks so much. I'll make this as quick as possible."

I took off the gloves I'd been wearing and tossed them into the trash can. Madelyn was sitting at a table in the far-right corner.

"How are you?" I asked, perching on the edge of the seat across from her.

"I'm good. I wanted to let you know that Brendan has gone back home to Cookeville. I think that his being away from Joey is good and that being back home with Mom and Douglas is even better."

"I'm glad. I know you're hoping he'll return to school."

She nodded. "I'm pretty sure Mom and Douglas will make him enroll somewhere—if not at the college he'd been attending, then somewhere closer to home."

"That's great. I'm really looking forward to meeting your Brendan one of these days, as opposed to Joey's."

"I'm looking forward to that too. By the way, I resigned my position in Cookeville and had accrued so much vacation time that I don't have to work out a notice."

"Fantastic!"

"Yeah. I've got an interview for a paralegal position at a law firm in Abingdon tomorrow morning. Wish me luck."

"I wish you all the best. What can I get you for lunch?"

She went with the special of the day—baked ziti with meatballs and garlic bread.

That night, several of us gathered at the big house for dinner. Roger and Jackie were there, as were Ryan, Homer, Sarah, John, Mom, Aunt Bess, and me. We had fried chicken, party house rolls, macaroni and cheese, green bean casserole, potato salad, and butterscotch cake.

We were all seated around the table enjoying some lighthearted conversation when Roger asked Mom, "Hey, Babe, would you pass the potato salad?"

She frowned. "Sure, sweetheart."

He laughed. "I'm calling you Babe, as in Babe Ruth . . . the Sultan of Swat."

"Oh, ha-ha. Very funny. I still worry that I hit that poor woman too hard."

"Too hard, my fanny," said Aunt Bess. "Had I been there, I'd have knocked her plumb out into the yard. In my day, I was a pretty fair ballplayer."

"I bet you were," Roger said.

And given that encouragement, Aunt Bess was off, telling us about the best game she ever played in.

Recipes from the
Down South Café

Chocolate Pistachio Cake

Yield: 1 Bundt cake

1 package white or yellow cake mix
1 package pistachio pudding mix
½ cup orange juice
½ cup water
4 eggs
½ cup vegetable oil
¾ cup chocolate syrup

Preheat oven to 350°. Combine the cake mix, pistachio pudding mix, orange juice, water, eggs, and oil in a large mixing bowl. Blend to moisten, then beat 2 minutes at medium speed. Pour about ¾ of the batter into a well-greased and floured Bundt pan. Add the chocolate syrup to the remaining batter and mix well. Pour over the batter in the pan. Bake for 1 hour or until a toothpick inserted in the cake comes out clean.

Cole's Chicken Salad

(Contributed by Cole Hileman)

Yield: Approximately 7 cups

3 pounds of chicken breasts
¾ cup diced onion
¾ cup diced celery
1 teaspoon chicken base (we use Better Than
    Bouillon)
2 cups mayonnaise
salt and pepper to taste

Boil the chicken to an internal temperature of 165°. Let the chicken cool and cut it into small pieces. Mix the onion, celery, chicken base, and mayonnaise. Add the chicken and salt and pepper to taste. Refrigerate and serve.

Party House Rolls

Yield: Approximately 20 rolls

1½ cups warm water
½ cup shortening
¼ cup sugar
2 teaspoons salt
2 eggs
⅓ cup powdered milk
2 packages active dry yeast
5 cups sifted plain, unbleached flour

Preheat oven to 450°. Pour the water over the shortening, sugar, salt, eggs, and powdered milk. Add the yeast. Mix well.

Add the flour gradually. Mix well and cover with a tea towel. Let the dough rise for about 1 hour until doubled in bulk. Roll out onto a well-floured board and cut with a biscuit cutter. Dip in a mixture of warm melted margarine and shortening (50-50 ratio). Fold the biscuit over your thumb to make a Parker House roll. Place the rolls touching in the pan. Do not crowd or leave any open space.

Let the dough rise again, covered with the tea towel, for about an hour or until doubled in size. Bake at 400° for 15 to 20 minutes until golden brown.

Butterscotch Cake

Yield: 1 cake

1¾ cups brown sugar
¼ cup butter
1½ cups milk
3 cups sifted cake flour
½ teaspoon salt
2 teaspoons baking powder
½ cup shortening
1 teaspoon vanilla
3 eggs, beaten

Preheat oven to 350°. Combine 1 cup brown sugar, butter, and ¼ cup milk in a saucepan. Heat, stirring constantly. Cook until a small amount will form a hard ball when dropped into a cup of cold water. Remove from heat.

Heat the remaining milk and stir into the syrup mixture. Cool.

Sift the flour, salt, and baking powder together. Cream the shortening and vanilla with the remaining brown sugar. Beat the eggs until light, and add to the creamed mixture. Add the dry ingredients and the butterscotch syrup mixture. Beat thoroughly. Bake in a greased and floured loaf pan for 50 to 60 minutes.

Butterscotch Icing

Yield: Approximately 2 cups

1 cup brown sugar
2 tablespoons butter
¼ cup milk
1 tablespoon light corn syrup
2 cups confectioners' sugar
¼ cup shortening
¼ teaspoon salt
3 tablespoons hot milk

Cook the brown sugar, butter, milk, and corn syrup until a small amount of the mixture forms a hard ball when dropped into a cup of cold water. Remove from heat. Cream together the sugar, shortening, and salt. Add the hot milk and then the butterscotch mixture. Beat until smooth and thick enough to spread onto the cooled cake.

If you are enjoying the Down South Café Mysteries,
keep reading for an excerpt of the first book in
Amanda Lee's Embroidery Mysteries . . .

The Quick and the Thread

Available wherever books are sold!

2 Just after crossing over . . . under . . . through . . . the covered bridge, I could see it. Barely. I could make out the top of it, and that was enough at the moment to make me set aside the troubling grammatical conundrum of whether one passes over, under, or through a covered bridge.

"There it is," I told Angus, an Irish wolfhound who was riding shotgun. "There's our sign!"

He woofed, which could mean anything from "I gotta pee" to "Yay!" I went with "Yay!"

"Me, too! I'm so excited."

I was closer to the store now and could really see the sign. I pointed. "See, Angus?" My voice was barely above a whisper. "Our sign."

THE SEVEN-YEAR STITCH.

I had named the shop the Seven-Year Stitch for three reasons. One, it's an embroidery specialty shop. Two, I'm a huge fan of classic movies. And three, it actually took me seven years to turn my dream of owning an embroidery shop into a reality.

Once upon a time, in a funky-cool land called San Francisco, I was an accountant. Not a funky-cool job, believe me, especially for a funky-cool girl like me, Marcy Singer. I had a corner cubicle near a window. You'd think the window would be a good thing, but it looked out upon a vacant building that grew more dilapidated by the day. Maybe by the hour. It was majorly depressing. One year, a coworker gave me a cactus for my birthday. I set it in that window, and it died. I told you it was depressing.

Still, my job wasn't that bad. I can't say I truly enjoyed it, but I am good with numbers and the work was tolerable. Then I got the call from Sadie. Not *a* call, mind you; *the* call.

"Hey, Marce. Are you sitting down?" Sadie had said.

"Sadie, I'm always sitting down. I keep a stationary bike frame and pedal it under my desk so my leg muscles won't atrophy."

"Good. The hardware store next to me just went out of business."

"And this is good because you hate the hardware guy?"

She'd given me an exasperated huff. "No, silly. It's good because the space is for lease. I've already called the landlord, and he's giving you the opportunity to snatch it up before anyone else does."

Sadie is an entrepreneur. She and her husband, Blake, own MacKenzies' Mochas, a charming coffee shop on the Oregon coast. She thinks everyone—or, at least,

Marcy Singer—should also own a charming shop on the Oregon coast.

"Wait, wait, wait," I'd said. "You expect me to come up there to Quaint City, Oregon—"

"Tallulah Falls, thank you very much."

"—and set up shop? Just like that?"

"Yes! It's not like you're happy there or like you're on some big five-year career plan."

"Thanks for reminding me."

"And you've not had a boyfriend or even a date for more than a year now. I could still strangle David when I think of how he broke your heart."

"Once again, thank you for the painful reminder."

"So what's keeping you there? This is your chance to open up the embroidery shop you used to talk about all the time in college."

"But what do I know about actually running a business?"

Sadie had huffed. "You can't tell me you've been keeping companies' books all these years without having picked up some pointers about how to—and how not to—run a business."

"You've got a point there. But what about Angus?"

"Marce, he will *love* it here! He can come to work with you every day, run up and down the beach . . . Isn't that better than the situation he has now?"

I swallowed a lump of guilt the size of my fist.

"You're right, Sadie," I'd admitted. "A change will do us both good."

That had been three months ago. Now I was a resident of Tallulah Falls, Oregon, and today was the grand opening of the Seven-Year Stitch.

A cool, salty breeze off the ocean ruffled my hair as I hopped out of the bright red Jeep I'd bought to traipse up and down the coast.

Angus followed me out of the Jeep and trotted beside me up the river-rock steps to the walk that connected all the shops on this side of the street. The shops on the other side of the street were set up in a similar manner, with river-rock steps leading up to walks containing bits of shells and colorful rocks for aesthetic appeal. A narrow, two-lane road divided the shops, and black wrought-iron lampposts and benches added to the inviting community feel. A large clock tower sat in the middle of the town square, pulling everything together and somehow reminding us all of the preciousness of time. Tallulah Falls billed itself as the friendliest town on the Oregon coast, and so far, I had no reason to doubt that claim.

I unlocked the door and flipped the CLOSED sign to OPEN before turning to survey the shop. It was as if I were seeing it for the first time. And, in a way, I was. I'd been here until nearly midnight last night, putting the finishing touches on everything. This was my first look at the finished project. Like all my finished projects, I tried to view it objectively. But, like all my finished projects, I looked upon this one as a cherished child.

The floor was black-and-white tile, laid out like a gleaming chessboard. All my wood accents were maple. On the floor to my left, I had maple bins holding cross-stitch threads and yarns. When a customer first came in the door, she would see the cross-stitch threads. They started in white and went through shades of ecru, pink, red, orange, yellow, green, blue, purple, gray, and black. The yarns were organized the same way on the opposite side. Perle flosses, embroidery hoops, needles, and cross-stitch kits hung on maple-trimmed corkboard over the bins. On the other side of the corkboard—the side with the yarn—there were knitting needles, crochet hooks, tapestry needles, and needlepoint kits.

The walls were covered by shelves where I displayed pattern books, dolls with dresses I'd designed and embroidered, and framed samplers. I had some dolls for those who liked to sew and embroider outfits (like me), as well as for those who enjoy knitting and crocheting doll clothes.

Standing near the cash register was my life-size mannequin, who bore a striking resemblance to Marilyn Monroe, especially since I put a short, curly blond wig on her and did her makeup. I even gave her a mole . . . er, beauty mark. I called her Jill. I was going to name her after Marilyn's character in *The Seven Year Itch*, but she didn't have a name. Can you believe that—a main character with no name? She was simply billed as "The Girl."

To the right of the door was the sitting area. As much as I loved to play with the amazing materials displayed all over the store, the sitting area was my favorite place in the shop. Two navy overstuffed sofas faced each other across an oval maple coffee table. The table sat on a navy, red, and white braided rug. There were red club chairs with matching ottomans near either end of the coffee table, and candlewick pillows with lace borders scattered over both the sofas. I made those, too—the pillows, not the sofas.

The bell over the door jingled, and I turned to see Sadie walking in with a travel coffee mug.

I smiled. "Is that what I think it is?"

"It is, if you think it's a nonfat vanilla latte with a hint of cinnamon." She handed me the mug. "Welcome to the neighborhood."

"Thanks. You're the best." The steaming mug felt good in my hands. I looked back over the store. "It looks good, doesn't it?"

"It looks fantastic. You've outdone yourself." She cocked her head. "Is that what you're wearing tonight?"

Happily married for the past five years, Sadie was always eager to play matchmaker for me. I hid a smile and held the hem of my vintage tee as if it were a dress. "You don't think Snoopy's Joe Cool is appropriate for the grand opening party?"

Sadie closed her eyes.

"I have a supercute dress for tonight," I said with a laugh, "and Mr. O'Ruff will be sporting a black tie for the momentous event."

Angus wagged his tail at the sound of his surname.

"Marce, you and that *pony*." Sadie scratched Angus behind the ears.

"He's a proud boy. Aren't you, Angus?"

Angus barked his agreement, and Sadie chuckled.

"I'm proud, too . . . of both of you." She grinned. "I'd better get back over to Blake. I'll be back to check on you again in a while."

Though we're the same age and had been roommates in college, Sadie clucked over me like a mother hen. It was sweet, but I could do without the fix-ups. Some of these guys she'd tried to foist on me . . . I have no idea where she got them—mainly because I was afraid to ask.

I went over to the counter and placed my big yellow

purse and floral tote bag on the bottom shelf before finally taking a sip of my latte.

"That's yummy, Angus. It's nice to have a friend who owns a coffee shop, isn't it?"

Angus lay down on the large bed I'd put behind the counter for him.

"That's a good idea," I told him. "Rest up. We've got a big day and an even bigger night ahead of us."

About the Author

Gayle Leeson is a pseudonym for Gayle Trent, who also writes the national bestselling Embroidery Mysteries as Amanda Lee. She lives in Virginia with her family and is having a blast writing the Down South Café Mysteries.

Ready to find
your next great read?

Let us help.

Visit prh.com/nextread

Penguin
Random
House